OLD

BONES

OLD

BONES

A Novel by

Greg Picard and Wendy Picard Gorham

workshopforwriterspress.com

A Workshop for Writers Press publication

Produced in conjunction with Bittercreek Enterprises
Durango, Colorado 81303
www.bittercreekenterprises.com

Cover design by Greg Picard and Wendy Picard Gorham
Cover photo courtesy of Bryan Picard

Other Books by Greg Picard

Other books by Greg Picard and Wendy Picard Gorham

Coming Soon…

Music CDs by Greg Picard

All available now through amazon.com

For Randall Hogue

The Ranger's Ranger

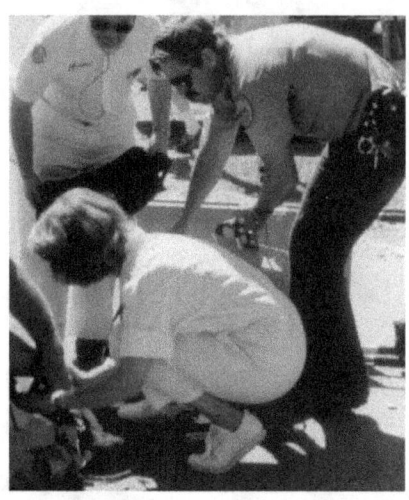

We Miss you.

In October of 2003 Cuyamaca Rancho State Park and Julian, as well as much of the outlying Eastern San Diego County, was destroyed by the massive Cedar Fire. This book takes place sometime before that event, and it is to the special people in those small communities of Eastern San Diego County, and especially to our Julian friends and neighbors and the extended state park family, that we dedicate this story.

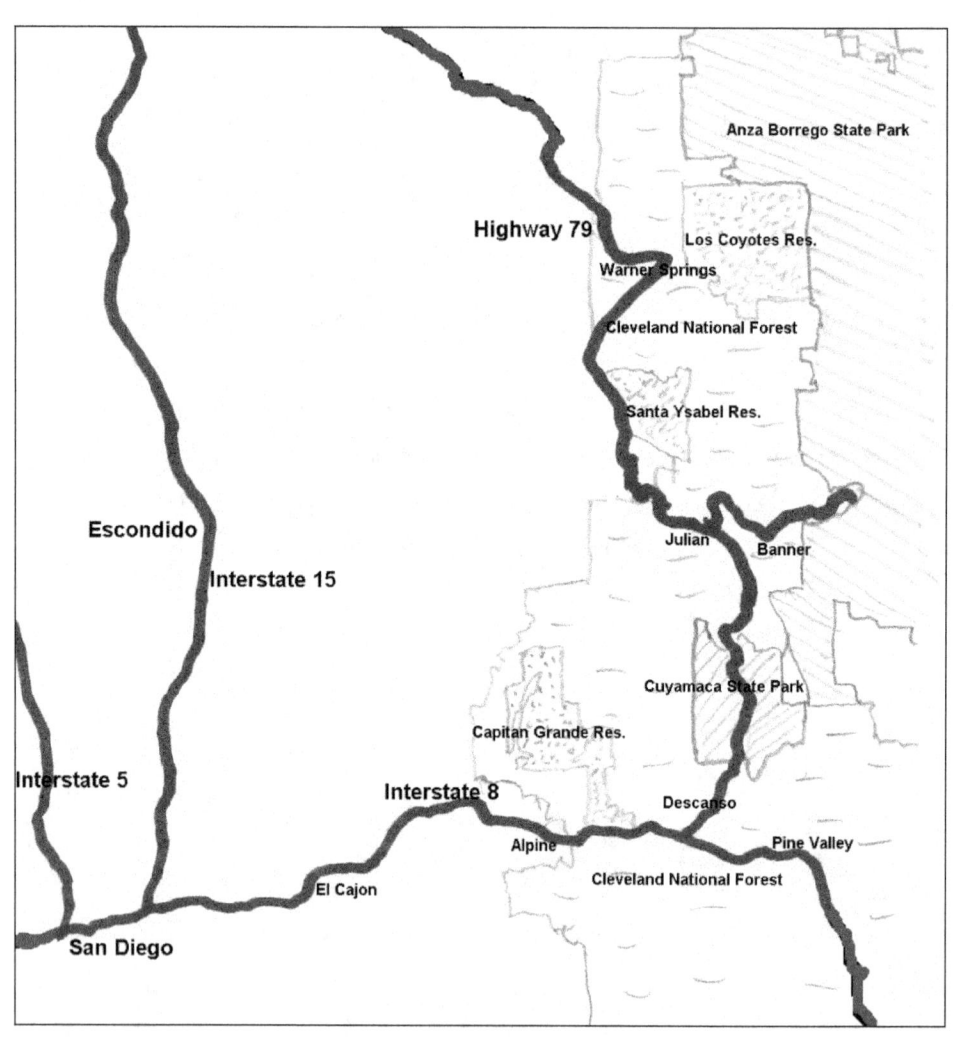

Chapter 1

Thursday, August 15

Like most days in the park service, Chris Becker was driving. Everyone thought rangers walked all day in the woods and led some kind of idyllic outdoor existence, but in truth most of their work was done from offices or their pick-ups and jeeps. Time and staffing levels just didn't permit wandering in the woods and talking to the animals. Still, the view of the scrubby chaparral grading gradually into pine and oak forest had its perks.

The sun broiled in through the open window and foretold another hot day in San Diego County. The day was clear, and he rolled the window lower to let the air cool him. His blond hair was long enough to tangle in the wind, and it reminded him that he should get a haircut. Long haired rangers were in fashion in the 70's and 80's, but the appeal with the current administration was fading fast. He was lucky he could keep his moustache and beard. Most police agencies frowned on such personal statements of style.

He spent the time driving old Hwy 79, back from Julian to the park office, noticing the wildflowers in the ditches along the road and remembering how she had loved them so much. She would always giggle

9

when she saw them and take hundreds of pictures of them. How many pictures of a flower do you need? She seemed so childlike in her joy. He ached inside with the memory. How long does it take to finally not remember each happy moment when someone is gone?

It had been nearly twelve years now since Lori had left him--had left them--and it still hadn't gotten any easier. In fact it was still quite complicated. The memory of the break-up, and the feeling that if he had just been or done something different it wouldn't have happened, kept trapping him in the whirlwind of memories that gripped him now.

Her choice to walk away from everything still perplexed him. In retrospect he could see how different they had become. Call it mid-life crisis or not, all she wanted now was trips to Tahiti and Cabo San Lucas, fast sports cars, gambling, and wild parties. No wonder she abandoned her daughter and wound up in Monaco living with a blackjack dealer. How could he compare to that, when he was most at home alone on a trail in the woods.

Keeping his mind focused on the fact that he had a job to do and a daughter to raise worked only so long before some other seemingly insignificant detail would flash across his mind and suck him down into depression. The nights alone in bed were still the worst, and he would think of the warmth of her skin against him. Too warm, to be exact, and he had continually wound up with no covers on in the morning. Sleeping now was at least thermally less difficult.

Difficult described a lot of things for Chris Becker today, not the least of which was how he would lay out a plan to stop the car burglaries that were still plaguing the West Mesa parking area. As the Chief Ranger, law enforcement fell to him along with all the other duties in the Montane Sector parks involving the visiting public. Park work was becoming more complex and urban in its character every year. Crime statistics in State Parks had nearly doubled in the past decade. More automobiles and better roads facilitated access. Visitor numbers increased as cities and suburbs expanded out nearer to park units. Now the chain of events and string of bad behavior often led right back to the nearest metro area and frustrated investigations that in the past had been pretty simple.

He didn't know exactly who was behind the latest rash of thefts, but he had a strong suspicion they were related to someone outside the rural east end of San Diego County that the park occupied. There were repeated reports of seeing a low-slung, chrome encrusted, red Chevy cruising the lot a couple of the times on the days that there had been a break-in. He was familiar with most of the vehicles in the back-country of the county and this wasn't one of them. It sounded more like something out of Logan Heights than Descanso or Julian.

The air cooled as he drove up the mountain, and he wished he were going for a hike up the 6500 foot shoulder of Cuyamaca Peak instead of driving up to the Park office. He knew he'd be grilled about what he was going to do to stop all these thefts by his boss, Superintendent Dick Savage. Savage didn't like complaints, and he was getting a steady ration of them lately from visitors who were tired of coming back from a horseback ride only to find their windows smashed and valuables missing.

"C601 – Montane" The radio broke the steady hum of the Cherokee's engine.

"Montane – 601, go ahead."

"We have a visitor in here who has a report you need to hear about something he's found on the trail." He could tell it was Val Simpson, his supervising ranger who ran the day-to-day operation for him.

"I'm down at Green Valley, it'll take me a few minutes to get there."

What now he thought? Val was probably one of the most talented and hard-working rangers he had, and she rarely needed his help handling things. Truth be known, she had a better feel for the operation than he did sometimes, and someday she was going to make a great Chief Ranger or Superintendent.

*   *   *

11

The headquarters at the Montane Sector was unique as facilities in the California State Park System went. Called the Dyar House by employees and visitors alike, the building dated back to the early part of the 20th century when the bulk of land in central and eastern San Diego County was used for cattle ranches. Even after the park was created the cattle operation leased the right to graze the park for many years, and on the surface the reasoning was that it kept the vegetation in check and lowered the fire danger. Now the two story stone ranch house was the nerve center of Cuyamaca Rancho State Park and Palomar Mountain State Park. Val Simpson stood just inside the porch entrance.

"What's up?" Chris asked, looking for rattlesnakes cooling beneath the step as he entered the Dyar House office. He could see that Val seemed tense just by the way she was holding her body. He towered over her at 6' 2" but her manner always made her 5' 4" frame seem bigger in some mysterious way. She was a 20-year veteran of everything parks could throw at a person, but he could tell something had her wound tightly now.

"We have a report of a body discovered on the Azalea Trail. Caucasian male, about 30…apparently pretty torn up. I sent Eric to secure the area and told him we'd be up there ASAP." Eric Larson was barely 21 and was newly out of the year-long ranger training program. He did well in the police academy and was doing well so far at Cuyamaca, but Chris wondered if he was up to a potentially big investigation so soon.

"Did you notify the sheriff's office already?"

"Yes, and I have the guy who found the body in my office."

"OK, do you have all the information you need from him for your initial report?"

"Yes, and …"

Chris cut her off, "Where's Elaine? Let's get her in here to babysit the witness until the Sheriffs' guys get here. I'm sure they'll want to do their own interview. We need to get up there with Eric. Make sure you bring the good camera and a ton of scene tape."

Just then Ranger Elaine Patterson walked in. Tall and perfectly formed, Elaine tended to 'suck the air out of the room' when she entered, but the jury was still out in Becker's mind whether she could do her job well enough. At least she could keep the witness from leaving. In fact, that was one of her problems. All the guys seemed to hang around her to socialize, both from the staff and the visitors. She rarely seemed to get her job done in a timely manner.

Val explained what they needed her to do and Chris headed back out to his Cherokee, followed a few moments later by Val making her way toward the newer half-ton Ford Bronco. For some reason at that moment it struck him funny that she had the big vehicle and he had the small one. Larger-than-life. That's what she was all right.

When they arrived at the Paso Picacho campground, Eric's vehicle was parked at the head of the Azalea Trail, and he had already taped the entrance off with police line tape. Though it was close to the campground, the trail was a darkly overgrown area heavy with brush and massive oak trees overshadowed by ponderosas and occasional incense cedars. It only took them a minute to find Eric about 500 feet up the trail.

"It's not pretty" Eric said. He was sweating heavily, and Becker suspected it was more shock than heat. Looking closer at the young man, Chris thought Eric was probably a bit nauseated, too. "The guy's a real mess. I marked my path line to him when I checked for signs of life. Here, I pulled his wallet and wrote down his name and other info for you. I put it back in the jacket pocket where I found it. Other than that, I put tape across the far side of the scene about 100 feet away and then just backed out the same path I took and came back here to keep anyone out. The other end of the trail still needs to be secured. He's thoroughly dead, and Chief, there's lots of blood, but from what I could see it looks like puncture marks on his neck. It's not sliced or stabbed."

Val interrupted, "What do you mean, like bullets or an ice pick?"

"Nope. Like a bite mark."

13

"OK, let's get Elaine up to the other end of Azalea as soon as the sheriff takes over the witness, and meanwhile Val, you go up and secure the trail until Elaine gets there" Chris said, as he turned to follow the trail to the victim's body.

When he got close enough he saw the flag markers Eric had used to ID his path into the body. He stayed back under a large oak in the shade and looked the whole scene over. The trail was extremely dry and tracking would be difficult. Ordinarily, he was a fairly capable tracker, but this was probably beyond his limit. The sides of the trail were heavily covered with oak leaves that hindered the tracking process, plus the soil on the trail was rocky, packed hard and baked by the sun. Still, he scanned for anything that would stand out. He could make out a few faint partial shoe prints in some dust and fine soil, and a large number of raccoon tracks. He conjured an image of a highly agitated pack of raccoons protecting a discarded peanut butter sandwich and could hear the evening news lead in his head, "*Giant mutant raccoons bite hiker to death at Cuyamaca, pictures at 11:00.*" Well, the sheriff would want pictures of all of the tracks. The light would be better later on, once the sun was a bit lower, and the techs could get good shots of the tracks then.

Given Eric's opinion about possible bite marks, Chris radioed back to headquarters and asked Elaine to call the area lieutenant for Fish and Game and ask him to respond. He was banking on him getting there before the sheriff's investigators. He'd wait for Lt. James before moving in closer. Cuyamaca State Park had recently been plagued with cougars stalking humans and livestock, and even one fatal encounter where a female hiker had been killed and partially consumed. That lion had been shot shortly after the attack, with much controversy over whether it had been the right cat until stomach contents had proven to contain parts of the victim. This kind of stuff always brought out the animal rights loonies and the environmentalists in droves, and Chris wasn't looking forward to the experience again.

The local press hadn't been easy to deal with either, especially with their penchant for sensationalizing everything. Suddenly, he was wishing he

14

just had his car burglaries to worry about. Fortunately, it was only ten minutes before Lt. Frank James showed up.

"Sounds like you've got yourself a nasty little mess here to deal with," James said. Lean and looking like a character out of a Larry McMurtry novel about the Wild West, Frank James was working the end of a long career in Fish and Game enforcement. Just a few more years and he would hang it up. Chris couldn't look at him without thinking of the actor Sam Elliot.

"Eric says he took a quick look at the body and believes he saw bite marks. Take a look at the ground here, would you," Chris said, "I haven't done an exhaustive examination, but so far I can't see any cougar tracks anywhere. What do you think?"

James followed Eric's flags, and, moving in slowly, he leaned over the body.

"It's obvious there is some bruising from the bite, but the teeth marks are clear and consistent with what a lion might look like." As he finished his examination, James stood up and backed away to where Chris now squatted at the edge of the trail and said, "ground's pretty hard here, but I see a few partial prints that could be a cat. Lotta blood covering up sign makes it a bit of a problem, but hopefully we can sort that out."

"I suspect the sheriff will approach this as a murder until proven otherwise, just like last time. We'll be here for hours with lights and forensics guys doing their scientific investigation stuff." Chris nodded at what James was saying. The last cougar death took eight hours of CSI work before the scene was released.

"I better go get us a deer and a tracking collar from somewhere to leave here when they finally take the body, so we can catch this cat when it returns to feed. It's probably out there watching us right now waiting for us to leave." Chris knew James was referring to a technique where the victim's body is replaced by a deer in the hopes the animal will come to feed on the kill it thinks is there and take the deer as a substitute. Not a perfect solution to catching the culprit, but it offered a reasonably high probability of catching the right cat if it happened soon enough. Chris thought to himself how sad it

15

was that wildlife-human interactions had degenerated to the point that you had to develop a technique to catch killer cougars.

"I've got a good sized herd that is usually over on East Mesa that will probably have one that I can cull out," James said, as he started back down the trail. Becker cringed inwardly at the thought that one of "his" deer would have to die in order to catch the cat, but Fish and Game had total authority over the deer and could make that decision at will.

He flipped his cell phone open as he walked back to where Eric was manning the control point. Dick Savage would have to be notified. Becker wished he could leave him out of the loop, but he knew he'd pay for it if he didn't alert him to what had happened as early as possible. The press would be there soon, and Savage would love the notoriety of making his comments on camera. At least that was one of the good things. Chris hated the press and the way they endlessly picked at things and generally got in the way. It also frustrated him that they seemed to spin stories to their liking, rather than to portray the actual facts. The only problem now was figuring out where Savage was.

Becker headed back to his Jeep and sat inside while he used his cell phone to notify the superintendent.

"Sorry to bother you Dick, but we have a sensitive situation here and I suspect you want to know." He filled him in on the details, and Savage agreed to come back from the meeting he was in at the regional headquarters in San Diego. Chris suggested he do the press conference in front of the park office so as to keep snooping reporters away from the area where the forensic team would be working.

Becker looked at the piece of paper Eric had given him with the victim's name. Technically, he shouldn't have messed with anything prior to photos and other evidence gathering, and Chris would have to remind him of that.

"Well Mr. Hess, I'm sorry you had to die here today. But at least I'm glad the sheriff will be doing the next of kin notification," he muttered under his breath as he started the Cherokee.

16

Chapter 2

"Would you like fries with that?" Alicia Becker asked, while secretly trying to calculate how much money she would have if she actually could get a nickel for every time she had uttered that loathsome phrase. After working the last three summers for Mr. Wong at the Hillside Resort restaurant, she had probably said that line enough times to be able to pay for her first semester of college. But, while there were lots of fries, sadly there were no nickels. So, it fell to Alicia and her part-time wages to help pay for the long-awaited college classes that would soon begin.

"No, thanks, I think I'll skip them this time," the plump middle aged woman smiled sheepishly, "and could I just have a glass of water? Thanks, Hon'."

"Thank God for dieters," Alicia mused silently, as she took the menu from the woman's outstretched hand, "cross one order of fries off my to-do list."

Unfortunately, that order of fries wasn't going to make much of a dent in that to-do list, which was growing considerably as the start of the fall semester at San Diego State

University was fast approaching. At the forefront of that list, and consequently at the front of her mind, was her inability to decide on a minor. English majors didn't technically have to declare a minor, since the major required so many units in itself, but it seemed such a waste to not assemble the remaining class units into something collectively.

RIIIING! The phone blared into the otherwise low pitched drone of the diner's voices. She rushed to answer it.

"Hello, Hillside Resort and Fine Dining, this is Alicia, how may I help you?" Again, she was wishing for nickels. The "Resort" part of the name of the establishment was sort of a misnomer, as this was a very low-budget affair, which was why she was hostess as well as waitress.

"Hey kiddo, it's Dad."

"Oh, hi, what's up?"

"Well, something has come up at work and I won't be home until late. Can you fend for yourself for dinner and whatever?"

"Yeah, I'll just have the cook make me a doggie bag. Is anything wrong?"

"It's complicated and I'm in a rush. I'll tell you all about it in the morning, okay?"

"Sure Dad. Oh, I better go, Mr. Wong is giving me dirty looks. You know how he hates us using the phone for personal calls."

"Okay. Hey, don't forget about registration tomorrow. Don't stay up too late, and be careful coming home in the dark. We've had a death and I'll be here with the sheriff for quite a while. And Alicia, stay inside tonight until I get home."

Though he was little more than a mile or two away from the restaurant, Becker stood, cradling the phone against his head, looking uneasily in the direction of the empty wild spaces that separated his daughter from where he was at the moment. If the lion was out there, it was still hungry.

"I love you, Dad." She was seventeen and eleven-twelfths, and he was still protective like she was a little kid. But, truth be told, she didn't really mind. He had been father and mother to her for going on six years, and she knew that she was the most important thing in the world to him.

"Love you too, Allie," and then a click and he was gone.

His reference to registration jogged her memory. Another thing on her to-do list was to make sure Mr. Wong remembered that she had asked for tomorrow off. She quickly surveyed the dining room. It was decorated in what Alicia referred to as "early lumberjack": wall to wall wood paneling, red and white-checkered napkins and placemats, and white stoneware plates with pictures of woodland creatures on them. She loved animals and nature, she was a park ranger's daughter after all, but in terms of design, one did have to draw the line somewhere.

It was only 5:30, so the dinner rush was only beginning. She quickly checked on the two tables that had already been served and found them happily munching, so she brought the water to her newest customer, who was primping her hair and putting on pink pearlized lip gloss while looking into a tiny hand-held mirror. She assured her that the rest of her order, minus the fries, would be out shortly, then she scooted quickly in the direction of the office in search of her boss. Alicia wondered if the woman at the table was expecting someone to join her, or if she just wanted to look nice for her meatloaf sandwich.

She knocked four times on his office door, waiting a few seconds between each knock. She read the polished brass nameplate on the door in between each set of taps, just to have something to do. *Daniel Wong, Proprietor.* She suddenly realized how incongruous that nameplate looked, all shiny and curlicued, against the rugged hewn planks of the door, like a china doll in a logging camp. After one last knock, Alicia decided he wasn't there. Her choices were to scour the premises looking for him, or sneak into his inner sanctum and check the work schedule he kept posted on a bulletin board behind the door. After weighing her options and deciding that a quick peek was the fastest and most sensible plan, she turned the handle and peered into the darkened room.

The light switch was just inside the doorframe, camouflaged in a wooden switch plate cover against a background of knotty pine tongue-and-groove paneling. The office, like the rest of the establishment, was surrounded in dark wood walls, but that was where the similarities ended. Once inside, the rustic motif ceased and an overwhelmingly eclectic mélange of styles assaulted the senses. The musky smell of a half-burned stick of incense competed for olfactory dominance with a peppermint studded candle left over from Christmas. The battered gray, four-drawer metal filing cabinet was papered on one side with reproduction "I Love Lucy" posters, while a chubby Buddha and a miniature pagoda perched precariously on top, next to a stack of ancient Marvel comic books.

Daniel Wong seemed an odd combination of Asian mysticism and kitschy Americana. However, there was one thing her employer took very seriously. His antiques. His tastes were wide and varied, but he knew quality when he saw it. She had seen him unpack a Native American Kachina doll he had once received from a dealer. He handled it like a newborn baby. In the corner of the office, under the window, he also had a Limoges tea set and an inlaid Russian tea cart from before WWII, which Alicia had to admit she had secretly pined for, ever since the day she had first interviewed for the job at Hillside.

"What are you doing in there!" She had just flicked on the switch when an angry voice behind her boomed into her ear. She knew immediately and without question that it was Mr.Wong, and that he thought she was stealing from him.

"I'm sorry. I was looking for you," she fumbled. "I wanted to make sure that you remembered I had asked for tomorrow off. I have to finish up my registration." Alicia was hoping that the look on her face would convey the plight of the college freshman more than the guilt of an employee caught where she shouldn't be.

"Table three needs their drinks refilled, and table seven hasn't been given their bill yet. I pay attention to what you say, I know you want tomorrow off, even though it isn't your regular day." His disapproval at her disruption of his perfectly planned schedule was clearly evident on his slightly wrinkled fifty-something face.

"Oh, great, okay, um…sorry about the tables. I'll get right on that." As she moved to take care of the customers, she thought, not for the first time, how high strung and oddly secretive her boss was. Looking over her shoulder before she rounded the corner from the back hallway to the big open dining room, Alicia could clearly see Mr. Wong peering intently into his office, probably checking to see if she had moved any of his precious knick-knacks.

The rest of the evening went fairly smoothly. After attending to tables three and seven as instructed, Alicia sat two more tables' worth of guests over the next quarter of an hour. They were about ready for their bills as well, when she realized it was nearly eight o'clock. Her shift would be over in half an hour. If she was going to get something to take home for dinner, she better order it now.

Alicia gave the two tables their bills, telling them to take their time, and walked toward the kitchen trying to formulate a game plan on the way. The cook who was working tonight was fairly new to the area, and Mr. Wong had only hired him a few weeks ago. However, it hadn't taken Marcus Lundee long to show he had other interests at Hillside Resort than just flipping burgers. He had asked Alicia out after only the second shift they worked together. She barely knew his name, and she didn't operate that way. She had let him down easy, or at least tried to, and now she had to carefully rehearse any interaction they might have in order to avoid giving him any reason to think that she had changed her mind.

"Hey Marcus," she began, trying to sound lighthearted, "do you have a few minutes to throw together a chicken salad for me, to go?" The best perk of working at Hillside was getting 50% off all food purchases for yourself within an hour before or after your shift.

"Sure. How about I make two and we go sit out by the lake and eat in the moonlight?"

Well, so much for carefully rehearsed and aloof. Too bad he was so pushy and forward, because he was nice looking if you like the scruffy, "I shop at Vampires-R-Us" kind of look, which she usually didn't go for, but Marcus pulled it off fairly well.

"Oh, gosh, thanks for the offer, but I have to get home. My Dad is waiting for me." *Lie. I will burn in Hell.* "Besides, I have an early appointment down the hill tomorrow." *Lie again.* She didn't actually plan on being at SDSU until eleven o'clock at the earliest. She planned on making as much of her remaining summer vacation sleep-in time as possible. Soon enough she'd have to get up at 5:00 a.m. to get a parking space at school by 7:00.

"Too bad, we could have had fun." Marcus let the implications hang there in the air between them. "Oh, well, another time. Do you want some garlic bread, too?"

"Huh?"

"With your chicken salad?" Alicia thought she saw a slight upturn to the corner of his lips. He was enjoying the fact that he had somehow gained the upper hand in the conversation. Now she just wanted to extract herself as soon as possible.

"Yes, thanks, that would be great." She wasn't sure he even heard that last word since she had turned and already started walking away before she finished speaking. A quick getaway was her only hope now.

When she got back, it was clear both tables of customers had been waiting several minutes for her to take their credit cards and finish up their bills so they could leave. That task completed, she tidied up the cash register area, took her apron off, and put away her order pad, pencil, and the extra straws she always carried in her pocket. On the way to the restroom she clocked out.

"It is a miracle anybody is asking you out the way you look at the end of the evening," Alicia glared at herself in the mirror. Her ponytail, which had started the evening tidy and professional, now had unruly tufts of her long, wavy auburn hair escaping around her ears and down the nape of her neck. Alicia was tired, and she looked it. She wiped down the counter and picked up a few paper towels that had been haphazardly thrown on the floor. After using the facilities and washing up, she left the Ladies' Room, flicking off the lights on her way out.

The lights in the hallway had been turned off already. Mr. Wong was a real stickler about using electricity sparingly after hours. She saw that his office light was still on, and as she passed by the partially open door, she leaned in, "Goodnight, Mr. Wong. I'm going home now."

"What! Oh, is it that time already? OK, goodnight." As he said this he was also obviously hunching over the paperwork on his desk, covering it with his body, as though he were a paranoid student trying to keep a neighbor from copying answers on a test.

Alicia stepped back into the hallway.

"What a weirdo," she thought to herself, "like I care about his stupid paperwork."

The kitchen was dark as well as the dining room. She grabbed her coat and walked out the door to the lighted front porch. There, leaning against the porch railing was Marcus, a red and white checkerboard bag in his hand.

"Here is your salad and bread," he barely extended his arm, bag in hand, toward her without getting up, and without looking away from her for a moment.

"Thanks." *Don't make eye contact. Don't show fear.* She felt like she was trying to save herself from a mountain lion attack. *This is stupid. He's not a lion. He's not going to attack.* Alicia quickly thrust out her hand, grabbed the bag, and spun around to face the parking area. She was sure she could feel his eyes boring holes into the back of her faded denim jacket. She walked to her Ford pickup, hoping her uneasiness didn't show, and fired up the engine. Just before the door slammed behind her, she heard the unmistakable sound of the striking of a match.

As she backed out of the parking space, she allowed herself a quick look at the porch. Marcus was still staring at her, that same slight smile playing at the corner of his mouth, a freshly lit cigarette dangling limply from his right hand, sending grayish-white tendrils of smoke across his shoulder-length black hair, and into the quiet night behind him.

The drive home was incredibly short, and of that Alicia was supremely glad. She was starving, and had been experiencing a very unladylike growling in her stomach for some time. She was convinced some of her customers must have heard it as she brought them refills on tea or extra BBQ sauce for their chicken fingers. Finally, relief was in sight and that salad was calling her name. Her home, a peaceful but rather bleak looking park-owned dwelling dating back to the Korean War era, wasn't more than a mile or so from the Hillside Resort. She could walk to and from work if she had to, although thankfully that had never actually happened. She pulled up the long asphalt drive and parked on her side of the wide turn-around in front of the garage.

This was the part she hated—getting out in the dark, open night and going into the empty house all alone. Some people would have seen it as relaxing, a time of solace; some personal space to unwind and be free of the parents for a while. Not Alicia. Not at night.

She had a ritual for situations such as this. She wasn't OCD, but she could see that someone watching her might wonder. She looked all around the dark meadow surrounding her mud-brown house and the detached garage, which stood some 20 or 30 feet away. After letting her eyes adjust to the pitch black, she was soon able to discern shapes—trees, rocks, the dark mound of the woodpile against the wall of the garage. Once her eyes were acclimated, she got her keys at the ready in her right hand and grabbed the to-go bag and her purse with her left.

She walked purposefully to the door, unlocked it, shoved her way in, and breathed a small sigh of relief. The first hurdle was over. Now to check the rooms. She turned on every light in the house as she went room to room looking in closets and behind doors to make sure no one else was there. Once satisfied, she made sure every window and door was locked and settled down to eat her long-awaited dinner.

She chided herself inwardly, wondering how long this overly acute sense of self-preservation would continue. But she knew that there were some good reasons for why she was so careful. Even at the tender age of 17, she had seen how dangerous life, and people, could be, even out here in unspoiled wild places—sometimes especially out here in the wild. But she had also seen how people could let fears like this control them. *I don't want to become some crazy old woman living alone with 60 cats,* she thought as she vowed to try to relax a little.

After spreading out her feast on a wooden tray and settling down on the worn, tan tweed couch in front of the TV, Alicia was finally able to relax. She flipped through the channels until she found what she was looking for, *The X-Files*. It was either that or a re-run of *Star Trek*, which would have been fine too, but tonight Mulder and Scully were finishing up solving a case that was started last week, and she was dying to see how it was all going to turn out. This was one good thing about evenings home without her dad, she had the remote control all to herself.

Chapter 3

Friday, August 16th

It looked like August's sun was going to burn a hole right through the roof of Chris Becker's cabin as it laser beamed its heat across the clear morning sky. He sat at the beaten and scarred pine table across from Alicia, looking at his coffee as though it were an alien life form, his tall frame bent low over the table. He had spent the night dreaming that he was moving all his household goods once again and awoke with a backache to prove it. In the early days of his career the department randomly moved everyone after three or four years in one spot. It broadened experience, but more importantly it kept the nicest parks from being locked up by long-timers. Becker found moving just plain annoying.

"Earth to Dad! I said do you want some cereal?" Alicia was busy scratching her black and white calico cat, Sadie, behind the ears with one hand and waving the granola like a checkered flag with the other.

Becker came out of his trance with a sigh.

"No, I'm just going with coffee this morning. Something about looking at that Hess guy's body yesterday just takes away my appetite. I never can eat much for a while after dealing with stuff like that. Car crashes, whatever, it all just takes some time to get used to what happened. It's a shock to the psyche to see a person's body like that." He almost said, "reminds you of your own mortality" but thought better of it.

"So what exactly happened?" Alicia hadn't seen him when he got home around midnight and so hadn't discussed the events of the previous evening with him yet.

"We found a body of a man recently killed on the Azalea Trail just outside of the Paso campground. We're not sure, but it looked like a mountain lion kill again." Chris said as he stared into his reflection on the surface of the coffee, as if Nostradamus himself was going to appear with an answer to both the car burglaries and the dead hiker.

"Allie, I want you to be extra careful around here. Lieutenant James, from Fish and Game, put down a deer in place of the body again, but as of midnight last night he hadn't had even a peep out of the tracking device on it. Nothing's come near that deer." The thought that a cougar with a taste for humans was still out hunting in an area so close to where he and Alicia lived was unsettling. It was tough enough to protect park visitors. He didn't want to have to worry about his daughter taking out the trash and getting jumped by a lion.

He had seen lion tracks in the snow last winter by the back door, so he knew for sure the cats were not uncomfortable coming that near the house. He suspected the Boy Scout camp across the meadow was leaving the garbage accessible in the dumpster, too. It wouldn't surprise him if they were deliberately leaving food out to feed the animals in some misguided attempt to bring them into the camp for the kids to "experience nature." It wouldn't be the first time.

"Why are all the lions doing this here? Isn't it a little strange to have people being stalked and bitten and now two of them killed by different cougars?"

"We can't say for sure it's a cat yet. The sheriff and the Fish and Game necropsy unit will have to make that official call, but the bite marks were consistent with a lion. We couldn't see anything else as a cause of death," Chris said, as he added cream to his coffee and stirred it slowly.

"So, why is it happening?"

"Cats… are hunters. Mostly, they hunt and sometimes they reproduce and then they hunt some more. Their recreation is hunting and their survival is hunting. Pretty much their whole life is hunting. The deer population has been dropping for years, and the fire protection removes prime meadow feeding areas when brush and trees eventually fill them in. Then people come in and build houses and remove more habitat. If the cats can't get enough deer they eat something else. When you fill an area with brush and hikers you're just asking to be dinner."

"Yeah, Dad, but that still doesn't answer the question of *'why here?'* The same loss of habitat is happening all over the country, and yet *we're* having all the problems with cats."

"Well, that's not entirely true. Colorado has had one death and a few attacks, and Northern California had one fatality near Auburn and a possible cat kill near Oroville in the last few years. Then there are people who just go missing in the woods and are never found, so we don't know if their cause of death could be cougars, too."

"Still, it should be happening everywhere, Dad."

It was hard to argue with her logic. There was something odd about the anomaly of so many attacks in San Diego County. They had shot four lions here already in the past four years. This one would be number five if they found it, and if they didn't find it soon, they wouldn't keep the search up. They would just figure the cat left the area, and with a cat's range being anywhere from 15 square miles to 200, it could be anywhere. No way could they justify shooting just any lion. PETA would have a field day with them, and the TV channels would eat up that kind of story even more than the death of the man they found yesterday. It just didn't do in liberal, green California for preservation organizations to appear that they were wantonly killing the very things they were there to protect, and the department was extremely sensitive to bad publicity.

Chris decided a change of subject was in order.

"You need to be thinking about registering for your classes at SDSU today, not why pumas are taking out hunting licenses on people. When is your registration time?"

"I don't exactly have an appointment, but I was told that if I want to see someone about my schedule, I should get there before lunch. I guess Fridays in summer break are short days for most staff and teachers, so I think I need to get there by 11:00 am. Also, I probably need money to pay some fees, like parking permits and stuff like that."

Chris had forgotten all about the school fees after all the issues at work this week. Money was tight on his meager state wages, and just keeping the cars repaired and food on the table was difficult enough sometimes. Alicia didn't make enough money at the restaurant to cover all the tuition cost, and Chris had agreed to take money out of his account to make up the difference.

"Tell me how much it is and I'll write a check."

"I don't know what the exact amount will be, especially since I have to buy books too. Can you give me two signed blank checks?"

"You promise you won't go buy a bunch of new record albums with them," Chris said, mockingly.

"Dad! You're showing your age. Nobody even has records anymore."

"Actually, you might have a problem getting them to take a check with my signature on it if they ask for identification." Chris hadn't thought of that before. The world was getting too complicated.

"Take my credit card then, I guess. They won't give you grief about ID on that." What a sad commentary on our society that is, he thought. "Have you decided on a minor yet? "

Alicia traced one of the scars in the old dining table and took a moment before she answered. This had been a sore subject since her father had been pushing her to study one of the hard sciences.

29

"Dad, I really want to major in English and minor in *anthropology*. Anthro is scientific. Anyway, I'll just drop the Intro to Biology that I registered for on the phone last week, and add Anthropology instead." Alicia was very grateful that universities had switched to phone and online registration from the in-person fighting for classes that her father described having had to go through. Unfortunately, switching minors this close to the semester starting did require some face-to-face time with the powers that be.

"Well, it's sort of a science. Anyway, it is your decision, but jobs are hard to come by in those fields. I can't say as I blame you though. The last thing I want is for you to do something you can't stand. I know it hasn't seemed like that when we've talked about it, but I wanted to make you aware of the long term impact of your decision."

Chris couldn't help but look in Alicia's green eyes and see the little seven-year-old girl who had chased snakes and bugs around the Mojave desert with him so many years ago, or the awkward and gangly twelve-year-old in new braces he had looked at and wondered what she would be in another eight or ten years. Now that time was getting so much nearer. How did she grow up so fast? The freckly little girl face had turned into the face of a young woman, lip gloss and blush replacing the Chapstick and dirt smudges of just a few years ago. It sometimes hurt to look at her. He turned and drained the last of his coffee and put the imitation birch tree cup in the sink.

"O.K., I've got to get to headquarters and meet with Warden James. Hopefully, there is some good news this morning about the cougar hunt."

"Yeah, I need to get my stuff together for school and get ready."

"It's an hour drive if there's no traffic, so you better give yourself some extra time," Chris said, as he slipped on his Stetson and Sam Browne belt. The Smokey Bear hat was a royal pain, and in the wind its flat brim tended to take flight like a Frisbee, but it was a statement. The department pushed rangers to always wear it. "I'll see you tonight and maybe we can make those buffalo burgers, and Al, it's your turn to cook and wash the

30

dishes!" Chris grinned as he twisted his blond moustache, pleased that he'd remembered their Friday night agreement.

"Yeah, yeah…" Alicia disappeared into the hallway of their tiny cabin and headed for her room. Chris could hear her rooting around for her backpack and purse and again felt that disquiet in his mind of the transition of a little girl to a woman. He wondered if every father felt this way, or if raising her alone had given him some special burden. He adjusted his gunbelt and Stetson hat and stepped out the door. As he shut it behind him he yelled back into the house.

"My credit card is on the kitchen table…don't lose it!"

He heard a faint "I won't" from the bedroom…not without a hint of exasperation in the voice. He imagined the eye roll and head toss that went with it and smiled to himself.

State Park patrol vehicles were generally kept at the shop yard out of the general public eye. Chris made a habit of taking his home, since he lived in the park, as did the other two resident rangers in case they were called out late at night. The Jeep Cherokee was the cheapest four wheel drive unit the department could find on the market and had a few years on it already, but Chris was glad it was at least an improvement over the first beat up pick-up he had been assigned when he started as a ranger with State Parks, nearly eighteen years ago. It had had 106,000 miles on it, and was a slant six engine with a 1,000 pound fire pump and tank in the back. Its rust, dents and scratches gave it character, which made it fit right in when its two wheel drive left him stuck off road in the mud. He had once taken it down along a creek bed and buried it up to the rims in soft sand. As a wet behind the ears rookie, he had no idea how to rescue himself.

One of the crusty old maintenance workers saw him stuck there and stopped. The rift between maintenance and peace officer rangers was still raw when Chris was hired. They had previously all been one group, and the resentment over the split in job duties took decades to heal. Rangers with their shiny badge were considered primadonas, and maintenance felt second-class.

He remembered how the maintenance employee took one look at him by the creek and laughed, then started Chris's fire pump to wet the sand around the tires. The water firmed the substrate and Chris drove out with no trouble. Chris never forgot the lesson. Every person, no matter what job they did in the department had their skills, and their importance and dignity should be respected.

This morning his Cherokee was covered with dew from the night before, in spite of the day's summer heat. He wedged himself in and after cranking it over, rolled out of the driveway onto Highway 79. As he did so he noticed a deer on the highway about 100 yards up toward Cuyamaca Lake. It was struggling to get up and it was clear to Chris the animal was injured, probably hit by some commuter with no time to care what happened to it.

He turned north to check it out, and when he got there the animal was clearly floundering with a bloody gash and two legs snapped at the shoulder. He knew there was no hope for a deer like this and parked his Jeep with the light bar flashing to warn oncoming traffic. His only other alternative was to call the wild animal rescue people west of Julian, and they would pick it up and set it out in their compound for their cougar to finish off. He wasn't in the mood to deal with them today, and he didn't want to prolong the animal's suffering, so he drew his pistol and considered the bullet trajectory, since the area behind the deer was the Boy Scout campground. After adjusting his aim he fired one round and dispatched the animal.

While he was dragging the carcass off the road toward the brush, another car came by at about 50 MPH. It nearly ran him over in spite of his warning lights and a clear line of sight. The woman driving was gone before he could even yell at her. At that point he was pretty sure he had euthanized the wrong 'mammal.'

"Brain dead jerk driver," Chris muttered and headed back to his car thinking he had living and dead deer everywhere and the lions had to pick on his hikers! What a mess. His job was nothing if it wasn't abundant with low pay and variety. It still bothered him that there were a relative

32

abundance of deer and yet cougars were becoming more of a threat to people. Sure, deer numbers had declined after the fires of the 1950s and 1970s had created all the big meadows that were now just inedible coyote brush and manzanita, but large deer herds were still to be found.

Something different was going on. Maybe it was just too many people moving into the more remote areas and too many people visiting parks. Still, people shouldn't be the preference for cats. They just didn't fit the lion's visual profile of four-legged prey. He slammed the Jeep door and snapped the light bar off as he turned around and headed back south to headquarters. By now, Frank James was probably already pacing in front of the office.

*   *   *

Alicia checked her watch and grumbled as she hurried back down the hall toward the kitchen. She wouldn't admit she had a tardiness problem, and instead preferred to classify herself as "temporally challenged." She had battled it her whole life, and some days she was just doomed from the very beginning. Apparently this was one of those days.

The credit card's silver glisten flashed at her from the kitchen table as promised. She snapped it up and tucked it carefully in the inside zipper pocket of her small leather purse. She looked at her watch again—10:01. So much for leaving herself extra time. She sincerely hoped this was one of those days when there was no traffic.

As she was about to open the front door, backpack and sack lunch in hand, the phone rang.

"Of course. Perfect timing."

As was her rule, she waited to see who it was, just in case it was her dad.

"Hey, it's me. Tag, you're it!" And then a click and dead air.

Alicia smiled to herself. Michael. In a world that felt like a game of poker most of the time, occasionally the Lord would give you a good hand.

Her dad was one. Michael was the other. From the minute they met in seventh grade there had been something, a strong connection. Not romantic, although everybody thought that's what it was, but something else. It was like they were family, like those crazy stories you hear of twins separated at birth only to be reunited as adults. It had been hard since she had moved to Cuyamaca and wasn't able to see him much, so she was happy that he got his home base posting with Americorps in San Diego.

"Sorry Michael, can't talk now," her lament carried into the warm mid-morning air as she pulled the heavy green front door closed behind her, and turned the dead-bolt securely into it's slot with her key. The best part about family was being able to blow them off and know they will still love you.

Chapter 4

Chris always loved the drive to park headquarters. Highway 79 wound through beautiful stands of old Live Oak and Black Oak and forests of Ponderosa and Incense Cedar. In spring, the huge meadows were filled with pale blue larkspur, lupine and bright orange poppies. Along Cold Stream, in the tight curves descending from the campground at Paso Picacho, visitors were stunned to see huge sycamores standing sentinel duty along the highway. Horse and hiking trails paralleled the highway and then headed off into the backcountry. The park's 26,000 acres gave an incredible opportunity for solace, and its dedicated wilderness areas were a rarity in Southern California.

More than once Chris would watch visitors from San Diego arrive and express wonderment at the vastly different scene from the one in San Diego and Orange County's congestion and urban sprawl. In winter at 5,000 feet it was not uncommon to have a foot or two of snow and freezing temperatures. One could hike to almost 7,000 feet. People from the beach communities of Southern California would routinely come up in winter completely unprepared in shorts and wearing their flip-flops. It was a mystery land to the uninitiated and occasionally resulted in tragedy. The tortuous roadway was a death trap to the incautious, and its large wilderness swallowed up unprepared hikers routinely in winter or summer.

Native American peoples had flourished in its oak forests and left behind evidence of their habitation in numerous locations jealously guarded by park staff. Archeology was a part of the park staff's responsibility, just like protecting the flowers and the animals and the visitors themselves, but archeology was poorly funded. One person was available to work on studying and preserving nearly a million acres of parkland archeological resources out of the Regional Headquarters in San Diego. Consequently, pot hunting and searching for arrowheads was popular and hard to prevent. Chris passed near one of the most outstanding village sites as he pulled into the headquarters meadow area that was shared with the San Diego Schools County Outdoor Education Camp. As he drove up the road to the rough-hewn stone ranch house used as the headquarters building, he saw Lt. James' Fish and Game truck and was once again jealous that it was a far nicer vehicle than his.

Like the shiny new truck, there was something enviable in the look of the man as well. Frank James was the epitome of the wild-west cowboy. Tall, with a flowing, dark moustache, you expected him to be wearing a low slung six shooter and a trail-worn, sweat stained horseman's hat with a red bandana, instead of his DFG issued ball cap and .40 calibre Smith and Wesson semi-auto. He leaned against the granite rock wall of the Dyer House and looked as though he would have belonged there when it was built nearly four decades before. He looked up from his coffee cup as Chris pulled into the parking space next to the building.

"You stand that close to the basement steps, if you're not careful Frank, you'll have a conversation with Pedro, our resident rattlesnake."

The warden checked around his feet. The steps led down to the 'archeological archives,' which more accurately could be described as the trash heap in the basement. Department funding never was provided for secure protection for some of the priceless records and Native American artifacts poorly cataloged and held in storage there. Some were on display in the small museum on the first floor, which at least provided some degree of protection, but the lack of care in the basement was nothing short of criminal in Chris's mind. And more than once he had gone to look for something down there and found the rattler settled in the shade at the bottom of the cool cement steps.

"Put a Stetson on it and solve your staff shortage. At least nobody would mess with the pile of stuff you crammed down there in the dark."

Lt. James knew a lot about the park. He had been assigned to Central San Diego County for many years, and had started his career as a park ranger in Southern California, before switching over to Fish and Game to get the higher pay they somehow warranted in the gerrymandered mess that was the State pay scales. With unions and lobbyists and a legislature that could barely figure out how to pay for a cup of coffee, it wasn't likely to ever be a fair or well-organized system with equal pay for equal work.

"Frank, you've been around too long and you're getting cynical to boot. Besides, you know the only snakes we allow in the department are the spineless management guys in Sacramento."

"They aren't all in Sacramento Chris, I can name a few a lot lower down."

Chris knew he was referring to Dick Savage, the Superintendent in charge of Cuyamaca and Palomar State Parks. Savage was liked by very few who ever had to work for him, but like many managers, his ruthlessness often made him very popular with those above him.

"I'd watch what you say around management, my friend."

"I'm not afraid; I'm not looking to go anywhere else. I'm on cruise control. I keep telling you I've only got a few years left, and I can do that standing on my head. And your management can go stick it…"

Chris cut him off, "Nobody's perfect Frank. Did you find anything more about the puma? Has the collar started signaling movement?"

"Not as of yet, which kinda bothers me. See, lions don't go far from a kill when they make it, unless they've eaten their fill. The body didn't have much gone except a bit of the scalp, so I figure a cat should have been right close, probably watching us all take a piss in the woods there while the sheriff was doing the forensics gathering yesterday. The cat should have been right on it the moment we left. It would have gone back and seen the bloody deer carcass and been pleased as punch."

Chris still shivered at the thought that they had been watched the whole afternoon and evening by a killer cat. Even with all the scene lights the local volunteer fire department put up, it was still a low visibility environment and people were walking in and out of sight all night.

"Another thing bothers me Chris. When I got there and looked around the victim's body, there wasn't a single animal hair on him. He had on a pretty dark shirt. Those light colored hairs should have shown up easily. No hairs. Not on his clothes, not around where the bite marks were...nothing. That's not normal. It's not impossible, but a cat usually leaves hair at a scene. You ever had a house cat? They can't walk through a room without leaving hair on something!"

Chris thought of his battle with all the white hair on his green uniform jeans every day from his cat at home. He could vacuum a canister a week from the floor alone.

"So, what? Are you saying it's not a cat? Are you thinking bear? We don't have bears here that we know of, and even if we did California's black bears are pretty docile."

Chris' question had caught Frank mid sip on his coffee and he muttered into the cup, "I'd expect a lot different looking scene from a bear and the bite marks would be way different. I'm not saying it wasn't a cat; I'm just saying it just doesn't fit completely like I think it should." The remark echoed disturbingly from the bottom of his coffee cup.

"Do you have time to come into my office and go over this a bit more with me? I need to finish my report on it and you could help me with a couple details, especially considering what you have just brought up. Did you mention this to the sheriff's investigation team?"

38

"Those guys? They only had one plan, and that was to lay it off as an animal attack as soon as they saw the bite marks. They run their own show and aren't much interested in a country bumpkin game warden's opinion. I took off and found that deer to shoot so we could swap out the body and figured I'd done my part. The coroner and the DFG forensics lab will give us a clear answer on what killed him most likely. Fortunately, they didn't push to have the body checked only by the MD in the county morgue or we'd probably never have a clear answer."

Chris wasn't as negative about the Sheriff's people as Frank was, so he made a note in his mind to call them and fill them in at the homicide squad. He unlocked the back door to the Headquarters building and they walked in. The reception/dispatch room was dimly lit and he opened the blinds before they headed upstairs to his office. The walls were dark paneled and gloomy. Their heavy boots echoed on the wooden steps as they climbed to the second story offices. Chris had his office at the head of the stairs and they both barely fit in the small room. No luxury for Chief Rangers. Only recently had he finally gotten a padded office chair. Guests still sat in the straight backed wooden one he had used before. He flipped on the fluorescent fixture overhead and it quietly crackled and blinked to life, giving a cold and institutional illumination to the place.

As they sat down Chris asked, "Did you get the photos developed that you took yesterday?" Chris had hoped to get a broad perspective, photographically speaking, by being able to compare his shots with the ones Frank had taken. Besides, to be truthful, the 'good camera' Val used wasn't all that good, and he was always waiting for it to give out in the middle of an investigation.

"Yeah, I found a one hour photo place that was still open late last night in El Cajon and had one of my wardens drive all the way down there and back rather than wait to do it in Alpine this morning."

"We'll have to rely on your shots for the time being. I'm waiting on Val to bring ours in sometime today." He couldn't bring himself to add that Val would be bringing them in from Alpine. One of the drawbacks to living in the Park was no nearby photo developing, along with no pizza, no gas station, no…

Lt. James opened his briefcase and pulled out a fat pack of 4x6 photos and began to sort through them and lay some out on the desk in front of Chris.

As he slapped the last one down he said, "One other thing bothers me too."

Chris was curious why Frank hesitated, "What?"

"Well, it's not anything I can be sure about. It's just that the bite marks bother me."

"Just looking at them bothers me," Chris said. The gore and blood and the glassy eyed, half-lidded stare into eternity that the victim wore was enough to weaken any stomach.

"It's more than that. Bite marks vary from animal to animal. Just like us, their teeth are different. The spacing is unique as they grow, and it is unique between juveniles and adults, and it is very unique in distinguishing it from any other animal on the planet."

"Good, you've convinced me they are unique. We'll give this one a gold star award for oral hygiene from the American Dental Association for being special when we catch it. I'd give it a free bag of cat food but as we can see, it's already eaten."

"No, you're not getting my drift, partner. There is something unusual with this uniqueness, and I can't quite figure it out."

Chapter 5

The creamy white stucco walls and red-brown ceramic tiled roofs of Hepner Hall, Adams Humanities, Storm Hall, Nasitir Hall and all the other buildings speckled on the sprawling SDSU campus were daunting to Alicia even before she had gone inside any of them. Upon entrance, however, she was completely overwhelmed. While she had been to the campus once before, taking an orientation tour with her father and several other students and parents last spring, the college application process had been so streamlined that almost everything could be accomplished through the mail, or over the phone. So, here she found herself, staring at a maze of doors and hallways with no idea where to go. No tour guide this time. No dad either. She hated feeling like this, like a country girl in the big city, but the truth be told, that's what she was. Alicia felt completely lost in a sea of other students who seemed to know exactly where they were going.

"This is ridiculous!" She actually said this out loud. A young man passing by her on the other side of the hall looked at her curiously.

"Sorry, not you…" but he had already forgotten her and was on his way toward the outer door.

41

This time she was careful to reprimand herself silently, *"Buck up Buttercup, you've gone through much worse things. You can do this."*

Alicia started tentatively down the hall to her right, looking for signs of authority. Happily, her search was short and within minutes she found herself in line for Student Services. It seemed odd that there were only five people ahead of her in line. She thought there ought to be more last minute changes like hers. Perhaps the relative vacancy of the office was due to the impending lunch hour. Only two service windows were open, the other four were closed tightly with little white signs dangling on them that read "Next window, please." This made the line move slower than she had first hoped, and by the time her turn came, she had been standing there for twenty-two minutes.

"Can I help you?" The young man peered above the partition separating his side of the counter from that of his customers.

"Hi, I sure hope so," she stepped up and put her small purse on the counter next to her, poised to rifle through it for any bit of identification or information he might ask for.

"Ok, well, are you a student here?"

"Yes. Well, I will be when the semester starts."

"And what is your social?"

Alicia was still not used to being identified by a number rather than her name. It felt impersonal and creepy, but she rattled it off to him none-the-less. She had the feeling that before her college career was over she would wish she could just tattoo the number on her forehead. Now that really would be creepy.

"Let's see, Alicia Nicole Becker, right?"

"Yes, that's me."

"I notice we only have a P.O. Box in Julian listed for your address."

"Well, yes, that is the correct mailing address."

"Right, but we need your physical address as well." His glasses and wildly curly dark hair made him look like one of the characters in *Weird*

42

Science. He peered at her above his horn-rimmed frames and waited with thinly veiled impatience.

She wanted so badly to answer with a smart remark, to ask him, "Why, are you planning on coming over?" However, it was clear that she needed this guy to be on her side, especially since what she was here to do might prove difficult enough without antagonizing those who could help her. So, she took a different tack.

"Oh, I'm sorry about that. We live out in the country where there really isn't any mail service…in a State Park, actually," she smiled hopefully at him. Sometimes that revelation was enough to spark a conversation and interject some real humanity into an otherwise cold business exchange. No such luck this time.

"Uh-huh, but you still have a physical address, so what is it?"

"Sure, its 27755 Hwy 79, Descanso, California."

"Thank you. Ok, everything else seems to be in order, so what can I help you with today."

"I would like to change my minor from Biology to Anthropology and then change my classes accordingly." She debated batting her eyelashes and smiling vacuously in an attempt to soften the blow of her request, but decided to go there only as a last resort.

"We'll see what can be done, but I must say it is fairly late in the registration period to be making such changes." His disapproving look made him appear much more fatherly than she would have expected his obvious youth to allow. For a moment he was forty-something instead of barely twenty.

"Any help you can give me would be great." She smiled, took an imperceptible step toward him, leaned into the laminated oak counter and waited, eyelashes at the ready.

He eyed her steadily, gauging her sincerity, looking at her as a guy looking at a girl for the first time. He appeared to be reserving judgment, for now.

"To be honest, changing your minor isn't a big deal, and dropping Bio 101 isn't a problem either. The part that gets sticky is adding the Anthro 101 in its place. That class is pretty popular, and currently all three sections of it are full." His eyes shifted from the keyboard to her face. She felt almost as if he were daring her.

"Isn't there anything that can be done?" Cue the eyelashes.

He hesitated and then said, "Well, there is always the possibility of getting the teacher's signature to over-ride the class size limitations. It's pretty simple, actually. All you do is take this form to the professor and explain your case. If they think you seem serious, they will usually accept you in the class." He handed her the form.

"Is that it?"

"Once Dr. Whiteside signs it, bring it back here and I'll get you all set up in the system." He seemed to be warming to her.

"Thanks. Where is Dr. Whiteside's office?"

"Oh, that's easy. Come over to the window and I'll show you." He opened the small swinging door that barred the entrance to the counter where his window was, and strode toward the huge bank of windows on the far side of the room, beckoning her to follow him.

"Ok, his office is in Storm Hall," he pointed as he spoke, "see, past the Library and Hepner Hall, on the far side of the campus."

She felt disoriented and tried to follow his gaze, but in truth her mind was swimming as he rattled off the names to her.

He seemed to tell that she was confused and not following his description, "No, over here," he put one hand lightly on each of her shoulders, and pivoted her slightly to the left. He let them linger there an instant longer than necessary. Definitely not her type, and Alicia wondered if he was warming to her too much?

"I have a break coming up in about 10 minutes, I could walk you over there if you want." Clearly warm had moved to hopeful.

She decided she had better extract herself tactfully, "Oh, I see it now. Thanks so much for your help, but I don't want to take any more of your time. I can find it, and then I'll be back with the form." She smiled, genuine but slightly vacant, trying to sever whatever emotional connection he was trying to make. "Thanks again." She looked over her shoulder after a few steps and smiled again.

"No problem. Remember, Storm Hall. Oh, and this office closes at 4:00, so…" his voice trailed off and he seemed to shrug the encounter off as he walked back to the counter and squeezed back through the spring loaded doors. Alicia heard him say "next" to the person at the head of the line as she rounded the heavy oak doorframe and headed down the busy hall.

*   *   *

It took her what seemed like forever to locate Storm Hall. She found herself wondering if she should have taken that clerk up on his offer of a chaperone, but in the end she made it to the threshold of Dr. Whiteside's office. She tapped lightly on the doorframe, and was greeted with a loud "Come in!"

"Dr. Whiteside?"

Alicia stepped into the room. She saw a man, well really mostly saw just his long-ish graying hair, because he was hunched over his desk working on something, and all that was visible from the door was the top of his head. The room was stacked with books and papers in disarray, and shelves on the wall held pieces of pottery and what appeared to be primitive tools.

"What can I do for you?" He looked up from his work, gave her a quick once-over, and bent down again.

In his brief glance up, she hadn't gotten much of an impression of the man. He hadn't really looked her in the eye, or even smiled.

"Sir," her father had always taught her to be respectful, "I just changed my minor to Anthropology, and I was hoping to add your Intro to

45

Anthropology class, but I was told it was full and I would need your permission to add it at this point."

He straightened fully in his chair and looked directly at her for the first time. He appeared to be sizing her up, and while she wondered what conclusions he was drawing about her blue jeans and t-shirt, she couldn't help but notice some things about him as well. For one thing, she may have to let go of her idea that all college professors wore suits and ties. Dr. Whiteside was living proof of that. He looked like something out of an old Western. His shirt was a creamy white with the classic pointed yokes and silver-edged, pearlized buttons of a western style dress shirt. Instead of a tie he had a black bolo with a silver steer head loosely cinched around his neck. On the credenza she noticed a broad white cowboy hat with a heavily beaded and feathered band.

"What's your major?" She expected more of a Texas drawl from someone dressed as he was, but his words were crisp, with a slight East Coast lilt to them.

"English."

"English, huh, well that's not a bad companion for Anthropology. Were you thinking Linguistic Anthro?"

"No, actually, I was leaning more toward Socio-Cultural."

"Oh, well, that would work too. Literature is socio-cultural at its core, right?" He smiled, a big, large-toothed white smile. In fact she was realizing that everything about him was large. Not fat, just large. His shoulders were much too broad for the desk chair in which he was now sitting. His arms were meaty and tapered to wide hands with short stumpy fingers that somehow reminded her of sausages.

"Yes, I thought the two would make a nice complement." It was true, to some extent, but it was also true that Anthro minors don't require many units, and English majors require so many units that a minor isn't even mandatory. She hated to be wasteful with the extra classes she had to take, and wanted to wrap them up in some usable package, and Anthropology had been the most appealing of the choices. However, now that he had

46

pointed out the correlations in the two disciplines, Alicia was starting to think this could really be a good choice.

Dr. Whiteside pushed his chair back and stood up, grabbing the shiny metal object that he had been working on off of his desk. He was tall, as she had suspected, and as he walked around the corner of the well-worn desk, she could see that very new looking black jeans and a pair of grayish-green ostrich skin boots completed his outfit.

As he took another step toward her, his hands went to his belt and he began fumbling with the buckle. In her mind flashed all the Hollywood stories of teacher-student affairs, and she wondered if he had misunderstood how far she was willing to go to get into his class. Worse yet, she was painfully aware that her slight 5'6" frame was no match for his bulk if this came down to a physical confrontation. Still, she thought she could make it pretty unpleasant for him.

"Dr. Whiteside..." her voice was less forceful than she had hoped and she took and involuntary step backwards.

"Here bring me that paper to sign. You have the form right?" Both hands were at his belt now, and she wasn't sure whether she should be getting ready to kick him in the shins or run, when he seemed to make some final adjustment and removed his hands to reveal the shiny object now proudly displayed at his midsection. He hadn't been getting ready to remove his belt, he had instead been re-attaching the belt buckle he had been working on at his desk when she walked in. From the pristine shine of the thing, he had been cleaning it, spit-polishing it presumably as there was no evidence of solvent.

"Pretty nice piece of antiquity, isn't it...and I got it for a song," he said.

Alicia released all the breath she didn't realize she had been holding in one great whoosh, "Sure is...here it is," and stepped up and put the papers on his desk.

He signed them in several unintelligible strokes of an honest to goodness ballpoint quill pen, and then smiled at her and reached his hand

47

out to shake. As his meaty paw engulfed hers, she found herself profoundly aware of how vulnerable she would have been if this meeting had gone the way of her imagining.

"I think you'll do well. Look forward to seeing you in class Miss…" he looked down at the form, "Becker. Now you'll have to excuse me, I have a tee-time in half an hour." With that he brushed past her to the hallway and held the door open for her until she passed through it and then locked it behind her.

"Thanks again, Dr. Whiteside." He nodded and was off down the hall. She stared after him for a minute or two. Not only was he breaking every idea she had about professors, but now she was wondering about golfers, too. She tried to picture him out on the links in that get-up. She chuckled to herself at the image and retraced her steps to the quad in search of a shady spot, figuring she'd better grab some lunch before facing the registration clerk again.

*   *   *

Alicia sat on a bench in the shade of a large pepper tree in one of the small courtyards of the campus reviewing her receipt from the bookstore. Things had gone fine at the registration office after lunch. Things had even gone fine in the bookstore, and she had found all the texts required by her teachers, most of them used and therefore a reduced price. Nonetheless, here she sat wondering what kind of math could explain how seventeen books had cost over $560! That averaged out to be more than $30 a book, and most were books someone else had already owned! She knew she didn't have that much in her account, and she was pretty sure her father couldn't afford to pay that much either, and yet the charge was there, on his credit card. She felt sick. She dreaded having to tell her dad how much she had put on his card.

Suddenly she could feel her purse shiver against her leg. Her phone was on vibrate.

"Hello," she said, sure it was her dad and that Murphy's Law had conspired to force her to tell him the bad news without any easing into it or preparation.

"Hey Nick." Only one person in the world referred to her by the shortened version of her middle name.

"Michael, I'm so glad it's you!" And she was probably the only person who hadn't switched to calling him Mike by the time he was in eighth grade.

"It's nice to be appreciated. I tried calling you twice at home, and once on your cell, where are you?"

"I've been at State trying to figure out my classes and draining my father's bank account. You know, a typical day in the life of aristocratic American youth such as ourselves." It was nice to be able to joke about it at least.

"Yes, I know exactly what you mean, I spent my 'typical day' framing a house." Michael had been in Americorps for two months, ever since the week after graduation. He had spent most of the intervening time working on rebuilding homes in Texas for Tropical Storm Allison victims. Part of his 'aristocratic youth' would involve at least three years devoted to this service based group in order to earn enough scholarship money for college. His father was a professional man, but there were three older siblings who had already cleaned out the college coffers, and his mother had been sick for the last several years. Any extra money the family had went to her care. So, in terms of higher education, Michael was pretty much on his own.

"Nice…good to know you are picking up some manly skills."

"Yes, and from the sounds of it, you may need to develop whatever kind of skills keep you from getting eaten by lions!"

"Oh, you heard about what happened at the park? I didn't know the media had gotten a hold of that on any national level."

"They didn't. I check the local news there on the internet sometimes, you know, just see what's going on in your neck of the woods. Anyway, there was an article about it. I was a bit worried about you. Is your dad

49

getting a lot of crap again from the environmentalists about this lion, like he did last time?"

"I don't really know. The whole thing only happened yesterday. They haven't even figured out what lion did it, as far as I know. But my dad is kinda freaking about me being careful outside."

"Like you are ever *not* careful!"

"Hey, what's that supposed to mean?!"

"Nothing, nothing. Oh, I gotta go. The boss is calling me. Break time is over. Keep me posted on all this stuff, and hey, do be careful, ...promise?"

"Yeah, yeah. Bye."

She flipped the phone closed, then flipped it open again, deciding she had better call her dad before she started for home. Maybe he wouldn't ask specific questions, and she would have time to ease into the subject of their destitution. Her fingers pushed the familiar sequence of numbers and waited for the connection to be made.

Chapter 6

Becker wasn't sold on Frank James' skepticism about the sheriff's investigation at the lion scene, but one thing that Chris had noticed in the aftermath of finding the body, which he didn't mention to Frank James, was that he was curious about what the victim was doing on the trail in the first place. He got all kinds of visitors in Cuyamaca, but he was struck by the fact that the victim was wearing a type of fancy dress shoe that simply didn't fit with the average hiker--not that it was unheard of for people to come up from San Diego expecting sidewalks in the wilderness. Chris had seen people in all sorts of dress, so anything was possible. Still, as he watched Frank James drive off in his irritatingly well-equipped agency patrol rig, he wondered about the lion attack victim's reason for being in the wrong place at the wrong time.

He knew if he were graced with good equipment and adequate staff he could investigate the cougar killing much more effectively, but his agency consistently took a back seat to active participation in cases like this. He considered what happened in *his* backyard to be *his* problem to solve, but he knew Dick Savage would be on his case if he even smelled a hint of investigation. He was supposed to be a Park Ranger, feeling ferns and conducting nature walks. *"Old school"* managers never could accept the full peace officer status that had been conferred on rangers, even though it had happened twenty years ago, nor did they want to waste precious park budgets on investigative activities. Still, if he were careful, he might at least find out a little about the victim without arousing too much curiosity from upper management.

He could hear a door opening and muffled footsteps in the office downstairs as he got ready to leave. If he got going right now he could beat the Superintendent coming in the office and maybe find out a little bit about this fellow on the trail before he got completely shut down.

The downstairs office was still green with reflected light, from a reluctant to rise morning sun barely peeking through the Dyar house's thick oak trees. The office clerk put her purse in her desk and she turned and smiled at the sound of his footfalls.

"Mornin' Chris," she was round faced and her ruddy complexion gave the impression of always being freshly and vigorously scrubbed.

As Becker came down the last step of the stairs he said, "Jane, I'll be out on some errands most of the day. Let Val know when she comes in that if she gets any information back from Fish and Game, or the Sheriff, she is to call me right away."

"Do you want me to tell Dick where you can be reached?"

"Just tell him I had several stops to make, and I'll be back this afternoon."

She forced the desk drawer shut on her oversize leather bag and looked up at Chris. Jane was no dummy and probably suspected he was up to something, but he wasn't going to ask her to lie for him.

He purposely kept it vague as he added, "I'll be out in the field all day on the radio if you need anything."

Jane was opening windows in the cramped, dingy office as he took off in his Jeep for El Cajon. The victim's ID showed him with an address there, and since Chris had found no phone number on the body, he figured it was as good a place as any to start. The sheriff would know more, but as proprietary as they could be with information he was reluctant at this point to give them any reason to warn him off the death investigation.

Highway 79 was relatively clear, and most of Interstate 8 was a smooth trip as well, until around Fletcher Parkway, where the traffic thickened like butterscotch pudding on a hot stove. The crowds and smog of the city were depressing to Becker, even though the San Diego area was probably better than most of the west coast metropolitan towns.

August usually cooked the sulphurous concoctions from the over-abundant cars into a dusty haze that muted all the colors, but today was fairly clear as the coastal breeze revealed the green leaves and flaming red blooms of the oleander forming an ornamental barrier between the East and West bound lanes of the freeway. This lush but poisonous plant had somehow been elected as the greenery of choice for Southern California freeways, and Chris wondered if it should have been the choice for the state flower instead of the poppy. But he couldn't stay cynical for long. The day was lovely and the breeze had cleared the air and allowed San Diego to show off the relaxed tropical beauty for which it was famous. Even the sky was a pure crystalline blue for a change.

Fortunately for him, the place he was looking for was just off Fletcher where it paralleled the freeway, and he soon found the address. It was a run-down 1970s style box of two story apartments with a nearly dead lawn and faded green stucco walls that would soon be in need of paint. The building ran the length of half the block, which if he was generous, could be described as lower middle class. It had a small, dark entry alcove on each end. Occasional small houses separated other apartment complexes in a neighborhood that was clearly under the stress of urbanization and economic dislocation.

Chris checked the mailboxes and verified that Xavier Hess was in fact listed as a resident of the *Remington Arms Apartments and Suites*, at least according to the Marks-A-Lot handwritten #29 next to his name on the box, before heading up the open staircase to the second floor residence. As he walked along the outdoor hallway, he noticed two bikini-clad young

53

women reclining on somewhat dilapidated folding chairs in the central courtyard below. In years past, Chris would have enjoyed the view more, but now all he could think was that it was a shame such attractive girls were so dedicated to getting an early start on baking their skin into polished leather. Not that it mattered much to him since he had been dating infrequently of late, and an evening out with a woman seemed more like a job interview than a social opportunity. For him, it was rare to make it to a third date.

"I am definitely getting old," He muttered under his breath as he turned away from the view and checked the numbers to the right of each door. There it was, #29. The shades were drawn on the apartment window, and as he was about to knock a second time a short, red-eyed woman of about thirty pulled the curtain back to peek out.

"Mrs. Hess?" When she nodded he continued, "I'm Chris Becker from Cuyamaca State Park. I'd like to talk to you about your husband for a few minutes if I could."

The uniform opened some doors and definitely closed others. This time the curtain fell back and the door pulled open.

"Thank you for speaking with me, I know this must be a hard time for you." His voice trailed off and he realized his hands were fumbling with the non-regulation State Park ball cap he had unconsciously removed from his head as he had begun speaking. Funny, the automatic gestures that came in the presence of so raw a grief.

The woman looked lost to Chris, in the way that starving African children have that vacant thousand-yard stare. She didn't say a word as he stepped inside the darkened living room. The place appeared small and crowded with knick-knacks and wall hangings of various kinds. The effect was positive, in spite of the small space. A tiny kitchen opened on the living room with a hall that Chris assumed led to a bedroom and bathroom.

Her voice was soft, but with a tobacco huskiness far advanced for her age. Chris guessed she must have started smoking when she was about ten. "The sheriff's investigators were here yesterday evening to tell me about my husband. They said he had been killed by a mountain lion."

54

"The facts seem to support that possible theory Mrs. Hess, and I'm just doing some follow up for my report on the case. I'm so sorry about your husband. Was he a guy who liked to hike in the woods a lot?"

The woman took a seat on the leather sofa. "Xavier, no, he was a construction contractor and rarely had time for anything but work. If he took a walk around the block in the evening it would have been a surprise to me. I can't imagine what he was doing up there unless it was something about work. He was always out trying to get projects to bid on. Even at night he would meet with project managers to discuss jobs."

Chris wondered about a man meeting at night with project managers. Could this guy have been up to other nighttime "conferences" and telling his wife it was for work? The thought came unbidden and he had no reason to think that about Hess, but it wouldn't be the first guy to be meeting the local coffee shop barista for a late-night drink, or an unobserved hike in the woods. He sat down in the chair opposite the sofa. "So, do you think he could have just stopped to stretch his legs for a bit in the park?"

"No, if my husband wanted to stretch his legs it would have been under a table with a beer on it. He just wasn't that sort of active outdoor-type guy. Is the park bidding out any jobs for paving contracts that he might have been checking on? He didn't share a lot about his business with me on a day-to-day basis." She began to root in a half full pack of Camel Lights. "A few years ago I used to work on the books, but I finally quit that to go back to school." She snapped the lighter.

"Was there anyone that might have had a grudge with your husband?"

Her eyes widened. "I thought he was killed by a cougar, are you saying he wasn't?"

Chris was upset with himself for getting her disturbed and off track this way. He mentally kicked himself for asking the question.

"No, but since the autopsy report isn't in we just have to ask routine questions for my report just to be complete and avoid being criticized for not doing my job carefully."

She seemed to accept that, even if Becker didn't.

She took a deep drag and said, "Enemies?" she exhaled slowly, "It's the construction industry. Everyone is mad at someone most of the time. You don't get your job done on time and it affects some other guy's company. They are always yelling at each other over something. Then there are the guys who just do lousy work and you have to go out and do it over when the customer isn't satisfied."

He shifted his gaze from her face to the rest of the apartment. Hess's wife was pretty plain looking, much like the furniture, but Becker couldn't help but notice that in spite of the ordinariness of the apartment, the knick-knacks were unusual, and he realized many were Native American pots and art. The rug on the wall was an ornate Navajo design and if he guessed correctly was an original worth a fair amount of money. He wondered about the ceramics and their value.

Chris had made the mistake of stereotyping this young guy and his wife into "construction worker types," something he was always cautioning Alicia against. He'd figured them for off road motorcycles and nights at the bars. Maybe they were contractors by day, and burgeoning art collectors by night. Mrs. Hess had said she had gone back to school. Maybe it was to pursue a degree in Art History or Native American Studies. Or, it was just as plausible that they had inherited these things from some eccentric old uncle and were selling them off to pay for her college classes. He wondered what other stereotypes and pre-judgments he was setting himself up for on this case. Just the fact that he was calling it a "case" was a pre-judgment that it didn't deserve.

"Do you have children?"

"No, we talked about family, but we wanted to wait until I finished school and the construction business was going well. We haven't been doing very well on the construction bids, and several equipment breakdowns have cost a lot of money in the last two years. I finish my last year at San Diego State next spring and was looking forward to a job for a while before having a baby."

56

She swept her limp dishwater blond hair from her eyes, and Chris could tell the woman was near tears so he changed the subject.

"That is a beautiful wall hanging you have there. Is it Navajo?"

"Yes, it's a Navajo camp rug from the early 1900s. It's not a particularly valuable one, but I like its pattern and colors. My husband was fond of collecting artifacts like these wherever he could buy them. Sometimes we'd go out and…"

She stopped, and Chris wondered if it was emotional memories or if she realized she was about to say something she shouldn't. He waited, but she left it unsaid.

"So, did your husband's company specialize in paving?"

"Yes, but we often made most of our profit in excavation work and lately were doing more of that in small projects all over the county. Xavier may have been up there looking at one of them when…" She trailed off without mentioning her husband being killed.

Chris figured this was about as much as he could hope to get from her at this point without knowing more about her husband's official cause of death. He had hoped for more, and he still hadn't satisfied himself about why Hess was out on the Azalea trail.

"Well, I guess that's about all at this point Mrs. Hess, we'll be in touch if we know more and if we manage to catch the lion. We still have a team out there searching."

"Do you have children, Ranger Becker?"

Her question caught him off guard, and he paused at the door. "Yes, ma'am, I do. A teenage girl, and oh boy—what a time of life that is!"

"You must have started out young with your family. You and your wife made the right decision," she said wistfully.

Chris suspected that her husband was the one who wanted her to finish school and not have children. Being in business for yourself, and buying diapers too, wasn't always easy. Throw in the occasional art purchase, and that could be a real financial strain.

Chris smiled and extended his hand to her, "Thank you for your time, Mrs. Hess. I'll be in touch."

"Pamela," she smiled and put her small, soft hand in his and shook his almost imperceptibly. "Thank you for coming all the way out here. Xavier was a stickler for details. He would have liked it that you were trying to get your report right. Somehow that makes me sort of feel better." Her smile weakened, and she looked away as her hand went limp and dropped to her side.

Clearly she was spent. Chris put his hat back on and tipped the brim slightly in her direction, all in one fluid movement, walking quietly out the door and shutting it behind himself. He felt oddly chivalrous. She somehow saw him as a champion for her husband, getting the details right and all that. He only hoped the details wouldn't reveal something that would hurt that poor woman more.

Hurt. The subject of children and a wife had set him to thinking again about his own situation. Obviously, Lori hadn't thought it was the right decision to have a child. Once again, he wondered what she was doing at this very moment. As he drove toward the Interstate his cell phone rang, and he glanced at the caller ID, and smiled to see that "the child" in question was on the line.

"Hey, Dad, I finished the registration stuff and I'm going to be heading home in just a few minutes."

"How did it go?"

"I'll tell you all about it when you get home, but basically everything is working out OK."

"Good, I'm in my work Jeep and we need milk. Would you pick some up before you get back to the house? You know I don't like doing personal stuff in the Cherokee, and I'm not sure, but I may have to work a little late tonight again." Chris knew he would have to catch up on the office work he had left undone in order to interview Mrs. Hess or he'd hear about it from the boss. His monthly reports were already overdue, and he knew Savage would be expecting a nice clean "accident" report on the lion killing.

Chapter 7

The serpentine roadway of Interstate 8 stretched eastbound in front of Alicia as she motored back towards the mountains. She hated her father's aversion to stopping for groceries or other necessities while in his work vehicle, and she hated it even more that ever since she had gotten her driver's license, that duty had invariably found its way into her jurisdiction. To make matters worse, she had been so engrossed in the Sue Grafton book on CD she had been listening to on the way home that she had not only missed her intended stop at the Vons on Los Coches road, but had also flown by her fallback option of the Daniel's Market in Alpine. She had been in that autopilot mode where all roads lead home. Now she was cursing herself as she made the turn-off to Highway 79 and began the winding journey up to Cuyamaca.

"Well, off to Julian it is," she muttered to herself, grudgingly acknowledging that her only viable option now was to drive all the way to the Park, past her house and the Hillside Resort, Harrison Park, and all the intervening 15 miles into Julian to do her dreaded marketing.

In truth, it wasn't such a bad idea to go into Julian. She could get the mail and get some groceries at Jack's. Maybe she could even get a treat to bring home to her dad…to soften the blow of the cost of her books.

"Yes…ha, ha, I'll use his sweet tooth to my advantage," she did her best evil sorceress impression, but felt rather foolish speaking to herself in exotic voices, and consequently spent the rest of the trip to town in silence.

After rounding the bend by the Lookout Point and passing Jess Martin Park, the first of her errands presented itself. At the intersection of Hwy 79 and Hwy 78, the large gray structure of the Julian Post Office loomed to her right. She turned into the parking lot and found a space close to the entrance. She emptied the box in record time, not even bothering to sift through the letters and bills and junk mail to see what might have her name on it. Instead, she threw it unceremoniously onto the seat next to her and edged back onto the road, turning left and heading into the main section of town. Parallel parking was not her strong suit, her dad always said her attempts reminded him of docking maneuvers on the Space Shuttle, so instead of embarrassing herself trying to do that, she opted for the small parking lot in the rear of the store.

Her time that day at the College had been used wisely, but somehow the day had drifted by. As she entered Jack's Grocery, she noticed her watch and was surprised to discover that it was already 4:10 pm. In terms of shopping, this was a perfect time. All the townies would have gone home by now, but the working stiffs stopping by to pick up a few things on their way home wouldn't be arriving for another hour, so she should have the place pretty much to herself. In terms of dinner, though, this was bad. She had to get back home and start cooking something. As her dad had so gleefully reminded her this morning, it was her night to cook, and she had no idea what to make.

She was staring blankly at the cuts of meat encased in the glass display cabinet when the checker on duty called from across the room.

"The pork chops are good today, and I bet your dad might like them. I can give you a quick recipe if you want."

60

Alicia spun around, startled by the familiar voice, tinged with the slightest hint of an accent, "Marina, hey, how's it going?" She covered the ten or so steps separating them in a second or two. "I haven't seen you for a while, what's up?" She wondered if Marina was right about her dad liking the chops. It was kind of strange for anyone else to estimate what her father would like. Alicia was so used to being the only one thinking that way.

"Not much is going on for me. How about you? College must be starting soon. Are you excited?" Marina's smile was broad and white, with just the slightest hint of a dimple on one side. The effect of this against her café au lait skin was quite nice. She was a pretty woman, but not shockingly beautiful. Perhaps her most striking feature was her dark brown hair, thick and loosely braided over one shoulder.

"Excited or scared…I can't decide which it is! Either way the butterflies in my stomach are the same!" Alicia made a fluttery gesture in front of her mid-section and a half-pained expression on her face for emphasis.

"Oh, Alicia, you'll do fine, don't worry. It must be hard for your dad to see you growing up so fast, though."

That was the second time she had mentioned her dad, which was odd because they weren't really friends. Sure, they knew each other, everyone in town knew everyone else, at least by sight if not by name, but Alicia was pretty sure that Marina and her father had never said more than a dozen words to each other.

"I guess. He doesn't really talk about it that much, but sometimes he looks kind of sad and I wonder if it's about me, or my mom." Alicia let the words drift off into nothingness, wishing she hadn't brought up her mother. It was too painful and private to talk about, even with someone as nice as Marina. "Anyway, he will probably wish I had already grown up and moved away tonight when I have to show him the bill for the books I put on his credit card!"

"Ah, yes, I remember those days. School books are so expensive. I struggled with the burden I was putting on my parents by going to college.

61

After two years I took a break to help the family, but then my father got sick, and I met my husband, and my Casey was born. Before you know it you are thirty-two! I never went back to school. Enjoy it while you can Sweetie…life sneaks up on you fast!"

There were a lot of gaps in that story that Alicia wished she had the time to ask about. Especially what had happened to Marina's husband. That was a huge mystery. What she didn't need to ask about was how much Marina loved her son. That little three-year-old cutie was the center of her world; Alicia had witnessed that for herself plenty of times when Marina and Casey would come in for a late lunch on Saturdays. They always got the special, an order of onion rings on the side, and washed it all down with a huge chocolate shake. They split everything fifty-fifty, down to the last slurp of ice-creamy goodness. Alicia had never seen anyone who looked like a husband, or an ex-husband anywhere around. Come to think of it, she had never seen Marina with any man. She wore a ring on her wedding finger, but it was silver with a feather motif and a large oval amethyst in the middle. Not exactly a typical wedding ring.

For now the status of Marina's romantic entanglements would have to remain a mystery because she had begun rattling off instructions for her special pork chops.

"Do you need me to write that down for you, or can you remember?"

Alicia couldn't admit that she had daydreamed through the first half of the recipe, so she just shook her head, saying, "Better write it down to be sure. In fact, while you do that, I'll just grab the last few things I need."

Marina nodded and smiled, but she was already muttering to herself as she scribbled on the back of an old coupon. Alicia only caught a few words before she was out of earshot, "Pre-heat oven to…" She smiled to herself. Somehow the brief conversations she had with this kind woman made her feel simultaneously good, and kind of sad. Sad in that they were in passing and far between. She wished that there was a woman in her life, and wondered for the hundredth, or perhaps thousandth time if her mother ever thought of her.

After grabbing a loaf of bread, half-gallon of milk, and some oat bran cereal she went back toward the register to check on Marina's progress. She found that there was another customer who had recently come in, and that Marina was ringing up the carton of cigarettes the young man had bought. She could tell at a glance that it was Marcus Lundee. His black hair and leather jacket were unmistakable. Alicia ducked back behind the aisle, hoping the bags of tortilla and potato chips would shield her from his view. She hated herself for hiding from him. It was like she was some frightened schoolgirl hoping the big bully wouldn't take her lunch money. That thought was enough to propel her forward. She raised her chin and brushed her hair from her face, and tried to look as aloof and detached as possible. She felt she would have been supremely successful, had it not been for the unfortunate collision of her basket with the Cool Ranch Doritos. Several bags cascaded to the floor around her.

Alicia's mind registered the little shriek Marina gave as though it were far away. For a brief moment she stood there in complete silence, unmoving, in disbelief. She wished the floor would swallow her, and her basket, and the blasted Doritos in one big bite. But of course, that did not happen. What did happen, was, in fact, far more astonishing. Marcus, without a word or a look, put his carton of cigarettes on the counter, strode over to her, picked up all seven bags of Doritos in one fell swoop, stuffed them back on the empty shelf, then walked back to the check out and retrieved his smokes. It all happened so fast, that Alicia had barely realized what his intention was before he was done and on the other side of the room again. This was completely unexpected. Marcus did not strike her as her idea of a perfect gentleman. She stood there dumbfounded, wondering if perhaps she had misjudged him.

Marcus took the two or three steps to the door backwards, and nudged the door open with his right hip, waving to Marina with his free hand as he leaned back on the door to open it fully. Then, just as his body began to turn away and head out the door, he finally looked at Alicia. His dark eyes bore straight into hers. His expression was unreadable, and then slowly that

63

familiar slight upturn of his lip. That smile. It always made her feel like a mouse being toyed with by the neighborhood cat. And then he winked at her. She could feel the blood coming up to her cheeks, and she knew from bitter experience that her face was now becoming bright red. As much as she loved the auburn tinge her scant Scottish heritage had given to her hair, she detested the way it made her face so quick to flush. She further despised the fact that the last thing Marcus had seen was her blushing, and he knew he was the cause of it.

Alicia walked, with the air of one defeated, to the cash register. As she placed her purchases on the counter, Marina finally spoke.

"Well, Sweetie, you sure know how to make an impression on a man."

Alicia looked directly into Marina's eyes and saw the mirth thinly veiled there. "You are laughing at me!" she exclaimed, her indignation somewhat genuine and somewhat exaggerated.

"No, I'm not…not really. It was a funny situation, but I know it wasn't funny for you. I was laughing more at the silent exchange between you and that boy. I've never seen Marcus do anything chivalrous, and I've never seen you blush like that before! Do you two know each other? More importantly, do you two have something going on with each other?" The mirth in Marina's eyes had changed to a conspiratorial inquisitiveness.

Now Alicia's indignation was full and sincere. "Absolutely NOT!! He is the most infuriating person I know! As if it's not bad enough that I have to work with him at Hillside, now I have to be subjected to him during my errands as well!"

"Oh, Sweetie, I'm sorry. I shouldn't have teased you. I didn't realize there was a history between you."

"It's not much of a history. He just started working at the restaurant a month or two ago, but he sure has been giving me the 'full court press' ever since," Alicia said, as she reached into her purse and produced a twenty dollar bill and handed it to Marina.

"Well, I'm sorry that he is giving you a hard time, but if today is any indication, it looks like he really likes you," she finished counting out Alicia's change and handed her the bag with her items.

"Lucky me."

"You may want to give him a bit of a break. I think he's had a rough time of it lately."

"What do you mean?"

"I'm not sure of the exact situation, but I think his mother is ill and his dad doesn't seem to be in the picture. He mentioned something to me about looking for a second job. I actually told him that the boss was looking for someone at night to take deliveries and clean up after closing. He's been working here for a while."

"I had no idea."

"Just something to keep in mind next time he is making you crazy," Marina's smile was gentle and had that motherly twinge to it. Alicia got the distinct impression she was being taught some sort of lesson. She didn't have much time to ponder the implications of it though, as Marina was escorting her to the door and giving her a quick hug.

"The recipe is in the bag too, Sweetie. Let me know how your dad likes it, OK?" Alicia watched as the older woman turned and ambled back into the store. She realized, after a moment of standing on the sidewalk trying to look for her car, that Marina had ushered her out the front door, when she had parked in the back. This meant that she would either have to walk back through the store, or around the corner and down the block to access the parking lot on foot. Since she planned to visit the Julian Pie Company anyway, which was situated just past the corner of the block Jack's was on, she decided to walk there instead.

As she rounded the corner onto the planked walkway in front of the pie store, the faded red screen door opened to reveal a round-faced girl with mouse-brown hair streaked with peroxide blond.

"I saw you coming from the corner. What's in the bag?" Dawn Mills was the kind of girl you might call 'pleasantly plump,' although she wouldn't have said there was anything pleasant about it.

"Just stuff for dinner. It's my night to cook, but I don't have time to make dessert, and I sure could use one tonight."

Dawn looked at her blankly. Sometimes Alicia felt like she had to do most of the heavy lifting in this relationship.

"I was thinking about a pie or something." She waited.

Finally Dawn got what she was hinting at, "Oh, well, there are a couple that didn't sell from yesterday. I could probably give you one of those. They are too old for us to try to sell tomorrow."

"Oh, that would be great. I don't want to get you in trouble though." This was the portion of the conversation involving the obligatory apologies and 'are you sures' that she always went through every time Dawn gave her a pie, which at this point was about twice a month. Alicia might have felt guilty about this if it weren't for the fact that she had single-handedly enabled Dawn to pass twelfth grade English, even though Alicia herself was only in the eleventh grade at the time. She figured that these pies were fair payment for an entire year of tutoring.

"No it's fine. What do you want. We have apple, Dutch apple, or Strawberry Rhubarb?"

This was a no-brainer. "I'll take the Rhubarb. Thanks so much. You're a lifesaver! My Dad's gonna freak when he sees the bill for my books!"

"Oh, that's right, you've got the college thing starting soon. See, that's another reason I'm glad I'm taking a couple years off. At least I have some spending money. No matter how much you work, you're going to be broke paying all those bills and gas, not to mention all the time you have to spend studying. I couldn't do that. I need to party while I'm young."

Alicia resisted the urge to try to explain the relative value of partying and working in your uncle's pie shop, versus working hard and going to college so you could someday have a rewarding career. It would have been lost on the girl anyway. She just had very different priorities.

"Speaking of partying, Vic and I were out yesterday morning on that same trail where that guy died! Can you believe it? Freaky!" Dawn had to shout that last word, as she had gone into the back room and was digging in the refrigerator for the rhubarb pie.

"What were you guys doing up there?" Alicia didn't realize until after the words had escaped the confines of her mouth how lame they made her sound. Obviously she could guess what Dawn and her 23 year old boyfriend had been doing out alone in the wilderness. Sadly, Dawn decided to explain it to her.

She popped back around the corner from the store room. "Oh, well Vic got some weed from some guy he knows, and so we were up there trying some of it before I came to work." She got a box from under the counter and put the pie into it. "I mean, we were doing some other stuff too…" Dawn let the sentence trail off, but shot Alicia a knowing look.

Alicia felt her stomach actually turn at the thought of doing "other stuff" with Vic Morrison. She felt sorry that Dawn thought so little of herself that she would go to such lengths to make a guy like her.

"Aren't you worried about someone seeing you up there?" Alicia was pretty familiar with Azalea Trail, and it was a popular hiking spot for park visitors. It wasn't unlikely that you could cross paths with several other hikers on any given day.

"Not that early on a weekday. It was like 8:00 or something. On weekends we are more careful, or whatever. Anyway, nobody saw us. There were only two other guys on the trail that day and they were so pissed at each other they couldn't have cared less about what we were doing."

"They were fighting?"

"Well, not punching each other or anything, but yelling and stuff. We had to pass near them where the trail splits. They weren't that close to where we were on the footbridge but I could see the one guy's face and it was really red and he gave me a dirty look. The other guy had his back to me, but his fist was clenched like he wanted to hit something."

"It's strange to think that while you and those guys and whoever else was on that trail yesterday, some hungry mountain lion was looking for breakfast! You're lucky that lion didn't find you and Vic out there."

"Yeah, tell me about it. I was really freaked when I heard that some poor guy was killed on the same trail I was on that very morning!"

The door opened and an older couple walked in. It was clear they knew what they wanted and were in a hurry. Dawn shifted her focus to her new customers as she slid the rhubarb pie, packed securely in its box, across the counter. "See ya, Allie."

"Hey, thanks Dawn, I'll see you later." Alicia took the pie box in one hand and her bag from Jack's in the other and headed for the door.

Chapter 8

Alicia was just pulling the pork chops out of the oven when she heard her father's park truck pulling up the long driveway. Peering through the small window situated over the time-worn enamel sink, she could see he was bent over and walking slowly. He looked tired. This did not bode well. If he was already in a bad mood, it wouldn't be improved by her day's expenditures. She glanced hopefully at the pie on the counter, as though it were somehow a magic talisman.

His key was in the door now.

"Hey Allie, I'm home!"

"Hi Dad. Dinner is ready in five, OK?"

"OK, just let me go get my boots off and wash up."

She heard his briefcase clunk down and the water running in the bathroom before he came back.

Chris was not often an outwardly religious man, but tonight he chose to say grace before they ate. For some time after, there was nothing but the contented sounds of chewing. Then, after the initial hunger was satiated, the inevitable question came.

"So, how did it go at the   college today?"

"How do you like these pork chops?" Alicia's last desperate attempt to delay the conversation was met with a confused stare from her father.

"It went fine." Defeat. "I was able to get my minor officially changed to Anthropology. That was kind of weird in itself. I had to have the permission of the professor, and boy was he an interesting character! Anyway, my schedule is all worked out."

"Great. How about the books? Did you get everything you needed?"

She knew what he was getting at. "Yes, but I guess what you really want to know is how much did what I need cost, right? Well, I guess there is no point dragging it out. The bill came to $563.98. I'm so sorry."

The clouded look that came to Chris's eyes contradicted the words that came from his mouth, "Oh, Kiddo, don't feel bad. I know college books are expensive, but I have to admit that they have sure gotten worse since I was in school."

"Is this going to be a problem for us? I could try to get a few extra shifts from Mr. Wong until the bill is paid off."

"Thanks, but it wouldn't be good for you to start school off exhausted and over worked. You need to start college putting your best effort forward, not scrambling to work overtime. We'll be OK, don't worry."

They ate in silence for a while longer. Then Chris answered her question out of the blue, "I like them fine, actually."

"What?"

"The dinner, the chops, I like them just fine. Where did you get the recipe? It's new, right?"

"Yes, actually. I got it from Marina over at Jack's. She made a special point of saying she thought you would like them, so I guess she was right." Alicia was somewhat surprised to see a slightly embarrassed grin briefly sweep across Chris's face.

"I can't imagine what would make her think that," he said, and then, making a complete change in the subject, "I'm just glad to have some good food after the day I had."

"Oh, what happened?"

"I spent the morning interviewing our victim's wife in town. The poor woman is distraught and emotional. It was just sad and depressing to talk to her about her husband. Top it off with the fact that I didn't find out anything useful, and I'm even more confused. He doesn't seem like the kind of guy that belonged out there on the trail in the first place." Chris, and all law enforcement personnel, had it drilled into them as cadets in the academy that sharing investigative information with their families would be a great temptation and should not be done, so he figured he had gone about as far as he could with telling Alicia about his day.

"Enough about my day, did I notice a pie in the kitchen?" With the lack of space, it was impossible to hide any surprises in it. The small cabin's kitchen was often joked about as being made for elves and gnomes since it was only about 8'x10' and obviously the expectation was only men would live here, and everyone knows they never cook. Anyway, rangers were expected to eat bugs and pine nuts while they were in the woods all day, so who needs a functional kitchen?

"Yeah, at least I was able to get a free Strawberry Rhubarb pie to help take the sting off the day for both of us. Let me go get it sliced."

After they each had their giant slabs of the tart pastry in front of them, Alicia looked up suddenly, "Oh, I forgot to tell you what Dawn told me."

Chris had cut a large chunk off the tip of his piece of pie, and it was now poised on the fork, hovering in the air, "Alicia, is that where you got the pie? You know how I feel about that girl, and about you hanging out with her."

"Dad! It's a small town. I can't avoid everyone here, especially when they work at places I need to go. Dawn's an OK person, anyway. I don't know what you have against her. Besides, I got the pie for free!"

Chris had heard enough rumors about how wild Dawn was from some of the staff who lived in town, and he had seen the extremely suggestive way she dressed. Plus, she had been a smoker since high

71

school, which was a clue he couldn't ignore about her attitudes and what she thought of playing by the rules.

"I've heard enough about her behavior from the deputies and some of my staff that it's clear she's on her way to trouble. The Julian sheriff's deputies broke up a drag race out on highway 79 at one in the morning last month, and she was one of the kids out there. Allie, you are known and made by the company you keep in life."

"I just got a pie from her, Dad, don't get all weird about it."

He didn't answer. Maybe he was over reacting. Raising kids was too hard. There was so much to know and understand, and so many influences outside the home that he couldn't control. And raising a girl was just plain foreign country to him. He sat and chewed his pie.

"So, do you want to hear what she told me, or not?" Alicia didn't mean to sound so cheeky, and her father was gracious enough to let the small show of attitude go unchecked.

"Alright, let me have it. What kind of antics is she up to now?"

"Well, I don't know if you would call them 'antics', and it certainly isn't going to help my side of the argument much."

"You started down this path, so let's hear it."

"OK, well, Dawn and her boyfriend, Vic, were up on Azalea Trail the morning of the lion attack! It's scary to think that someone I know could have been the victim instead, if not for the fickle finger of fate being pointed at someone else."

"And what were they doing up there I wonder. They don't strike me as the robust, naturalist types." Chris raised one eyebrow and smiled a tight-lipped smile of disapproval.

"You aren't going to arrest her or anything, are you?" Alicia was just coming to the realization that she was about to tell the chief ranger of the park about known illegal drug use within park boundaries.

"No, besides, you haven't really told me anything concrete. However, I do think you should tell her to be careful up there. She could

72

easily get caught, if not by me then by some other ranger, or more likely some hikers."

"I think she barely escaped getting caught yesterday, actually."

"What do you mean?"

"Oh, she said that as she and Vic were walking back down the trail after they…" Alicia paused and pursed her lips and looked uncomfortably down at the floor, "…after they had gone as far as they wanted on the trail," she tried not to laugh when her dad rolled his eyes, "anyway, they walked near a couple of guys arguing near the footbridge."

"Did you say the footbridge? What time was this; did she say?"

"It was about eight or so in the morning I think. She and Vic were just hanging out before she had to go to work. She was wondering if one of those guys was the guy who got killed."

"Did she see them close enough to make an identification?"

"I don't know. She didn't act like she recognized either of them, but maybe she remembers what they looked like."

Chris didn't know where this information would fit in, but he knew he had to run it down. If he could show Dawn one of the pictures of the victim that he had, perhaps she could identify one of the men she saw. It might somehow shed more light on why the guy was out there. Dick Savage would tell him it was not important for an animal mauling death, but it still bothered Becker why this guy was there. Little details mattered, and this one was out of place.

Chapter 9

The shrill ring of the phone next to her head pierced through Alicia's dream world and yanked her to wakefulness. Her eyes stared blankly at the ceiling as the second ring sounded. By the third, she had turned her head to read the time displayed in cool blue LCD on her bedside clock radio.

"8:10, who would be so cruel as to call me at this time on a Saturday morning?" Her voice was altered with a sleepy raspiness that sounded odd to her. She cleared her throat, "Hello."

"Hello, Alicia. This is Daniel Wong." His voice was tense.

"Mr. Wong? What's wrong?" She stifled a laugh. This was starting to sound like the dialogue from some bad "B" movie. "I mean, why are you calling?"

"Auralia, the weekend maid, called in sick, and it is absolutely imperative that I have someone to clean the rooms this morning. I can't get ahold of Juanita, besides, she has already maxed out her hours for this week. Can you come in early for your shift and clean the rooms, especially room 3? I'll buy your breakfast if you can be here in 20 minutes."

Alicia wanted desperately to say no, to stay in her warm bed and savor the last Saturday of her summer. Besides, she absolutely hated cleaning the bungalows that the restaurant owned. She knew she had agreed to be back-up maid when she had taken the waitressing job, but so far she had only had to vacuum and make the beds of one of the four rooms when the regular maid had suddenly gotten the stomach flu halfway through cleaning. Now Mr. Wong wanted her to come in and do a full cleaning on all the rooms that had been stayed in that week in preparation for the weekend tourists. She hated cleaning her own mess, but other people's was positively disgusting! Then she remembered the bookstore credit card bill looming on the horizon. The extra hours would help make a small dent in the sum, and that was worth a bit of suffering on her part.

"OK, but what is the big deal with room 3?" Mr. Wong was such a skinflint that there had to be a good reason that he was greasing her up with a free breakfast.

"I'll tell you when you get here."

*   *   *

Amazingly it only took Alicia 18 minutes from hanging up the phone until she was standing in front of an impatient Mr. Wong. She couldn't believe the phone and her dressing didn't wake her dad. Her father would have been speechless at how quickly she had jumped out of bed, brushed her teeth, pulled her hair into a high ponytail and thrown on her jeans and a pale green T-shirt. Done. Nothing fancy. No point in getting dressed up, or showering for that matter, if one was shortly going to be elbow deep in scrubbing bathtubs and changing sheets.

"Good. On time. Now, you have 30 minutes to eat, and then come to my office for instructions." Wong double-checked his watch and nodded in satisfaction. Apparently his day seemed to be back on track. "Tell the cook what you want for breakfast." He turned on his heels and fairly marched back down the hall toward his office.

75

Alicia watched his retreating form, shrugged, and headed for the kitchen. As she rounded the corner into the kitchen she expected to see the kindly middle-aged face of Roger Kennedy, the long-time day shift cook at Hillside. Roger had been there longer than anyone, even Mr. Wong who had purchased the establishment nine years ago from the previous owner. Instead, however, she was greeted by the slick black ponytail and starkly handsome face of Marcus Lundee. He glanced up when he heard her approaching footsteps, then looked back down at the grill, barely registering her presence with a nod of the head.

"Where's Roger?"

"Don't know. Wong called me in to work a double shift for today. I think Roger is down the hill. Something about his sister."

"Oh, I hope she is alright." There was an awkward silence.

"So, the boss said to make you breakfast on the house. What did you do to deserve that honor?" The twisted grin and raised eyebrow was obvious on his face.

"Oh, that's my bribe for coming in and playing maid for Mr. Wong today."

"Really…now that's something I'd like to see." Marcus' grin was wide and suggestive.

"Oh, no, no!" She was blushing. Again! If this boy was trying to put her off balance every time she saw him, it sure was working. "That didn't come out right. He called to ask if I would clean the rooms because the maid is out sick."

"Ah, well that explains the outfit." He was giving her the once over.

"What do you mean?"

"Well, you just don't usually come to work like that. I mean jeans and a tee is not your usual preppy khakis and polo shirt." He was bent over the grill again.

"I am not preppy!" She didn't know why she was offended, but somehow she didn't want Marcus to imply that she was a goody-goody. "I wear that to work because it is comfortable while still looking nice."

76

"Don't get so defensive, I didn't say preppy was bad. Jeans and a tee aren't bad either. You look great in both. I was just surprised because you look different from your usual."

He wasn't smirking, or laughing, or even looking at her. As her brief flash of irritation subsided, she became aware of something. He was paying attention to what she wore. He noticed when she wore something different. And he had just given her a compliment. She had no idea what to do with that information, but for the moment she decided that the safest thing to do was change the subject.

"Well, I better order. I'm on a strict time schedule apparently."

"OK, what can I get you?"

"How about a ham and cheese omelet and a side of fried potatoes? If I'm going to get a free meal, I may as well shoot the works. I'll have a chocolate milk, too, but I'll get that myself."

"Cool, coming right up." She didn't know if he was trying to be aloof after sharing his appreciation for her looks, or if she was reading into the situation, but whatever the case, the moment of tension between them had subsided.

Alicia got a large glass and filled it to the brim with the cold milk. She took it to the corner booth in the dining room and went back to check on her meal.

"Order up," Marcus said as she entered the kitchen pick up area.

"Mine? Already? That was quick. Thanks."

Taking the plate to her table, she spent the rest of her allotted mealtime happily munching on what turned out to be a very tasty omelet and perfectly spiced potatoes. She was somewhat surprised at Marcus' skill in the kitchen, and even more so at the radish rose he had garnished her plate with. She picked it up to examine it more closely. It appeared to have been carved all in one piece from a perfect little red radish. This was not something she had seen him do during the regular dinner rush, so she could only assume it was a special gesture for her, if in fact he had done it at all. It was possible the boss was trying to add a little class to the joint and had somehow bought them in bulk. She didn't have much time to wonder about it, though, as Mr. Wong was striding purposefully toward where she was seated. Impulsively, she wrapped the little vegetative sculpture in a paper napkin and dropped it in her purse just as he reached the table. He sat down right next to her, instead of across the booth as one normally would. This invasion of personal space was disconcerting and Alicia instinctively scooted several inches back, trying to re-establish some boundaries. The attempt proved futile, however, as Mr. Wong leaned conspiratorially toward her before he spoke.

"Alicia, as I said before, it is imperative that the rooms be cleaned, most especially room number 3."

"Yes, you said that before. You also said you would explain what the big deal is about room 3 in particular. Did the last guest trash the place or what?" Alicia's patience for suspense was wearing thin.

Wong glanced about the room, making sure no one was watching or listening in on their conversation. He had the air of a man ready to divulge state secrets, and Alicia had to admit he had officially piqued her interest.

"What I am about to tell you must remain strictly between us, is that clear?"

"Yes, sir. Of course."

"In going over the accounts for the week, you know, the cash register receipts and the guest register for the bungalows, I recognized one of the names as being the same one released to the media yesterday. That is to say that I realized that the last guest to stay in room 3 was the man who was killed by the mountain lion out in the park!"

Alicia couldn't contain her surprise, "Xavier Hess!" Her voice had risen sharply and Mr. Wong put a finger to his lips to silence her, and looked around the room again to see if anyone was paying attention to them now. When he was satisfied that they were still being ignored he removed the warning finger but still mouthed a silent *shhhh* before letting her speak again.

"I don't believe it!" This time Alicia tried to match his hushed tones.

78

"Well it is true, and it is terrible. The thought of a man so close to death staying in one of my rooms is very disturbing. His aura must be cleansed before I can rent the room to anyone else. This is where the urgency comes in. There is a party of six coming in this afternoon, and they are set to be housed in rooms 2 and 3. You have to do a regular cleaning of all the rooms, then completely remove all traces of this Hess person, scour the room, throw away all the linens and replace them, and cleanse the aura all before your shift starts at two."

"Are you serious?" He could have interpreted her incredulity to be based on his expectations of her cleaning abilities, or at her astonishment at his superstitious nature, and he would have been correct on both counts.

"Quite." He slid to the edge of the bench seat and stood up in one very economical movement. "You'll find the cleaning supplies and new linens in the utility closet next to the men's room. Please place the soiled sheets, bedspread, towels, and shower curtain in a black trash bag and place it at the back door of the kitchen. You'll find a new replacement bedspread and shower curtain on the top shelf of the closet, and you can replace the towels and sheets with freshly laundered ones." Before turning to go, he carefully laid the set of master keys on the table and then looked sharply at her, "you have five hours, so step lively."

*   *   *

Rooms 1, 2, and 4 had occupied her until nearly 12:30. They had required only regular servicing, but vacuuming and wiping sinks and mirrors, and scrubbing toilets, and changing linens for three rooms was still very time consuming, especially for someone not used to the routine. Now, here she was on the threshold of room 3, and an odd sort of expectant feeling had come over her. She thought Mr. Wong was very strange for being so concerned over the psychic debris left in the room, or whatever he was freaking out about, but Alicia had to admit, as she stepped through the door, that there was definitely something strange about being in the private space of one who had so recently met such a violent demise.

Something else strange had been nagging at her since her brief discussion with Mr. Wong this morning, too. She had been so surprised to hear that Mr. Hess had been staying in this very hotel the night before his death that she had forgotten to ask herself why. Hadn't her father told her the night before of his sad task of talking to Hess's widow at their home in El Cajon? So, if he lived less than an hour away, why on earth would he have gotten a motel room here the night before he was killed? If he knew he needed to come here, why not drive up in the morning? Her curiosity got the better of her, and instead of delving right into stripping the bed and piling up the towels, she decided to do a quick survey of the room instead.

Alicia felt like her childhood hero, Nancy Drew, as she tip-toed carefully around the room. It was clear that the bed had been slept in, by someone who tossed and turned it seemed. The closet was empty. No luggage meant that this was intended to be a short stay. Or maybe there was luggage in Hess's car? Her dad never mentioned that. She walked around to the other side of the bed and noticed a small scrap of something half hidden under the bed skirt. Reaching down, Alicia picked it carefully up between her thumb and forefinger. Upon realizing what it was, she was very glad she had left her rubber gloves on. Dangling from between her fingers was a pair of leopard print thong underwear, edged in black lace with a little black satin bow in the front.

"Ew, ew, ew! Yuck!" She wished desperately for one of those orange biohazard trash cans you find at hospitals. Instead she opted for a clean, empty trash bag from her supplies.

"Well, that answers that question. Cheating jerk!" She felt genuinely sad for the poor woman who thought she had lost her husband two days ago, but had apparently lost him to another woman some time before. At least now his renting a motel room was explained, and with it any sense of mystery or intrigue. Now she was just disgusted and wanted to get the room cleaned and behind her as soon as possible. She decided to start in the bathroom, thinking it is best to get the worst over with first. She entered the open bathroom door and flipped on the light. Staring back at her from the mirror were at least a dozen dark red lipstick kiss marks.

"Oh, give me a break!" This love nest thing was getting to be a bit too much, and Alicia was beginning to wonder what loathsome thing she would find next. One thing the "lip" love note seemed to indicate was that the woman in question had not gotten to say goodbye to Hess in person. Perhaps he had still been sleeping when she left, or maybe it was the other way around.

Fortunately, there were no more surprises in the bathroom and she was able to scrub the surfaces and mirror and replace the linens with the new ones without any further distractions. It wasn't until she began dusting the wood furniture pieces in the bedroom that she came across something else that looked interesting. Mr. Wong provided a pad of paper and a pencil next to the phone in each room. She had checked all of them today, tearing off any used sheets and placing them back nice and neat on the dusted night table. Then she noticed there was a small piece of what she thought was paper on the floor that she must have missed earlier. Picking it up she found what she thought was from the paper pad was actually the inside of an old-fashioned matchbook cover. The matches and striking surface had been torn off and all that was left was the cover. One side was advertisement, and on the inside she found a pencil scrawled note.

"*Azalea ¼ m. ft. br. 8*" She wasn't sure what it meant, but the hair on the back of her neck was suddenly standing on end. Alicia stuffed the matchbook cover in her jeans pocket. This was actually a clue—worthy of Nancy herself. Suddenly it occurred to her that she ought to save the panties as well, and she cringed as she rooted around in the trash bag for them. She knew she needed to call her dad, but she had to finish with this room first. She looked at her watch. It was 1:23 pm. She rushed to strip the sheets off the bed and replaced them with clean ones. She took the new comforter, beige with big blue flowers, out of its plastic packaging and spread it over the bed as well. Just as she was plugging in the enormous vacuum, Mr. Wong tapped on her shoulder from behind.

"Ahh!" She actually jumped in the air she was so startled. "Mr. Wong, don't sneak up on me like that!"

"I didn't sneak up on you…you should be more aware of your surroundings. Anyway, I wasn't trying to scare you. I wanted to bring you this." He extended his hand to her, and in it was a small ceramic item.

"What is this?"

"An incense burner. I want you to light the incense and let it burn once you have finished here. This will complete the cleansing process." He handed her the stick of incense and a box of matches, then turned and walked toward the door.

"OoooKaaay…" she didn't quite know what else to say. What she wanted to say was that he was being ridiculous and that all this little smelly stick was going to do was drive away guests, but 'OK' seemed the better choice if she wanted to keep her job. "No problem."

"Good, now get back to work, your shift starts in half an hour and we've been busy today." And then he was gone.

Chapter 10

Becker awoke Saturday morning to the thud of the back door screen as Allie left for work. He wondered why she was leaving so early and wished she had closed the door a little quieter. He was scheduled to give a campfire program tonight and was going to sleep in a bit before going in to work late. It was one of the fun perks of the job.

He had all his slides assembled in his projector and was going to sing a few campfire songs and then spend the rest of the program telling the campers about the Kumeya'ay Indian peoples and their culture. This small group was historically known to inhabit much of the interior portion of southern California and down into present day Mexico. Many of the native peoples still lived their ancestral lifestyle somewhat intact in the interior portions of Northwestern Mexico to this day. It was difficult for Americans to think of Mexico as a land of past and present all rolled into one, for many areas outside of the towns and larger cities still remained much as they had been hundreds of years ago.

Chris dropped his feet on the cabin's cold tile floor. Carpet was a luxury the park service was reluctant to expend money on for mere employees. So the park offices were

83

nicely carpeted, since the same standards applied to state senator's offices, while employee housing was uninsulated, poorly repaired, and cheap vinyl tile was often installed throughout the house. At least in summer it wasn't so bad, and he could break down and buy several large area rugs if it really bothered him that much. What was really bad was that it had finally taken legislation to force the removal of asbestos from the houses. The mice in the attic didn't mind, but it irritated Becker. He was also worried about the old World War II post and knob wiring that was deteriorating in the walls and attic. Last month, he had found a mouse electrocuted in the breaker panel box when it bridged two of those old wires.

After a quick shower and some coffee he was in a better mood. He hooked up the projector and ran through the slides for his campfire one more time, and then tuned his guitar, taking the time to play a few country songs and one or two by James Taylor that were favorites. Sometimes the campers even liked to sing them if they were really in the mood. He tried to shy away from the traditional and very ancient campfire tunes in favor of more modern stuff, but since fewer and fewer young people were spending time in the wilderness these days he didn't get much chance to use them. With all the competition from motorhomes, complete with movie entertainment centers and dish TV reception, he wondered why people even came to the park at all. A good wall mural would have sufficed just as well. Ninety-five percent of the people who did come never left the highway turnouts or the campgrounds. It's a wonder the cougars found anyone to attack on the trails.

Chris waited until almost 11:00 AM before driving to the park office. When he walked in, Val Simpson was waiting for him inside the door.

"I need to talk to you for a minute," she said as she cocked her head toward the stairs. Chris followed her up to his office and she shut the door behind her. He always hated when she shut the door, because he knew it meant trouble. Someone on staff must have done something that she didn't want anyone in the office to overhear.

"Must be bad if the door has to be shut."

"We've got a problem I thought you should know about. Unfortunately, a lot of it seems to be unsubstantiated second hand information."

"Aah, just what I love, good juicy rumors that get everyone in an uproar."

"Well, it's a bit more than rumor. The Maintenance Chief told me that we've had some stuff go missing from the shop yard, and his feeling is someone on staff is getting in there and taking it. It's the kind of stuff that you'd have to have a key to get in the shop building to gain access to. The funny part is that it's old stuff that they don't use much: A circular saw, some heat lamps and lighting, a lot of it probably due for replacement but not in really bad shape. It had been stored in the back room of the building."

"So you think someone came in and took stuff that he thought no one would miss."

"Yeah, and the kind of stuff you'd use for a building project of some kind. I doubt it is anything someone took to sell, because it is too old and worn out to get any real money for the effort."

"Any idea who is behind all this? I'm sure you have an opinion. Somehow, I doubt you would have come in to mention it if you didn't have at least some clue."

"Apparently, Ollie Mahlon was seen in there a lot recently with his personal van."

"I might have guessed. You know, Ollie isn't a popular guy around here. Are we jumping to conclusions just on that basis, or did someone actually see him load up stuff from the shop building?"

Ollie Mahlon, as the Resource Ecologist for the District, was unbelievably disliked by most of the staff since he had the power to invoke all sorts of environmental restrictions on work that was being done in the park under the authority of the California Environmental Quality Act. If you wanted to take a teaspoon of dirt, Mahlon could stop you by saying that a certain type of flower grew in the "area" and you would have to wait until spring so he could do a survey of the area and clear the project. By then, the funds for the particular project were usually gone, most often used up by the "review" process itself. Becker had been frustrated himself a number of times by these tactics.

Environmental protectionism was the new religion for some, and Ollie Mahlon was His Holiness, the Chief Cardinal in the Montane Sector. Under the wording of the law, not one molecule got disturbed without his say so, and he was fond of pointing that out to everyone. Chris knew the Maintenance Chief and Val Simpson had both butted heads with Mahlon, and Chris had refereed a few more screaming matches between them than he liked.

"There is a bit more. Apparently, Ollie took a swipe at his daughter last night after work, at least according to one of the park aids. Nobody filed a complaint, and she's probably scared to death of him. Also, twice this week I've had complaints of smelling alcohol on his breath when he's at work."

"Hold on a second, I get it. The guy isn't on my 'Best Friend Forever' list either, but let's not jump to conclusions too fast. After all, I've been in that shop yard pretty often and so have you. I've even seen Savage in there this past month a couple times. If we just base it on who's been seen there, then we are all suspects."

"Yeah, you're right, but I'm just sensitive toward people who may be taking their issues out on their kids."

Becker was taken up short by Val's comment, remembering something she once said about her alcoholic father and her unstable childhood. She could be projecting her past, but on the other hand when it came to Ollie Mahlon, he was curious.

"All right, Val, I'll have a chat with him about the alcohol, but until you can get some kind of real evidence about thefts or assaults there's nowhere to go on that. If you get a written statement about smelling alcohol on his breath, I probably can do a "probable cause/reasonable suspicion" blood test on him since he is covered under the federal law for random testing of drivers in the department. Better yet, if they can testify to slurred speech, gait impairment and the like I'm sure we can test him, but you need to get it when he's actually under the influence."

"OK, I'll work on it. By the way, you're still doing a campfire tonight, right?"

"Yes, at Paso Picacho Campground. How many campers do we have registered there tonight?"

"It should be pretty good attendance. We're full, and we even put a bunch of people in overflow for self-contained vehicles overnight. Group camps are full, too."

"Sounds like it will be fun."

She held at the doorway to his office and said, "How's school going for Allie? She get all her classes?"

"Yeah, no problems, except the textbook industry is out of their minds with what they charge for books these days."

"You're lucky. You're raising a good one there. You should be proud."

"I am...oh yeah...I am."

The park family. That's how it was in the small enclaves they lived in. Everyone knew everything about everyone. Chris knew, or suspected, who drank, who cheated on their wives, whose kids were failing out of high school, and whose kids were going off to college. For the most part, it was a good thing and was very supportive. Sometimes it felt a little close and invasive, Allie called it 'living in a fish bowl,' and for Mahlon it was about to be the latter.

Chris sat at his desk considering how he should approach Ollie about his drinking. It was no secret the guy was a tippler. At staff parties he was always pretty well lubricated, but proving on the job consumption was a bit more difficult. Still, all he needed was reasonable cause at a time when he could get him tested in town before he burned off the alcohol in his system. Mahlon had a short fuse so the conversation was not likely to be a pleasant one, and Chris decided he had better get it over with as soon as possible.

He told Jane that he would be out on patrol in the park rather than point out that he would be looking for Ollie. He already knew Mahlon was supposed to be doing an evaluation of a trail realignment project that had impacts on vegetation and on archeological resources. He knew the District Archeologist was out with him on the horse trail near the Sweetwater Bridge. In the years since the Boulder Fire in the 1970s, the park vegetative growth had become incredibly dense. Trail construction work was more complex as a result.

Plans had been drawn for years to do prescription burns to reduce the fuel load and return the park to its traditional fire dependent state. Chris was always frustrated that funding for fire staff was always a problem, as well as timing them with the proper weather conditions, and so only one extremely small test burn had been accomplished in the last ten years. Frequent small fires had historically burned at the hands of the Native Americans here, or from the summer lightning storms, which kept the area relatively safe from the huge firestorms that raged periodically through similar places in California now in modern times. This trail realignment project would reduce erosion from equestrians and the trail would also provide a tie-in to a burn unit as a fire line. Chris was hoping to get a burn done this fall once the trail was built. True to form, Mahlon was slowing things down. Even the archeologist sounded ready to consider the project. No small feat, as Cuyamaca was one of the richest repositories of Native American artifacts in California.

He pulled in to the parking area near the bridge over the brackish green flow of the Sweetwater River behind the compact pickup truck that Mahlon used. Assuming he would be somewhere on the East Side Trail or further up on the Harvey Moore Trail, Becker started to head that way. He had only gone a few steps when he heard Ollie Mahlon call his name from down in the riverbed below the bridge. This time of year the Sweetwater ran thinly, if at all. Vegetation growth had exploded so much along the drainages that all available water beyond the winter rain and snow was quickly sucked up and little was left to run in the dog days of summer, although Chris had

88

late summer pictures from after the Boulder fire that showed the river full from bank to bank. Generally, one could step across it these days even at the height of its peak run-off. Becker stepped off the trail and made his way to the riverbed.

"How's the work going on the trail environmental review?" Chris asked.

Mahlon stood up from the plants he had been examining. Hair that was almost white blond and blue eyes contrasted with a thick overweight build that gave him the look of a wrestler, yet he was quick on his feet and closed the distance to Chris quickly. "I think I've just about finished with the field work and should be able to write up the CEQA review in a day or two for Dick to sign. Mostly, we need to watch out for the larkspur that grows around here. It's not endangered, but it would be a crime to destroy it. Otherwise, we are just whacking through ceanothus and coyote bush."

Chris was surprised that Mahlon hadn't found an endangered lizard or fungus to stop the project. It was well known that he hated horseback use in the park and had advocated to end it. He found support from a growing number of archeologists who studied the area, as well, and claimed the horse trails and camps had been built on Native American village sites.

"That's good to hear, and I'm sure Dick will be happy for a quick resolution so we can get the work done before next season."

Chris wondered where the district archeologist was. He didn't want to discuss Mahlon's drinking with anyone else around.

"Where's Charlie Sims? I thought he was finishing up his archeology review on the project today as well."

"He went up the Harvey Moore Trail to look for more sign of artifacts, but he didn't expect to find anything. He's been over this trail a dozen times this year, but you never know what some horse's hoof will kick up. He just left about 5 minutes ago. You could catch up to him if you want, I'm sure."

"No, actually I needed to talk to you. I got a report that you have had the odor of alcohol on your breath while you were at work."

"From who? That's bullshit! There's no way I would ever drink at work. I use mouthwash for my dental bridge so I don't have bad breath. Maybe that was what they noticed?"

"I can't tell you at this point, because I don't know. It's an anonymous report, and frankly I don't care who said it because it doesn't give me anything to act on. I'm just here to warn you that it better not come to anyone's attention again or we'll march you right down for a blood test. Your random testing could come up at any time, as well. I'm just trying to..." Chris hesitated because 'put the fear of God in you' was what he wanted to say, but thought he should make it a little softer, "give you some friendly advice and information so you don't get taken by surprise."

"This is all lying crap, and I want to know who said it!" Mahlon's face was flushed with anger.

"If anyone ever acts against you on a complaint like this, you'll know who said it. Until then, it's just a word to the wise from a *friend*." Chris nearly choked on the word, but he needed to divert Mahlon from wanting to know who ratted on him.

"Personally, I think you should just let it pass and don't give them the satisfaction of knowing they got to you. Just go on about your business, and change your mouthwash to something else."

Chris didn't know what to believe about the mouthwash, but he knew he had never seen any outward signs of intoxication from Mahlon at work. Until he did, he figured to give him the benefit of the doubt. He was also concerned about the thefts from the shop and wondered how to approach the subject.

"Is that all you needed, 'cuz I've got to get back and make a few calls?" Mahlon had turned from Chris and was scrambling up the side of the shallow creek bed. Chris followed, considering how he might broach the other topic he had come to discuss.

"We've got another issue that I'm doing routine inquiries about, and I'm questioning a lot of people. A number of items have come up missing from the shop and your personal vehicle was reported in the shop yard a couple of times this week. I need to know what you were doing back there." Chris had expected a real explosion with this question, but Mahlon was surprisingly calm.

"I went back there to put equipment in my state truck that I had in my van."

Chris paused on the bridge. He didn't want to have this conversation with the back of the man's head, so he waited until Ollie stopped walking and turned around to face him before he asked his next question.

"What equipment was that?"

"Last week they were doing routine servicing on the truck and took it into town to have the work done. I had no vehicle to use, so I put the GPS and some large scale maps in my van and used it for work. I also had a crew of volunteers removing exotic plants and invasive brush that I was working with, so I had to load some shovels and picks and a lot of garbage bags."

The two began walking toward the road again. There was an uneasy silence between them, like each was wondering what the other was thinking. It all sounded legitimate to Chris, but it also gave Mahlon the opportunity to swipe the equipment when he was in there. It confirmed he was, in fact, in the shop around the time of the theft, but really didn't give Chris any more to go on than that. Probably not enough for a warrant to search, and considering this was just low value, worn out equipment that was about to be disposed of anyway, it didn't look like the investigation was going to go very far. Still, it was worth keeping in mind that Mahlon might be up to more than he said. He'd see what Savage wanted him do before he put any pressure on. He suspected he would be directed to write a theft report and get back to "park work," whatever that was!

Never a particularly friendly person, Mahlon seemed to have calmed down by the time they reached their vehicles. Still, he slammed his tools into his truck and spun in the gravel as he drove out to the highway. Becker left a bit more smoothly and headed toward Julian. He figured he had just enough time to go have a visit with Dawn at the pie shop. Perhaps he could

91

find out more about who was on the trail the day Hess died. He wouldn't mind telling her to keep away from Allie while he was at it, but he couldn't quite figure out how to do that without likely causing bigger problems.

Chapter 11

Chris was back at the office by lunch and ate his meager bologna sandwich and chips at his desk. Not for the first or last time he thought he needed to work on his diet and eat better. His questioning of Dawn was pretty useless, as she said she couldn't identify or describe either of the two men she saw since they were so far away. She thought the picture of Hess looked sort of like the red-faced guy she saw, but she just wasn't sure. She also told him she couldn't distinctly hear anything they said, just that they were yelling. He felt she was withholding information, but most likely it was that she was trying to prevent him finding out that she was up there smoking dope or doing some other illegal activity of her own. Chris figured maybe the dope was clouding her memory as well; regardless it gave him little more to go on than he'd had before.

Dick Savage was obviously in a foul mood when he came into the office Saturday afternoon just after Chris had finished his lunch. Perhaps the fact that he was working on a Saturday was the cause. The first clue was his lack of greeting to anyone as he slipped up the stairs to "the big office" and closed the door behind himself. If Val hadn't just shut Chris's door this morning, he wouldn't have been surprised if it couldn't close anymore, and since everyone was always coming in and out of his office it didn't make sense to ever shut it anyway. No one ever *wanted* to go in Dick Savage's office, so a door that shut for him was generally considered by most of the staff to be a good thing. Several staff members suggested barring it once he was inside. Today Chris knew that shut or open, he would have to go in and discuss the events of the past two days with the Superintendent whether there were bars on the door or not.

He still had a few reports on visitor accidents and petty thefts to review, so he stalled for time by finishing them up. The budget justifications he was working on for the next fiscal year could wait. California could be broke again by the time those were called for submission. It was insane how a state with such resources could have so many ninnies in elected office that couldn't balance a budget against tax revenues. He felt the whole government mentality was "spend without control" and make constituents happy with pet local projects so re-election was insured the next time around.

He remembered reading somewhere about how democracies only lasted until the populace had taxed all the wealth and voted themselves the entire treasury in benefits and perks. At that point no one produced any products or hired any workers and the society collapsed. From what he saw, Chris thought it likely. That chaos was not here yet, but someday it would come.

Becker snapped the last of his copy of the reports in a binder and put the remaining finished copies in his out basket. He was just about to grab his report on the death of Xavier Hess to take in to Savage when his phone rang.

"Ranger Becker," he answered.

"Hey Chris, I have the preliminary report from our Fish and Game forensics people on the lion killing autopsy." It was Frank James. "I guess they sat in with the county coroner when it was performed and they found death due to asphyxiation consistent with a lion kill."

94

"Well, I guess that makes it all tied up in a neat little bow for us," said Chris.

"Wait, I'm not done. Funny thing. You see, when they were all done, our Fish and Game biologist made a point to do some measurements on the bite marks and here's where it gets interesting."

"What was so interesting?"

"Remember I told you before the bite looked funny to me? You see, the lion likes to come up from either in front or behind and get a grip on the neck with its jaw. Sometimes, they make it and sometimes they don't. If it is a good killing bite, they get a good grip in front and all the teeth bite down and crush the windpipe. They keep holding for a long time just to make sure. If the bite is off a bit all the teeth don't dig in and you see only a few, which is what we have this time."

"So what's interesting about that? Are you making yourself a set of dentures from an impression for Snagglepuss?"

"Funny man, Chris, I am just really laughing. Would you get serious, this is interesting. The teeth that do show up on this have the same circumference."

"I sense I should understand something here, but I'm not following you, Frank."

"Look, when you bite into an apple and start chewing, your lower front jaw teeth have a circumference that is smaller than the upper ones. That way, things fit together when you bite down. It is similar with lions."

"So how is that important?"

"The measurements were funny on this guy. His lower jaw only had a few teeth catch in the flesh, but if the arc was extrapolated out, then it seemed too big to make a good fit."

"So what, we have a lion that needs dental work? Maybe some braces?" Something about this whole thing struck Chris as funny, "Get him in the movies and cap his teeth, too!" Chris was almost laughing out loud by now, but he realized the inappropriateness of his mirth and cleared his throat as a cover. "I'm sorry, it's been a long day. Now, what's a deformed lion got to do with anything?"

"Well for one thing, it will make it really easy to identify a lion as the killer if we catch one. I should tell you one thing though; our biologist said the coroner was not thoroughly satisfied with some features of the trauma and might be following up with further testing. Plus they're going to do a full toxicology screen which will delay findings probably another couple weeks."

Deformity in nature was part of its variability. This one seemed a little off the norm, but Chris was not a wildlife biologist. Maybe jaw deformity was more common than he thought. The Fish and Game scientists were always talking about unique dental patterns, so maybe it was a lot like humans. After all, how many murder victims had been eventually identified by their dental records being so unique. And what was this about "features of the trauma?" More unresolved details that just cluttered up what he was hoping would be a nice clean investigation.

"OK, Frank. Thanks for the update. Call me again if you have anything new that comes up."

Chris added the new information to his report and snapped his copy into the binder. He decided not to take the report to Savage just yet given the loose ends dangling. He knew better than to go to him now with his concerns about two mysteries. He was pretty sure he would be whipped like an errant schoolboy for wanting to follow up on the missing shop items, too. He was continually amazed at his supervisor's tunnel vision.

Chapter 12

Alicia tried to juggle the pail of cleaning supplies, the black bag full of the linens to be thrown away, and the laundry bag of linens from the other three rooms, all while holding her nose and trying to shut the door to room 3. The incense smelled horrible. She wondered why aura cleansing had to be so stinky. Finally she decided it couldn't be done, and resolved to do it in two trips. After placing the black bag out of sight on the side of the bungalow, just in case the new guests arrived before she had a chance to retrieve it, she picked up the laundry bag and cleaning pail and trudged back to the restaurant.

Wong was waiting for her by the rear entrance. "Just in time. You have 25 minutes before you have to be on the floor smiling and ready to serve, so you better do something with yourself." His glance travelled disapprovingly over her clothes and hair, and Alicia suddenly felt like some street urchin. "Also, if you are hungry, you'll have to do something about that too. This time only the regular 50% discount."

Alicia hardly knew how to respond. "OK." It seemed to her that lately, OK was about the only safe response she could give her boss.

"Give those things to me and go freshen up." Wong reached out his long, smooth hands, hands that had clearly never held a wash pail with the intention of using it, and took the bucket and bag from her and walked toward the utility closet.

"Thanks." And as she pushed open the bathroom door, she mentally calculated if she had enough time to clean up, scarf down some fries and a coke, and still get a call in to her dad. For some reason, that matchbook note seemed to be burning a hole in her pocket. Alicia chuckled to herself, maybe there was something to Wong's idea of 'psychic debris' after all. More likely she had seen too many cop shows, and in reality what she thought was evidence was weeks old trash.

Seeing herself in the mirror, she realized that her boss hadn't been insulting her about her looks, but rather telling it like it was. She was a mess. Her hair had come loose from the rubber band and was falling freely around her temples and ears. Her shirt was smudged in several places, and her face was flushed from exertion and the August heat. She kicked herself inwardly for not having brought a change of clothes.

"Oh well, just have to make the best of it." She said, trying to rally the spirits of the face staring back at her from the glass. Alicia rummaged through her purse and found a folding brush, kept handy for just such occasions. After patting her hair down with water from the sink, she expertly swept the thick mass back into a ponytail. She couldn't do anything about the stains on her shirt, her waitress apron should cover most of them anyway, but her face still needed some attention. The paper towel doused in cold water felt heavenly against her overheated skin. She wetted and re-applied the cold cloth several times to her face and neck until the heat flush had subsided, and she felt very much herself again. She had no time for full make-up, but instead slathered on some much needed lip balm and headed out the door, making a beeline for the kitchen and the promise of greasy goodness.

Alicia turned the corner and found herself alone in the kitchen. No Marcus. No smells of cooking. No fries? She peeked over the warming counter and saw several baskets of fries that must have been left from the lunch rush. She grabbed a basket and headed for the beverage machine. After filling her large glass with ice and Cherry Coke, she went into the dining room to find a secluded spot to sit and munch in quiet for a few minutes.

"Hey you," Marcus' voice startled her from a shadowed corner booth.

"Oh, hey yourself. Taking a break? Hope you weren't saving these fries for something, I'm starving!" She felt awkward but hoped it didn't show. Was she supposed to sit with him? Would it be rude to walk away? She didn't want to be rude, but she was too tired to endure the cerebral gymnastics required by a conversation with Marcus. He confused her and kept her off guard, and that required more energy than she felt capable of investing. Besides, she was still hoping for a chance to call her dad.

"Have a seat." Well that answered that question.

"OK, thanks." Alicia slid into the bench seat of the booth opposite her companion, and began quietly munching on fries and trying to think of something to say. She grabbed the ketchup bottle and methodically opened the lid, up ended the bottle and smacked the bottom end sharply, as though it were some errant child.

"You know, that's not the best way." Marcus said.

Alicia eyed him suspiciously. She had had bad experiences in high school with boys trying to be 'helpful' when in reality they were just trying to get a laugh. She remembered one particularly awful time that ended with her in the girls' bathroom trying to wash mustard out of her favorite scarf. She really didn't miss high school. At all.

"No really. Here, let me show you." Alicia loosened her grasp on the bottle, but not on her fear that this would end with her in the bathroom covered in a condiment. "It has to do with suction, or something. Anyway, if you hold it straight up and down like you were and bang on it, you will get some ketchup on your plate, but you are just as likely to get it on your lap too." Oh, here we go, thought Alicia. "But if you hold it more sideways and use a knife to just break the suction," he demonstrated as he spoke, knife in hand, gently coaxing the first bit into the neck of the bottle, "then it pours out evenly. No more explosions." And with that, he deposited a perfect swirl of ketchup on her plate and smiled up at her with satisfaction.

She wasn't used to him smiling broadly, at her or at anyone else for that matter. He leered. He smirked. He had even sneered and glared several times. But a genuine smile was new to her. It changed his face. He went from starkly handsome to warm and good looking. At any rate, the effect was so compelling she couldn't help smiling back. Not only did she smile, genuinely and appreciatively, but she looked right into his eyes. She never noticed the color before, but they were a soft blue, tinged with a hint of green.

"Thanks, I'll have to remember that," she said, still smiling and looking at him. In an instant, he seemed to become aware that she was looking at him, really looking at him. He shifted in his seat, averted his eyes and the smile instantly faded from his lips.

"No big deal, just something I learned when I was a kid." A palpable chill had descended on the conversation.

"Oh, well it's still cool." Alicia was having trouble keeping up with the changes in mood Marcus exhibited. She knew she hadn't had the energy for this when she sat down, and here she was, being proven right. She wondered, once again, what would make Marcus so distant and hard to connect with. Perhaps he was an alien sent here to study our social habits and interactions. Or better yet, he had been lost on a hike as a young boy and raised by wolves, and therefore was understandably socially incompetent. Whatever the situation, Alicia was growing very tired of these confusing exchanges with Marcus. In fact, at this very moment he was totally oblivious to her frustration as he sat staring sullenly across the dining room.

She took a deep breath, "Well, my break is just about over. Back to the grindstone." She took one last slurping sip of her coke, and picked up the empty basket of fries and soda glass.

"Wait." His gaze met hers again, and this time she clearly read pain in his eyes. There was true emotion here, like the smile. But this time he was aware. The smile might have been a slip, an accident, but there was something deliberate about the way he looked at her now.

That one word and the look on his face were enough to stop her cold. She simultaneously set the basket and coke back on the table, but didn't bother to let go of them. She waited.

He was looking at the table now, as though looking at her was too taxing. Or perhaps he couldn't look at her and say what he wanted to say. When he did speak, the words were rushed. "I was waiting for you, hoping we could have lunch together. I didn't mean to…you just looked at me with such…and your smile…." His words broke and he glanced up at her, perhaps to gauge her reaction. Whatever he saw there, in her silent and surprised stare, enabled him to go on. "Sorry. I just don't seem to know how to deal with people anymore."

She had no idea what to say. Who was this person? Surely he wasn't the cold and aloof Marcus she had come to expect, nor was he the confusing sometimes nice but mostly naughty Marcus she had dealt with of late. This was a broken Marcus. This was a real person who appeared to be offering some sort of olive branch.

"Who does, really." *Oh lame, so lame.* "I mean," *what a disaster,* "maybe it's the atmosphere, I hear this really isn't that great of a place to have lunch." She rolled her eyes in an attempt to exaggerate the humor in her statement, "I mean the food is pretty good, but the service is terrible." Self-deprecation was always good for a laugh.

"So what you are suggesting is a change of venue?" Some of the pain in his eyes had been replaced with something else.

"I guess so." Suddenly Alicia realized where the conversation was headed. *Shoot. Double darn. Shoot.* She had started down this road to make him feel better, not to help him ask her out.

"So perhaps we should try again somewhere else, like, where is there a better atmosphere?" The something else was hope.

"Don Giovanni's is quiet," she answered, referring to the quaint and actually quite tasty Italian restaurant that had moved into Julian only a year or two before.

"Sounds good. When?"

"My Dad and I try to spend Sundays together. Monday I start school, but I'm off Monday night."

"Monday night at Don Giovanni's, say around what time?"

"I guess I could be there by 6:30."

"Perfect." Yes, the look on Marcus's face was far less pained and far more hopeful than it had been moments before, and yes, she was pretty sure she had just asked herself out on a date. She could only pray that she wasn't going to somehow end up paying for it too.

Neither Alicia nor Marcus had to worry about where the rest of the conversation might have gone, for at that moment Mr. Wong left his previous post at the hostess table and marched halfway across the dining room and pointedly glared at the two of them.

"Break time's over, obviously." Alicia muttered under her breath.

"I'll take your dishes. I'm going to the kitchen anyway." Marcus had already begun gathering up her things along with the dishes that had contained whatever he had been eating before she arrived.

"Thanks. See ya." She favored him with a brief and somewhat uncertain smile, aware that they had turned some kind of corner, but totally unsure of what that really meant.

The rest of the afternoon went about as usual. Lots of glasses of water and asking if people wanted soup or salad and bringing clean forks and extra napkins. There were days she didn't really like this job. It was sometimes hard to be extroverted and energetic all the time. After her long morning of cleaning, she just wanted to go home and take a long bath.

It was approaching five o'clock. As the front door opened the bell attached to the heavy wooden doorframe jangled its familiar tune, and several people filed in from the afternoon heat. Glancing up from the recently vacated table she was wiping down, she could see that there were two separate parties, a family with two young children, and a party of three. It was the latter that particularly drew her attention. It was the Mahlon family.

State Parks was an interesting profession to grow up in. There was a connectedness amongst the employees and their families. Perhaps it was because rangers moved around every few years and it was sometimes hard to make friends, especially because park workers often lived in park housing, far outside of the normal town framework of neighborhoods. The surrounding park employees and their families were like a built in network. Instant friends. Actually more like extended family sometimes. Alicia had been hopeful that this would be the case when she and her father had moved there two years ago, and she had quickly been introduced to Veronica Mahlon. She was only two months older than Alicia, and they had been in the same grade at school. They had even shared several classes during junior and senior year, but their friendship had never blossomed as Allie had hoped.

Saying she disliked Veronica would be overstating it, but they weren't really friends either. Roni was one of those girls that liked to live a bit on the wild side, and she fought with her parents constantly. This was one of the first points of contention between them. Roni had assumed Allie hated her own dad, too. When she realized the exact opposite was true, she came to resent the relationship Alicia and her father had, and it compounded the differences that already existed between them. It became more than the fledgling friendship could bear. Now they were cordial to each other, but that was about it. Deep down, as much as Alicia disagreed with some of the choices Veronica made, she was sorry her family life was so full of struggle.

She made her way quickly toward the front and smiled her most professional smile. "Hello, Mr. and Mrs. Mahlon, Veronica, how are you? Would you like a booth or a table?"

"A table. I don't like being cooped up against the wall." Ollie Mahlon was overbearing even when simply asking for a table.

"Sure no problem." Alicia grabbed three menus, then turned her attention to the young family that had entered the restaurant at the same

103

time, "I'll be with you folks in just a moment," then turned back to the Mahlons, "follow me, please."

Chapter 13

Becker sat in his office, reviewing and filing the myriad piles of dog-eared citations and crime reports his rangers had written during the previous month. He was wondering how some of them could get a college degree and still not know how to spell. He got a kick out of one report that detailed a car stuck off road and how the driver found someone who used his "wench" to pull it out. He was almost finished when his phone rang.

"I have a request by the sheriff that we send someone to a disturbance call at the Hillside Restaurant." Jane's voice came on the line from the reception area downstairs.

"How come they don't send their own people? Hillside is outside of the park."

"Their dispatch says that both of the resident deputies are on an ambulance run and have a patient enroute to the hospital in El Cajon."

Becker knew that the four deputies and their sergeant covered a wide area in the back country with their nearest backup being down in Alpine or Pine Valley. They were also saddled with the only ambulance service in a 40-mile radius, since the volunteer fire department and the park service provided Emergency Medical

Technicians to respond but had no transport capability. It wouldn't be the first time the county made a request like this, especially since he usually had at least one of his own officers available within a very short distance of the call.

Being able to play nice with other agencies was an important part of the chief ranger's job. Besides, what went around came around. He had needed their help several times when none of his people could respond. Today was different only in the fact that he was the only officer in the park. Val was covering the field patrol and had taken a drug possession arrest down to San Diego for booking just an hour ago.

"I'll head on over there. Any more information about what the call really is about?"

"I'll transfer the dispatcher up to you."

The phone clicked and Chris knew the transfer was made. "This is Ranger Becker, I'll be responding. What's the nature of the call?" Chris could hear the background voices of other dispatchers in the call center taking calls as the woman on the other end gave him the details.

"Call came in just about two minutes ago that a man had come into the Hillside Resort Restaurant and was screaming at a woman. They felt like a fight was going to break out and requested law enforcement assistance. Sorry, that's about all I got out of them."

"OK, I'll be there in about five minutes. I'm going solo on this, so if you have anybody free can you have them roll this way, maybe get CHP started if you can't get one of yours? Hopefully I won't need them, but just in case," Chris let the thought dangle.

"I'll see what I can get rolling," she said in clipped tones, and Chris could tell she'd hung up before he could even say thank you. People who handled radio communications were like that. Courtesies like 'thank you' were implied, and about the only time you found them being used was by late night officers and dispatchers who knew each other personally and when business was really slow. Becker often joked that the Department of Parks and Recreation had only in the past few years graduated from using tin cans and string to communicate, so familiarity on park radios was a bit more common, but system consolidation was coming. Soon, all of their dispatch would be handled by a very impersonal someone hundreds of miles away.

Becker took the steps downstairs two at a time and belted himself in his Jeep as he rolled down the entrance road at Dyar. It was then that he realized Alicia was working at Hillside today. Whatever this disturbance was, she was likely involved. This thought ratcheted up the anxiety factor one hundred and ten percent. Rubber squealed as he turned onto highway 79 and accelerated north. His scanner was his only means of communicating with CHP or the Sheriff, and all it really gave him was something to listen too. He let it scan all channels since he didn't know which agency might respond. As he rounded the second "S" curve near the West Mesa Parking area he heard a CHP unit come up that he was enroute from Santa Isabel. Only about 20 miles away, they had had a fatal shooting incident there last year by one of the "chippies." He didn't interact with them as often as the sheriff's deputies, and Chris wondered which officer was responding.

By the time he pulled up to the Hillside restaurant he had still not come up with much of a plan, so he was cautious in approaching the building. He didn't want to get shot by some hot head who didn't want to confront a uniform. He exited his car quietly, and was glad he had opted against using the siren. He fairly tiptoed up the creaky wooden steps to the porch and edged his way along the wall until he could quickly look in from the side of the entrance door frame. He couldn't see much, but he could hear yelling. One voice he already picked out was Ollie Mahlon. *What the hell is he doing here,* Chris thought as he entered the main dining area. He was sure Mahlon should still be out in the field scouting endangered buttercups, or whatever was currently keeping him busy, not in the restaurant causing a scene. Besides, dealing with him twice in one day was more than Chris wanted.

Peering in again and craning his neck around to the side, he could see Mahlon yelling at his daughter and another young teen, while Daniel

Wong bounced around them yelling agitatedly that they had to "leave the premises." He didn't seem to be having much success, and he was trying to grab Mahlon to push him toward the door. Chris searched the rest of the room in vain, hoping to see Alicia and to know that she was alright. Not only was he worried about her safety, but he knew that his worry for her was a liability for him. He needed to focus now, and not knowing where she was did not help him do that.

"Hey, knock it off in here!" Chris shouted as he quickly moved deeper into the room. Sometimes all it took was a louder voice of authority to change the dynamics of a situation like this, and this time at least it got everyone's attention. Mahlon immediately clammed up, but Wong was still bouncing around like a paddle-ball out of control and repeatedly shouting "You must leave now! You must leave now!"

"Daniel, be quiet! Go sit down," Chris said, as he gripped Wong and pulled him to the farthest booth in the room and pushed him down into the seat.

"Stay here, and don't say a word." Chris turned his back on him before Wong could respond.

"Ollie, I want to talk to you outside."

Chris walked to the door and kept his eye on Mahlon the whole time. Mahlon was rooted to the spot.

"Come on Ollie, now! We need to talk."

Mahlon seemed to wake up and slowly moved toward Becker who let him lead the way outside. They stopped next to a huge oak that shaded the upper part of the parking lot. Chris could see the heat rippling off the blacktop on the rest of the lot. He imagined the same emotional heat radiating off Mahlon.

"OK, you seemed to have a lot to say in there. What was that all about?"

Mahlon hesitated, looked at his feet for a while like he was trying to decide whether he was going to tell Chris anything.

"It was a family matter."

"Well, you sure weren't keeping it in the family by raising holy hell in a public restaurant? Now what is going on?"

"My daughter shouldn't be hanging around that scum, Marcus!"

"What's wrong with Marcus?" Chris had no idea who this Marcus person was, but he decided that wasn't important at the moment.

"He's just a no good white trash punk. I think he does dope and I don't trust him. They used to go out a while ago and I figured we were through with him. I don't want her to have anything to do with him."

Chris hated domestic disputes, and when it involved park staff that he had to deal with in a professional capacity every day it made it even worse.

"Look, Ollie, if you go making a scene in uniform and get yourself arrested for assault you're going to wind up losing your job. It's not just paying a fine. The department will get involved, you know that. You need to keep your child rearing stuff at home."

Chris kept thinking in the back of his mind how if Mahlon got fired they would hold his position open for months or more to save salary. Development, maintenance, and resource preservation projects in the hopper would be delayed even more than they already were. If things went too long, funding would disappear for good projects altogether. He was glad this little brawl hadn't come to blows. Maybe he could make this go away.

"Why don't you sit tight out here for a minute in your truck. I'm going to go inside and talk to Wong and your daughter. OK? We clear on this? You sit tight."

"I'll be here." Mahlon nodded grudgingly.

Wong was still in the booth and Veronica had gone over to the bar and was sitting on one of the stools. Chris was relieved to see his own daughter sitting with her, trying to calm her down. The girl seemed to be crying. The teen Chris had seen earlier, who he guessed must be Marcus, was nowhere to be seen. Becker decided to tackle Wong first.

"Daniel," Chris said as he slid into the booth across from Wong, "I am sorry that Ollie got so upset in your place. It's good that there weren't many customers here to see it."

"Yes. Customers see this and soon I have no customers!! I don't want him in here ever again."

"Well, he's been a customer of yours quite a bit before hasn't he. I mean, why impact yourself financially by losing a customer. You'll probably, never have a problem with him again."

Wong stared at him warily as he continued, "You know it's pretty hard raising a teenager. You have any kids Daniel?"

"No kids, no wife. I am married to the restaurant."

"Well take it from me, it's a challenge, especially when they start to be interested in boys. Sometimes, you don't want to let them go." He inadvertently glanced at Alicia as he said this. "Ollie's just trying to be a good father and protect his kid, you know."

"Yeah, but he must not do it in my restaurant."

"I've told him to keep his family arguments out of the public eye. I don't think you'll have any more trouble from him."

Chris didn't give him the chance to file a complaint. He didn't want to put the idea in Wong's head, and he didn't think Wong really wanted to go that route either.

"I need to talk to Veronica a bit, and then we'll let you all get back to work, OK?"

Wong nodded and Chris went over and sat next to Veronica at the bar. Alicia knew her cue without being told, and discreetly moved off the red vinyl upholstered barstool and began wiping down the nearby tables with a damp cloth that she retrieved from behind the bar. Chris wished he could ask her to wipe the bar, too. It was sticky with residue from drinks and so he folded his arms at first and then decided to slouch in a more casual pose so he wouldn't seem angry.

"What's going on between you and your father?" He softly put as much sympathy in his voice as he could.

"He's being a jerk, that's all," she said as she whipped her long black hair out of her eyes. He could see she'd been crying and her eyes were red. The cop in him wondered about pot use, but chalked it up to tears. Still, pot could be a reason Ollie had been so upset.

"Isn't being a jerk part of the dad code? I'm pretty sure I read that somewhere," Chris said with a smile that he hoped would loosen her up a bit.

"He is all pissed about me talking to Marcus. He doesn't like Marcus, but he's wrong about him. Marcus is a good person. Besides, I was just *talking* to him. We both live in this podunk town, how am I going to *never* talk to him!"

"You've got a point there." Chris wasn't quite sure where to go with the conversation.

"Look, how about you and Marcus keep it strictly business and I'll talk to your dad and see if I can ratchet him down a few notches. OK?"

"Thank you Mr. Becker. My dad is all wrong about Marcus."

"Where is Marcus now?"

"He works here. He went back to the kitchen. I don't think he wanted to be around for all this. It makes him feel bad when my dad goes off on me because of him."

"Well, I don't blame him. Maybe I will go talk with him for a bit." Chris was curious just what this kid was like. Not so much for the sake of Veronica Mahlon but because his own daughter worked here. He threaded his way through the tables that separated the bar from the food preparation area in the back of the restaurant. He purposefully planned his path so that he would brush past his daughter on the way. He was trying to remain professional, but he needed to make sure she was OK. He patted her on the shoulder as he passed. She looked up at him. He saw concern, but no real fear as he searched her face. When she smiled at him, he decided she was fine for now, and he could get back to being a cop. He returned her smile, then pushed through the galley doors and found Marcus alone in the kitchen cleaning off the cook top.

111

"Sorry, you had to go through all that with Ollie and his daughter," Chris said as he approached. Marcus was intent on scraping and seemed to be beating the stove up pretty bad. Becker guessed he was imagining it was Mahlon. "Got any idea why he doesn't want you dating his daughter?"

"Whoa, not dating…dated. We dated. Past tense." He had paused in his scraping to look up in emphasis, but now he commenced to ravaging the stove again. "He's a colossal prick, that's all," Marcus grunted out with each scrape at the old iron grill surface. "I'm not dating her, we were just talking. Old friends, you know?"

"Seems like you must have done something to make him so upset," Chris said as he found a clean part of the tile counter next to the stove to lean against.

"Couldn't say what that might be. I think he just thinks his daughter is some kind of princess royalty and a working guy isn't good enough for her."

"OK, but I'd be careful if I were you. Mahlon has a temper. Maybe you might want to give his daughter a wide berth for a while. Probably best not to engage her in conversation."

"She's my friend. I'll talk to her when I want. If she doesn't want to talk to me that is up to her."

"Look, I can't say I blame you or disagree with you. I will make sure her father knows he needs to leave you alone, but I have to tell you it may not be worth the trouble you'll get from Ollie to go up against him. Just think about it."

Chris heaved himself off the edge of the countertop and said, "Let me know if he bothers you again, OK?"

"Sure, you can count on it."

Walking back out to the dining room, Chris waved and smiled at Daniel Wong, hoping that would be enough to indicate that things were pretty well wrapped up. Wong seemed to have calmed down, and for that Chris was very grateful. He wasn't sure what other tricks he could have pulled out of his sleeve if the man had still been as livid as he was when

112

Chris first got on the scene. Had that been the case, an official police report might have been unavoidable. Wong waved back distractedly, and seemed intent on seating a couple that had just walked in. Good. Back to business as usual.

Chris scanned the room, hoping for the chance to speak to Alicia. As he did, he noticed Rose Mahlon, Ollie's wife, at the cash register, apparently paying the bill, and leaving what he could only hope was a very large tip. It was funny he hadn't noticed her before. She was a striking woman—tall and willowy, with raven black hair that flowed like silk—but she was also one of those people who knew how to make themselves invisible, like a beautiful butterfly who learns to blend in with the flowers around her. Butterflies use this camouflage for defense. Chris had often wondered if Rose's motives were similar. He felt he couldn't leave without saying something to her, besides, Alicia was the one ringing her up, so he could have a moment to speak to her too.

"Hi Rose. In all the commotion I didn't know you were here."

"Chris, I'm sorry to make you come out here."

"Well better me than the Sheriff, to tell the truth. Ollie got lucky, and I told him so. I hope he takes me seriously and doesn't pull anything like this again." Chris wasn't sure how much influence Rose had with Ollie, but he wanted her to know that this was the last straw. Any other problems and Ollie was going to have some sort of official punishment.

"I know. I appreciate your help." She looked defeated and tired. He could imagine how difficult living with Ollie must be for her, and Veronica.

Chris walked her to the door and opened it for her. Looking out to Ollie's Suburban, he saw Ollie in the driver's seat, and Veronica sitting silently in the back seat. Rose moved gracefully down the old wooden porch stairs. He figured that would be a quiet ride home. Either very quiet, or very loud.

A warm hand slipped into his and broke his contemplation. He turned.

"Hey kiddo."

113

"Hi. I'm glad it was you who came when I called."

"You called?"

"Yeah, Mr. Wong wouldn't leave the 'scene of the crime' as he called it, and Marcus was part of it, so that left me. He sent me to his office to call 911. I never dreamed you would be the one who came."

"Normally it wouldn't have been. We all got very lucky this time."

"Dad, I have been wanting to call you all afternoon about something else. I found something."

"Allie," Chris looked at his watch and the little gold hands on the dial confirmed his suspicions, "kiddo, I can't talk right now. I'm sorry. I have that campfire program tonight, remember?"

"Oh, right. Well, afterwards then. Tonight."

"OK. Are you coming to the program?"

"I'll try, but I don't know how the rest of the night will go after..." she waved her hand around the room, indicating all that had transpired. "You never know what odd rituals the 'Zen Master' may make us do to cleanse the aura of the tables and chairs after this."

"What?"

"Nothing, I'll explain everything later. All will become clear, grasshopper..."

After he had gotten back in his Cherokee he took a quick turn through the campgrounds to do a routine check since Val was still not back in the park yet. He wrote out warnings on a couple of campers with dogs running loose and some idiots with a huge bonfire that was almost licking at the tree branches overhead. It always amazed him what people did when they were camping.

With the advent of motor homes and trailers, things had changed a lot in parks, but there were still those who felt the need to chop down the park trees for firewood, pick every pretty flower they saw, and swear their off-leash dog would never bite anyone. Those were the boring and annoying little violations that no ranger wanted to deal with. Chris only had to wait until after dark, when everyone started drinking seriously, then problems became

114

more violent and typical of the city values that many campers often brought with them. In a typical day he had averaged 10,000 visitors between the Cuyamaca and Palomar park units. With no more than two or three law enforcement rangers on duty on average it was woefully inadequate. In a similar sized town they would have two or three times that, at least.

The argument at Hillside with the Mahlon family and the warnings in the campground were taking him further from the mood he wanted for his campfire tonight. Programs like that were what gave the job its positive kick. The people who came to programs and hikes were the ones who really valued the park and on the whole wanted to have a good time with the ranger. Positive contacts like that were what made this job so different from routine law enforcement jobs. He slipped into his office and tried to avoid being seen or heard by his boss. That would ruin his day for sure. Unfortunately, Savage heard him when he hit the top of the stair and called out for him to come in to his office.

"I was just going to wrap up for the day and go home, so I'm glad I caught you." Chris felt like an insect in a web, with the spider approaching. "How is the report on the lion attack coming? Have they finished the autopsy and the investigation?"

"Pretty much. I haven't gotten their written report yet. Seems like everyone will be writing it up as a lion kill, even though there are some unusual elements that don't quite fit."

Savage jumped right on those comments. "What do you mean elements that don't fit? If they have concluded it is a lion kill why are you trying to make it something else? I've told you before, that's their job and you need to stick to yours! Besides, we don't need publicity that drags this stuff on and keeps people from coming here. It's bad enough that the public will have a murderous lion in the back of their minds without you trying to make this into something more. Our budget is tight enough as it is, and with the revenue generation program becoming more important here to supply our needs, we can't afford to lose a single one of those people who visit!"

Money. It was always about money with managers. Chris started to get red in the face but held back the fire in his tongue as he said, "The information I got was preliminary. Like I said, I haven't gotten the final written report and they could easily change their final ruling with the odd things that still have to be ironed out. I'm just keeping an open mind like we all should." His boss's eyes bored into Chris and he held his stare. Becker figured he'd get more argument, but Savage surprised him and said, "Just don't go looking to make this more than it is. I've got to go, but let me know as soon as you get the final ruling."

Chris turned to go without answering as Dick Savage gathered up some papers and stuffed them in his briefcase. By the time he got to the chair in his office he could hear the man's briefcase snap and his footfalls echo on the stairs. He let out a long breath, surprised that he had been holding it. He found himself wondering if he would be like his boss if he ever got the chance to be in charge. He pulled his slide tray out and fitted it onto the projector to run through his program once more before he packed up and headed down to the campfire center. It was late and he knew he only had a few minutes before he needed to be there to set up.

Chapter 14

By the time Chris got to the campground, it was after sunset. The campfire center was at the edge of a large meadow with thick worn and polished pine benches in need of a new coat of paint. Seventy-five years of bottoms had waited here for the ranger to spin some magical web combining the miracle of the great outdoors with entertainment and education in some inspiring fashion. A spider web covered plywood screen with faded white paint was functional enough to project slides on, and he pulled a heavy orange extension cord from the cabinet beneath it. He still had enough light to set up, but he had to rush. His unexpected detour with Mahlon in the afternoon had really thrown off his time schedule.

He went ahead and set the wood for the fire and got his projector and microphone placed at the ready. He didn't light the fire since one of the big treats was to pick a kid in the front row to light it. And to his credit, so far he hadn't set any of them on fire. People started to trickle in, and by the time it was dark he was able to warm them up and get them to sing along with him on a few tunes. He had tried to build a repertoire of songs that weren't too out of date, and so most commonly he tried to use John Denver songs that were heavy on the nature references. In reality, he didn't really care if campers sang along or not. He just enjoyed singing and playing, and had even started doing an occasional folk singing gig at the pizza parlor in Wynola once a month. Three or four songs usually were enough for the campers, and by then it was dark enough to light the fire and then open the floor up for questions about anything that the campers were curious about.

On this particular evening, he fielded some interesting questions including a couple about mountain lion safety and an upcoming park bond issue. He had to dance on both subjects since he didn't want to scare visitors too much about cougars, and the law prevented him from advocating a position while in uniform on how people should vote. He did make a point to tell them that Californians spent about one quarter of one percent of the state budget on their parks and, frankly, they all probably spent more on dinner at McDonalds.

He tried to make them laugh with a few environmental jokes and then he spent a half hour running through his slides and discussing the history of the Kumeya'ay Indians who had inhabited the park before white settlement. He marveled at how much simpler their lives were than what people in the park found contentment with today. He ended the program with another song. The appreciative applause was meager but genuine and so were the handshakes, as the weary audience thanked him and then wandered back toward their campsites. Chris was nearly finished stumbling through the darkness and packing up his gear when the radio on his hip crackled out his call sign.

When he answered Val Simpson said, "We have another lion incident, no injuries. Can you meet us at West Mesa parking?"

Chris cursed silently under his breath, as a familiar sinking feeling began to creep into stomach. Unbelievable. He was really beginning to dread these lion incidents. And two, so close together, well that could only mean trouble.

"I'm just finishing packing up my stuff at the campfire. I can be there in about five minutes." He tried to hide his consternation.

"OK, we'll wait for you. We lucked out this time. I have Lt. James here with me right now, too."

"Does Frank have the scent dogs with him, by any chance?" Perhaps a silver lining could be had after all.

"Actually, the whole hunt team is on their way at his request and should be here in about 15 minutes."

Becker was amazed at the rapid response, since getting a U.S. Department of Agriculture hunt team with dogs that were specially trained usually entailed a huge process and a lengthy response time. He packed his gear and arrived at the dirt lot along Highway 79 that allowed access to the West Mesa Trail.

"We had a bicyclist riding the trail and a lion tried to jump him," Val said as he exited his vehicle. "The guy was lucky. He jumped off the bike and put it between himself and the cat. Hollered his head off and threw rocks at it for a while until it headed off to the north along the trail."

Chris turned to Frank James who already had his hunting rifle out. "Val said you had a team on the way with dogs?"

"Yeah, they were down in Descanso going after a cat that apparently attacked and killed a guy's pastured horse early this morning. The guy has also lost 20 sheep over the past month, ten of them just slaughtered all at one time and not eaten. I guess the horse was enough to get the department finally actively involved, especially after your incident with the guy on Azalea. The team should be here any minute." James' own dog seemed anxious to begin the hunt. Chris was not so sure. Even though this was his third hunt since coming to work in the park, it was something he could never get used to. He also figured he had better call Alicia before this thing got started. Experience had taught him it could be hours before he got home. He dialed the number, but it went straight to the answering machine at home. He left a brief message. At least she would know where he was. He hoped whatever she had wanted to tell him could wait.

It was pitch dark. No moon and no breeze. One of those sticky nights that wouldn't cool off until midnight most likely. Scent should be good, so maybe they would get lucky. Maybe it would even be the snaggle tooth cat that had killed Xavier Hess, and they could put this whole series of events behind them.

The dog team and handler arrived as Chris was pulling his shotgun out of the rack and loading it with slug ammo. The handler pulled his dogs out of the truck and joined Frank James across the highway on the trail. Chris caught up and headed out with them, each man letting their bobbing flashlights lead the way. With the darkness cloaked all around them, Chris wondered if the lion could be just sitting on a tree branch right next to them as they passed. Hopefully, the dogs would be good at their job, but Chris couldn't help feeling vulnerable in a way he had never felt in any other situation. This was the supreme hunter they were tracking. The master of stealth and concealment, with hearing, vision and scent that was superior to all of them, save the dogs they relied upon. He felt more like prey than predator.

A sliver of moon cracked over the thick band of pines that surrounded them. The trail was broad and actually served as a road for park vehicles, though it was not surface treated in any way. The dogs were running free ahead and their clamorous barking echoed in and around the trees and boulders surrounding the trail sounding more like crazed wolves than well trained hunting animals. Chris had no idea what kind of sound they made if they had treed their quarry, but he was sure the handler would alert them if he felt the animals had picked up the scent or cornered the cougar.

They followed the road for the better part of an hour before the handler stopped and told them they needed to head out cross-country to follow the dogs. He was convinced they had picked up a scent trail and were close upon the cat. Apparently he was right because shortly before midnight, after a lengthy amount of bushwhacking on their part, the tone of the barking changed and became more frantic. The dogs were far ahead, so it took some time for them to close the distance in the rough country. When the men finally came up to the dogs, they had surrounded one huge pine about half way up the West Mesa in the wilderness area above the Fern Flat road not far below the 6500' Cuyamaca Peak. As Lt. James let his flashlight crawl its way up the tree, branch by branch, the anticipation grew. About half way up a cougar hugged the gnarled branch and hissed at the dogs below. The warden didn't waste any time unshouldering his rifle and taking the shot. The cat screamed and bolted straight up before tumbling out of the tree to the ground below. James advanced slowly and insured the animal was dead. Chris lamented that the animal had to die, but Fish and Game had given up tranquilizing years ago, since there was no place to move cougars to that didn't leave the Department liable for the animal's behavior, and no zoo wanted them.

"Not a very big one. Looks like maybe an 18 month-old teenager. Momma must have just kicked him out of the home territory." It was typical of females to keep their young around for up to two years and then chase them off to make their own territory. Male cats were only around for conception and would likely kill another cat under any other meeting circumstance. Females weren't much different after the young were old enough to fend for themselves.

James began prying open the cougar's mouth as the dog handler rounded up his animals and pulled them off their quarry so Frank could do his job.

"Well, at least we know the bicyclist really saw a lion and not somebody's house cat, but we've still got a problem. These teeth look perfectly normal, and I'm betting they won't match the ones on Xavier Hess's neck at all. I'd guess this cat's way too small, too," the warden said.

"Crap!" Becker couldn't help himself. This meant his case wasn't solved, there was still a rogue cat on the loose, and Savage would still be on his case.

"What do you want to do with the cat, Chris?" James was still holding the cat's mouth open.

"You guys will want to take a mouth impression won't you?" Chris said.

"Yeah, and maybe some saliva DNA and blood samples, but that's about it. If you guys want it for a museum mount or something you might as well take advantage of it. I'm sure no one will mind."

Chris thought about it and figured they could find money somewhere for the taxidermy. He was also more comfortable with this particular cat being an exhibit since it apparently hadn't killed anyone. Exhibiting "the" killer cat probably wasn't too politically correct.

"Sure, does Fish and Game have a freezer big enough for it until I can make arrangements?

"No problem. Once the biologist is done with it, I can keep it in the freezer at my place since I didn't get my deer last fall," James mumbled that last part with what Becker thought was a slight bit of embarrassment. Chris was more worried about the embarrassment the department might face if people felt that this mountain lion issue was a reason to avoid the park. No visitors wanted to feel that they were entering the heart of darkest Africa on their family picnic.

Chapter 15

Chris Becker woke up late on Sunday morning from the first really good night's sleep he'd had in weeks. He wondered if running around in the woods at night thinking you were about to be eaten was a good prescription for sleep. Actually, he was kind of surprised that he slept so well, as he was still mulling over the fact that, according to Frank James, the jaw didn't look like it belonged to the lion that killed Hess. Measurements would still have to be taken to confirm the facts, but it would be a disappointment if it didn't close the case and instead wound up giving yet another lion the reputation as a potential killer. Dick Savage would blow a gasket for sure if the news leaked to the press, and the local merchants were already poised to go on the warpath if the park shut down the campgrounds and trails for safety purposes, since their livelihoods depended on the park's visitors.

He stumbled to the kitchen and microwaved some of the previous day's coffee. He was off duty today, which was one of the perks of being Chief Ranger. He had spent 18 years working every weekend and holiday throughout the year, only being allowed to vacation during "rainy weekdays in November" as the rangers joked. It

123

had been a huge challenge to find weekend babysitters for Alicia when she was little, especially considering most Park housing is in the middle of nowhere. He was glad she was past that age, and also that he had risen enough through the ranks that he could be off duty at least some of the times when normal people had days off.

He fingered one of the dents in the old pine dining room table and wondered why Alicia wasn't up yet. Church started at 11:00am, and Allie was all girl. Getting ready on Sunday was a full on project with showers that often could be measured the way scientists measured eras of geologic time. He had done some of his amateur sketches and full paintings quicker than she could put on eye makeup.

"Allie! You better get your butt out of bed if we are going to get to town on time!" Chris yelled as he padded in his bare feet down the long hall to her room.

"You awake in there, or do I have to drag you out of bed?" When she was six he had been known to pull all her covers off and take them with him, just to motivate her. When there was no answer he cracked the door and peeked inside her room and was surprised that she wasn't there.

"Allie?" He checked the small bathroom in the hall but it was empty. He began to feel uneasy until he noticed through the window she was out picking some of the wildflowers that were growing on the small patch of meadow grass they claimed was a lawn.

"Hey, you know it's illegal to pick wildflowers in a State Park, lady! I need to see your driver's license please." She turned, twisted up her face and stuck her tongue out at him.

"I'll have you know I have influence in very high places Mr. Ranger. If you want to keep your job you better be nice, and you better be making a really good omelet for me, because it's your turn to cook breakfast."

"How about a Cheerios and milk omelet since we are both late getting ready?"

"Yuck!"

He made a mental note that he needed to mow the lawn if for no other reason than to lessen the fire danger around their cabin. He'd been ignoring it lately. He'd grown up mowing lawns for money as a kid and well into college, and he'd finally gotten to the stage of being tired of doing it. He went back to the kitchen and set out the cereal and bowls and then went down the hall to take a quick shower. When he was done and dressed Alicia was finishing up cereal and toast.

"I nuked some sausages for you. Did you leave me any hot water for a shower?"

"Allie, no one could leave you enough hot water for a shower if you were connected directly to the Old Faithful geyser! Hurry up or we're not going to make it."

Twenty minutes later they were in his primer gray Chevy pickup on the twisting highway motoring toward Julian and dodging cattle grazing on the highway from the ranch just north of the park. It was a 'fence out' county in the 1800s—people had to fence out unwanted cattle—and no one had ever changed the law. What few fences that remained were rarely maintained well enough to contain the livestock. Amazingly, in spite of the delays, both of the bovine and the human variety, they rolled into Julian with time to spare.

Julian was an anachronism in San Diego County. Purposely maintained as a quaint little gold rush town, its chief claim to fame now was the Julian Apple Pie. Apple orchards had legitimately succeeded the gold mining for a while, but few tourists realized that now most of the apples were imported, and only a few orchards were still even in existence. Most of the apples in the Julian Apple Pies were from anywhere but Julian, yet that didn't stop them from being loved, revered and consequently exported all over San Diego and Southwest Riverside Counties and beyond. The pastries themselves were as good as any other, maybe better, but what really sold those pies was the romance and mystery of Julian itself.

Extensive warrens of tunneling existed around the township and even one huge mine was contained within the Cuyamaca State Park

125

boundary. Buildings were maintained in the fashion of the late 1800s to early 1900s, and any day in summer and every weekend throughout the year the streets were crowded with vehicles from the coastal urbanites and congested inland valley communities looking for a day in the country. This lifestyle was great for the many retail establishments in and around town— for them tourism was lifeblood itself. However, the constant feeling of living in a fishbowl was difficult for locals during the weekends. Parking for church was a nightmare unless one arrived by 10:30, so Chris and Allie wound up parking almost up at the Eagle Mine and walking back downhill to the simple white wooden church on "C" Street.

He hadn't been on the mineshaft tour at the Eagle Mine just up the road from the church for a couple years and thought maybe they should do that after church. He still remembered the narrow low ceiling tunnels that made him feel like gophers must feel as they claw through the ground with the walls touching their bodies. It was almost the same at the Eagle Mine. Chris couldn't even stand straight in the tunnels until they got to the mine superintendent's "office" underground. It wasn't much larger than his bathroom at home, and sported a single candle to work by. When the tour guide turned out the lights, it was amazing how much one candle illuminated after the eyes were accustomed to the dark. Miners often conserved their candles when leaving the mine and would walk in the dark, dragging their foot along the rails the ore cars used. Cars would roll out to the dump-site by gravity and the miners would feel the rail vibrate as a car descended. Tunnels were so narrow the miner would have to scurry to one of the cubbyholes placed every few hundred feet and press his body into it before the ore cart ran him over...all in pitch dark. He wondered how many tunnels ran right under the town itself.

Chris and Alicia made it down the hill and up the granite steps of the church just as the organ began the first mournful strains of "Onward Christian Soldiers." They mumbled hushed greetings to the deacon at the door, and sat in an empty pew at the back of the small sanctuary. The benches were hard since the lumpy padding, encased in faded chartreuse

126

velvet, had ceased to perform its job years ago. The old upright piano was badly in need of being tuned, and God alone could help the voices of the choir…all four of them. Only a handful of people were in attendance. Infighting had decimated the congregation over the past two years. It was a pathetic thing to watch, and it reminded Chris that just going to church didn't make a person good. All the bitterness and mean spirited judgmentalism were as present here as in the workplace or any other arena of life. It shouldn't be here, but dealing with human beings made it inevitable.

Still, there were a couple of members Chris really respected—one was the pastor, which is why he still bothered to occasionally attend. He had never met a minister who was so down to earth and so humble. Unfortunately, it left him at the mercy of the evils that lurked in the hearts of many of the members. He doubted the pastor would last out the rest of the year. Word was out that the church board blamed him for the poor weekly attendance. Churches weren't much different than the park service or any other organization. They were organizations filled with people, both good and bad.

As the choir finished its last chorus, and the lone deacon passed around the wooden collection plate, Chris settled in for the morning's message. He found it an odd coincidence that the sermon was about child raising and the commandment to honor your mother and father, and wondered whether the pastor had heard about the dust up at the Hillside Resort with Mahlon and Veronica yesterday. The 'pine needle telegraph' could travel pretty fast in a small community.

"Well, I hope you paid attention and realize now that you must kneel in abject subservience to me until the second you turn eighteen," Chris laughed as they walked out of the church.

"Why yes, oh gracious master! I will plow all the fields and shear the sheep and tote the barge until that very day, which unfortunately for you is in exactly 19 days, 14 hours and about 34 seconds."

"Am I raising a mathematician here?"

"Hardly, just a rough estimate."

"Aah, thank God. I thought I'd never get rid of you," he snorted. "I think we should stop at Jack's and get some groceries."

"I just went to the store. What on earth do we still need?"

"Oh, I just felt like getting something special, like ice cream."

Alicia wondered if it was more to check and see if Marina was working. Something was going on there. She was sure of it. They walked down the steep slope of "C" Street and turned right onto Main. The shoulders were packed with parked cars and traffic was bumper-to-bumper moving about 5 miles an hour as people looked vainly for a parking spot. The Julian Historic District was a treat to most lowlanders who lived amongst the modern architecture of the urban coast.

The town was formed shortly after the Civil War by a few good old Georgia Confederate boys who were taken with its pine-fringed meadows. Named after Mike Julian, who soon discovered gold in the surrounding streams, the town flourished, with mining and agriculture being the mainstays of the economy. Several buildings along Main Street dated back to the turn of the 20th Century, with most originally being residences, saloons, a school, a jail, stores and hotels. The flavor was a mixture of old west and World War II architecture that catered to the bellies of its visitors with candy and pies. One of Becker's favorites was the old drug store with an authentic style soda fountain counter and 'soda jerk' that still served up its fare the same as the day it opened.

"So what kind of ice cream were you thinking of getting...Passion Fruit?"

"Huh?"

"You know, Love Potion #9 ice cream?"

"I have no idea what you are talking about. Do they really make stuff like that?"

"Come on Dad, you want to go see if Marina is working. You can't fool me."

"I do not. I just need an ice cream fix. Why would I want to see Marina? Just because she is beautiful and single and friendly isn't even

128

something I've ever noticed. You must have me confused with someone else."

Jack's Grocery was crowded with people like all the businesses on Main, though most were locals looking just to get groceries and escape back to the calm safety of their homes. Chris headed for the ice cream freezer and grabbed some peanut butter and chocolate swirl ice cream and then headed for the checkout counter. Alicia perused the adjacent isles, partly to make sure there wasn't something else they needed that she had forgotten, and partly to give her dad a little space, just in case he wanted it.

"Mmmm, that looks good. I love peanut butter and chocolate," Marina said as she rang up their purchase. "Is that all you are getting today?"

"Yeah, I just thought we'd celebrate a day off and indulge ourselves. I thought about doing the Eagle Mine tour or going over to the pool at Pinecrest. Just about anything to get away from the heat for a while sounds good. Have you ever been there?" Chris said.

"Yes, I take my son there to the pool a lot."

"I've never been, but since I've got ice cream that will melt, I guess that will have to do us for today."

Becker couldn't help but notice just how attractive Marina was. Long black hair, a perfect smile, and even with a full apron on he could see that her figure was classic. She had to have several guys after her, although having to take on someone else's kid sometimes slowed some of the men down. He wondered about asking her out, but was never very adept at that sort of thing.

"Well, maybe we'll see you there at the pool some other time? I get Mondays and Tuesdays off," she said.

"I only get Sundays and Mondays off, usually, so maybe we will cross paths some Monday."

Becker figured that was about as close to asking for a date as he could get. He wasn't quite sure what else to say, but he wanted to linger as long as he could. He struck on the only topic that seemed safe.

129

"I wonder where Allie has gone? We better get home before this starts to melt. Allie!" Chris smiled at Marina as he raised his voice and half rolled his eyes. "Allie! Come on kiddo, let's go." When there was no response, the smile on his lips faded to parental consternation.

"Don't worry, she can't have gone far—this place is no bigger than a postage stamp. Maybe she's in the back with Marcus."

"Marcus?" The consternation turned to confusion and then uncomfortable understanding. "Do you mean the Marcus that works at Hillside Resort?" He half hoped there could be some other Marcus with whom his daughter was holed up in the back room of the grocery.

"Yes, he started a while ago working a few days a week stocking shelves and cleaning. Anyway, they know each other, right? Maybe she is talking to him." Marina gave an encouraging little smile and waggled her finger in the direction of the storeroom as the customer behind him cleared her throat, obviously growing impatient at the delay.

Chris wasn't sure if Marina's smile was meant to encourage him to go to the back room to look for Allie, or to the Pinecrest pool to look for her, but either way he felt buoyed by the conversation, at least that part of it. The rest left him somewhat concerned. He had briefly considered the nature of Alicia's association with Marcus yesterday afternoon, but had never had the opportunity to ask her about it, and now he was worried that this seemingly volatile young man was alone with his little girl. He rounded the aisle of canned vegetables and saw Allie standing with her back to him, chatting pleasantly with the young man he remembered interviewing in the Hillside kitchen the day before. He was wearing a dark grocer's apron and leaning on a wide old push broom.

Alicia heard Chris approach and turned, "Hi, did you get what you came for?" She winked at him, impressed with her double meaning.

"Yes, ice cream, check. Now let's go, we don't want it to melt before we get home." He wasn't feeling playful, and instead gave her his best Do What I Say Now Young Lady look.

She was taken aback by his demeanor, but not so much that she forgot her manners, "Ok, sure, but I wanted to introduce you to a friend of mine. You met yesterday I hear, but perhaps not officially. Dad, this is Marcus Lundee, the night cook at Hillside, and apparently the new stock boy here. Marcus, this is my father, Chris Becker."

Chris wasn't quite sure what Alicia was doing with all this official introduction business. Hadn't he questioned the boy not twenty-four hours before?

"Nice to meet you Mr. Becker," Marcus said awkwardly, stretching out his hand.

"Likewise." He clasped the hand offered to him and shook firmly. He always felt he could tell a lot about a person by their handshake. Marcus' was firm and forceful. He was being polite, but he wasn't afraid or cowed by Chris. "C'mon, Allie, we gotta go!"

"Bye Marcus."

"I'll see you."

That phrase struck Chris a bit odd for some reason, and it stuck with him, even when they were out on the street walking back up Main.

"Why did he say 'I'll see you'? That's an odd thing to say for a teenager."

"What!"

"No, really 'I'll see ya', or just 'see ya' is much more natural. But 'I'll see you' is just so pointed, so specific. It bugs me."

"Oh jeez, do you always have to be a cop?"

"Trust me kid, dad radar trumps cop radar any day."

"He probably meant he'd see me at work. We do work together you know."

Chris didn't answer. Instead he stared at the sidewalk in front of him, occasionally glancing at the girl-woman at his side. He knew her better than anyone else in his life, in fact he knew there was something she wasn't telling him now, and yet his child was also something of a mystery to him. He hated to sound cliché, but he felt more and more that he was losing

131

her—college, boys and all that. She was growing up and there was nothing he could do about it except be so proud of her. Proud and sad. They walked on in silence.

They were past the church and turning right to head up yet another hill to reach the car when Allie cleared her throat.

"There may have been another reason Marcus said that." She spoke quietly.

"I'm listening."

"Well, I was going to tell you last night, but you didn't get home until…when did you get home, anyway?" She turned her face to meet his gaze, she might be getting older, but she wasn't getting any taller. At 5'6" she would always have to look up to see into her father's eyes. There was something poetic about that. It made up for the fact that she also had to ask him to help her reach things off the top shelf over the refrigerator.

"Long story. I'll tell you in a minute. Finish what you were saying."

"Well, I was asleep when you got home, so I didn't get to tell you that I am going to dinner with Marcus tomorrow night."

"What do you mean 'dinner'? Like a date 'dinner'?" Chris was doing his best to maintain composure, but he was not comfortable with this turn of events.

"Yes, at least I think so. That's why I wanted you to be introduced officially."

"Wait, you think so? What does that mean?"

"I don't know. Marcus is kind of strange. Sometimes he acts like we are friends, sometimes he acts like yesterday. We made an appointment to have dinner together, and he seemed happy about it. If that's not a date, what is it?" The look in her eye undermined her confident exterior, and he knew that she didn't need the third degree just then.

"Look. I'm sorry if I kind of seemed upset. He and I got off on the wrong foot I guess. To be honest, I'm not that comfortable with the guy, but I realize I don't really know him." Chris was trying to be diplomatic. "Look, do you feel comfortable around him?"

132

"Well, that's sort of a weird question. He's not dangerous if that's what you mean, but no, I don't feel comfortable around him. He is kind of dark and complicated."

"Oh, great. My daughter has a date with James Dean. Every father's dream."

"Dad!" They had reached their old Chevy pickup, and parted company, Chris going to the driver's side, keys in hand, and Alicia waiting patiently for him to unlock the passenger door. As they scooted in across the tan upholstered seats, both simultaneously buckled up and rolled down their windows as if on autopilot.

"Hey, I bet that ice cream has reached perfect eating consistency right about now, just melty enough to be really good. I think we still have some plastic spoons in the glove box from the last time we went to the McDonalds drive thru. What do you say?" Without waiting for a reply, Alicia began rooting around in the ample glove compartment's storage space, and emerged victorious with two cellophane wrapped spoons, one black and one white.

"Don't mind if I do." He took the black spoon, peeled the lid off the condensation covered tub, and gouged a huge swath from the middle of the pristine surface. "Aah, that hits the spot!"

"Hey, what about me?!" Chris barely had time to hand the ice cream container over before she stabbed in her spoon and scooped out a bite to rival the size of his.

Midway into their impromptu picnic, Alicia remembered she had been waiting to tell her father something since the previous morning, "Dad, oh my gosh, I almost forgot!" She had to put her hand over her mouth to avoid spewing ice cream spittle in his face.

"Take a breath Allie, what is it?"

"I tried calling you yesterday a couple times, but you didn't pick up, and then when I did see you it was that whole Veronica and Marcus thing, then you never got home," she shot him a glance that showed she had been worried, "and then we were scrambling for church."

"Oh, yeah right, before I left to get my stuff for the campfire program yesterday you said you wanted to talk to me. What's up?"

"Well, you'll never guess why I went into work so early."

"Yeah, you were gone even before me. That never happens." He smiled and winked, poking fun at her distaste for early rising.

"Hey, I'm a growing girl, and I need my beauty sleep. Anyway, I went there because Mr. Wong called in a panic because, get this, Xavier Hess stayed in one of the rooms at our resort the night before he was killed!"

Chris had clearly not expected a revelation of this caliber. His spoon full of ice cream, perched in midair, halted before its intended target by the complete shock he felt. He dropped the spoon unceremoniously back in the tub, narrowly missing his own lap, "What!"

"I know, weird huh?" She was beginning to lean closer toward him in her seat, and her eyes were getting rounder as she spoke, "wait, it gets weirder. So Mr. Wong is kind of a freak and worried about spirits and stuff, whatever, anyway, he needs me to come in and clean the room and cleanse the aura, if you can believe that. So, I go there right," she was leaning closer still, her eyes fairly popping out of her head, her voice increasing a decibel or two with each word, "and you'll never guess what I found!"

"Wait, what, you were in his room? Wong had you clean his room!" Chris' faculties had returned to him and he was thinking like a cop again.

"Well, yeah, I mean, the room had been used, it had to be cleaned. We had other guests booked. It's not like it was the crime scene or anything. There wasn't any blood if that's what you're worried about. And as I say again, I found something." Alicia was feeling somewhat deflated that her dad seemed to be ruining her big moment of revelation.

Chris saw the frustration in her eyes, so he struggled to contain his own, knowing full well that officially the repercussions for this mistake could be huge.

"Sorry kiddo, what did you find."

"First I noticed that the bed was mussed, not a surprise right, if someone slept there. But then I found a ladies leopard print G-string, so maybe there wasn't as much sleeping going on as I first thought, if you know what I mean." She cocked one eyebrow and tried to look conspiratorial.

"Yes, I know what you mean. It pains me to know that you are old enough to know what you mean, but go on, you have my full attention."

"Good, Ok, well, after the G-string, which by the way, YUCK, I went into the bathroom and found all these red lipstick kisses on the mirror, like she was saying goodbye to him." She looked at her father and waited a second for him to react, but he was silent, so she continued, "but that wasn't the most interesting thing I found."

"You've got to be kidding."

Alicia reached into her purse, thankful she'd had the presence of mind to transfer the matchbook cover and the panties she had found in the room from her pants pocket to a small Ziploc bag and put it in her purse before she, say, absentmindedly washed her jeans. *Could happen, she thought.*

"This is the most interesting thing I found." She placed the Ziploc bag in his hand, with the writing on the back side of the matchbook facing him, "this was on the floor near Mr. Hess' bedside table, the one with the phone. What do you make of it?"

Chris stared down at the scrawled writing, unable to put into words the thoughts spinning in his head. He flipped over the bag and saw the ad for a place called the Palomino Club on the front of the matchbook. One thought was clear enough to articulate though, "good job Allie, good job." The other thought was that Mrs. Hess had been a little short on details the day he visited her, and it was time they had another intimate "chat." The stress of her husband's death didn't seem a good enough excuse for Chris to explain to himself why she hadn't told him about Hess staying at the Hillside the night before his death.

135

Chapter 16

Monday, August 19th

It was dark. Not the kind of dark that one felt in the evening after sunset, but a dark that blanketed all sound and could be felt heavy and cold against the skin. Movement was slow and though conversation was taking place, no lips moved. The lips were supposed to be moving because there was no telepathic thought here, yet the lips didn't move.

His wife, Lori, moved through that darkness. Chris could make her out clearly and he sensed that the darkness must have held large pine trees and heavy brush along a trail as well. There was another presence, too, but he couldn't define it, though he was certain it was malevolent.

She was telling him she couldn't be with him any longer, and he was asking her not to go. She couldn't tell him why she had to go, just that she must, that they could never be together again. Sadness enveloped Chris in a way he had never known. It felt as if his heart was no longer inside his body, and that all that was left was a stiff wooden replica of himself. There were tears in her eyes as she moved away quickly down the trail. She kept saying "it's all my fault" as Chris screamed out for her to wait, but she kept on deeper into the darkened wood.

From that same darkness he sensed movement. Something unknown, the other presence. Then, suddenly it was visible and full blown and larger than life. A cougar that stood five feet high at the shoulders and at least ten feet long, and when it took Lori's head in its mouth it disappeared inside all the way to her shoulders. As it dragged Lori into the brush, Chris could see clearly that its movements were odd, jerky and almost machine-like reminding him of the clay models used in early horror movies. It even appeared that bolts held the shoulders and jaws to the body. He wanted to run and pull her free, but he was rooted to the spot where he stood.

He screamed her name, and as he did so he found himself in his bedroom breathless and sweating, with his heart beating wildly. As he realized it was only a dream, he sat up on the edge of the bed and held his hands to his face.

He had never dreamed of real people in his whole life. Lori became the one exception. She inhabited his nights in vivid Technicolor dreams once or twice a year, and always the sadness and despair accompanied the nightmares; for truly, they were nightmares. Always violent, always filled with longing and loneliness, always dark and foreboding. Lori was stabbed in a bar fight in one, crashed on a motorcycle in another. Always the feeling was, if she were with Chris, she would have been protected from these occurrences. This one, however, was different in that it somehow combined the events of the recent mountain lion attack into the scene. Perhaps, he thought, his anger and depression at her abandonment of him and Alicia had finally turned to revenge in his mind. It was unlike him, but who knows what the rivers of the unconscious would pour out, with more truth than that which was constrained by conscious intellect and moral judgments when awake.

The clock showed 5:00am and Chris knew he wouldn't be able to go back to sleep at this point since he had to get up at 6:00 for work. He quietly went to the kitchen and pulled down the coffee to put the grounds in the pot. As the coffee brewed so did his thoughts about the dream. Who ever heard

137

of a mechanical cougar? What on earth was that all about? Something else was wrong with the mechanical cougar, though Chris couldn't put his finger on it, and the images were all fading from memory the longer he was awake. Dreams were like steam. You could see them for a while, but they eventually faded, unrecoverable, into the atmosphere around them.

Why was Lori such a persistent feature in his thoughts after all these years? Surely, he had let go of all the pain and lonely memories long ago. Yet she still came unbidden into his sleeping thoughts at will.

Since he was up, he thought he might as well make breakfast, maybe a bit more than the typical weekday bowl of cereal. He found a year-old box of cinnamon coffee cake mix and poured it in a bowl. No bug or mold showed its face, so he figured it was still good enough to eat and began adding milk and eggs to it. He wasn't much of a cook, and poor Allie lived mostly off TV dinners, hamburgers, and spaghetti unless they were occasionally practicing how to be real cooks. On rare occasions he might have a woman briefly in his life who volunteered to cook them a meal, but Chris just hadn't seemed able to connect to any of them and they soon lost interest. He warmed the oven and slipped it in to bake. As he got the oven mitts out 17 minutes later and put them on he again thought of Lori, and how she had put her hands in these mitts to cook. "Things" always brought sad memories, and he reminded himself to buy new oven mitts next time he went shopping.

Alicia stepped into the kitchen just as he pulled the fresh smelling cinnamon coffee cake out of the oven. Her hair looked as if she had put it in a blender, and she shielded her eyes from the bright fluorescent light of the kitchen. The fuzzy pink kitty faces at the toes of her slippers allowed him the most fleeting feeling that she was still eight years old instead of practically eighteen. For a split second he thought he could actually feel his heart in his chest, and he understood again where the word "heartache" originated. Whoever coined that phrase had a daughter, a daughter who was growing up.

"Do I smell cinnamon? How long did I sleep? Is it Christmas?" The look of pure confusion answered Chris's question of whether she was being sarcastic or if she was still half asleep.

"No, it's not Christmas." His half-hearted laugh felt strangely more hollow than he had intended. He wasn't sure if it was the oddness of the hour, the darkness of the dawn compared to the blaring light in the kitchen, or the disquieting remnants of his dream.

"Well it isn't my birthday for a few more weeks, either." She was more fully awake now, "so what's with the coffee cake?" The strangeness of the situation was slowly dawning on her, and her mind was trying to make sense of it.

"Last time you made breakfast on a school day, you had gotten the job here. Oh, Dad, we aren't moving again are we?" The danger she perceived in the situation had wiped away all traces of sleep and her eyes had grown as big as saucers.

Chris's laugh was genuine this time, although he felt a twinge of guilt that her life had been one of shuffling all over the state. She was usually such a trooper, but her obvious panic belied the toll their transience had taken on her.

"Can't a dad make breakfast for his daughter without it being a federal case?"

"Yes, 'a dad' can, but you can't. Let's just say cooking is not your forte. Something is up, so if we aren't moving, what's going on?"

"OK, I had a bad dream," Chris was serious now.

"About Mom again?" Alicia knew all about his battle with the dreams.

"Yeah, about your Mom again."

Alicia hated to hear that defeated tone in his voice. After all these years he sometimes still seemed so broken.

"Motorcycle or bar fight?" She nudged him in the ribs in an attempt at joviality, realizing mid-jab that she was making fun of her own mother's

139

death, even if it was only her 'dream death'. This conversation was too weird.

"No, this one was really weird. A giant mechanical mountain lion stuffed her head and shoulders in its huge mouth and drug her off into the night." Chris stabbed a knife into the coffee cake with a little more force than was actually necessary to cut through the steaming pastry.

"Yikes!" Alicia couldn't be sure how much of her exclamation was due to the dream description or the fact that her dad was murdering breakfast.

"Now do you understand the dire need for the cinnamon coffee cake?" He plopped a huge piece on a plate and then slapped a generous dollop of butter on top.

"Absolutely, but no butter on mine, Dad, I prefer not to actually feel my arteries hardening. So, a lion ate her head, huh, what do you suppose Freud would say about that?" She reached across him to get a fork.

Chris looked askance at her as she opened the drawer, "Probably that it had something to do with my mother, which I can guarantee it did not! Besides, what do you know about Freud?"

"Mostly, so far as I can tell, that he was a nut-job obsessed with body parts. I started reading ahead in my Psych 101 textbook. Besides, Michael's father is some sort of therapist, so he has learned a bunch of 'shrink think' and always has an answer for what a dream means."

They each took their plates and headed for the table. Sitting kitty-corner to one another, they were both lost in the silence of enjoying a hot breakfast for a change. After several bites, Alicia's thoughts turned back to the conversation.

"So if it wasn't about Grandma," a slight smirk appeared at the corner of her mouth, "what was it about? Why was the lion a robot or whatever? That's the weird part. That part is what is really bothering me."

"That's the part that is bothering you! I tell you that your mother is decapitated in my dream and I don't do anything about it, and the part that bothers you is that the culprit is less than organic!" The sense of panic rising

140

in his throat was surprising even to Chris. Had he totally failed his daughter by not protecting her from the truth of his feelings, and dreams, all these years? She had been his best friend and confidant since she was a little girl, and it had always seemed like she could handle it, like she was wise beyond her years, but of late he had wondered.

"Geez Dad, don't have a coronary. You've killed Mom off a dozen or more ways over the years. I expect her to die in your dreams. It is your way of processing your grief. I get it. I have ways too. What doesn't make sense is that usually the modus operandi—"

"You've been watching way too much TV."

"—whatever, the MO is usually logical, believable, or at least possible. A car accident, cancer, you know, but never a science-fiction-super-Frankenstein-cat! That is just too weird, even for you. Besides, it is too much like what is going on in real life—you know, the dead guy. I think your subconscious is trying to tell you something."

"Who are you?" Chris didn't know whether to be impressed or worried by how clearly she was psychoanalyzing him.

"Hey, I'm a bona fide college student now," she struck her most professional pose and looked pointedly at him, then noticed her fuzzy slippers and the façade crumbled before his eyes. She slumped back in her chair and sipped the last drop of her milk in her glass, "besides, like I said, Michael and I talk about this kind of stuff a lot. We both have people in our lives who could benefit from a little psycho-babble."

"I'm not sure how to take that, but OK, assuming you are right, what pray tell, Miss College, is my subconscious trying to tell me?"

"Well," she appeared to be considering the question thoughtfully, and gearing up for a long dissertation when she happened to glance at the clock on the VCR, "Oh, shoot! Sorry Dad, I have to hurry if I am going to get to school in time to get a parking place. You would not believe how fast those lots fill up!" She was babbling now, rushing to clear her spot at the table.

141

As she scooted to the kitchen to rinse her plate, she paused and leaned around the door-frame to look at him. Chris was still sitting, sipping his coffee, eyeing her expectantly.

"Ok, if you ask me, there is something bugging you about the case. If you want a more detailed analysis, you'll have to wait until I get into Psych 102." A split second later he heard splashing water and the clank of fork on ceramic as the plate landed in the bottom of the sink to be tended to later.

As she passed back through the dining room, she kneeled down, planted a kiss on his cheek and hugged him quickly.

"Sorry you had a bad dream, Daddy."

"It's just a dream, don't worry about it, I'm not one of the psycho-babble people." As she fairly ran down the hall in her haste, he marveled again at her ability to be at one moment all grown up, and at the next moment his little girl.

Looking at his watch, Chris realized he had better get going to work, too. He interlaced his fingers and stretched his arms forward to prepare for the day and shake off the last remnants of the eerie feeling of his dream. He drained his coffee cup and took it to the sink.

Chapter 17

The sea of red brakes lights flowed before her like a fiery river, as Alicia inched down Grossmont Grade at an agonizing 12 miles per hour. She had never seen Interstate 8, five lanes abreast at this point, anywhere near this crowded. But, she had also never been out here at morning rush hour. She looked at her watch and the feeling of panic ratcheted up a notch, tightening the imagined knot in her stomach and quickening her pulse.

Her night's sleep was less than helpful, too. Her dreams weren't as ominous as her dad's, but she had tossed and turned and then wound up dreaming she was going to school and had attended the first day of an important class, but for weeks now she couldn't find it again. She had an important assignment to turn in soon for the class and somehow didn't even know the teacher's name or the class title. In her dream fog she wasn't entirely sure what she was supposed to do for the assignment and also worried that she had missed so many lectures that she wouldn't be able to pass the final exam. The eerie, post-dream feeling had dissipated in the shower, but the vague sense of disquiet had remained. She chalked it up to first day jitters.

"Where are all of you people going!" she yelled over the final strains of some Tom Petty song on the radio, and glanced at the LCD dashboard clock. The heartless green glow of the numbers answered back 6:48.

The perky sorority tour guide who had led the group of prospective students, that had included Alicia and her father, around the labyrinthine maze of the various campus buildings last spring had insisted on the importance of getting to the parking lot by 7:00 am. Alicia easily had another 6 or 8 miles left to go, which at this rate could easily take nearly half an hour. Suddenly, the full weight of realization hit her—this was just the first day. She had four more years of this. One small consolation was the fact that, for this first Semester at least, she had been able to stack her classes so that she had Fridays off from school. This left her two full days to work at Lakeside with a little time in the mornings for homework. Alicia was beginning to realize that college was going to be a big change.

It was 7:21 when she pulled into the parking lot on the South side of the Campus. She and her dad had scoped out several of the lots, and decided this one would be the best to access the areas of campus she would be using most. It required the least amount of walking, and was right near a Jack-in-the-Box, both of which put it high on her list. It must have been high on everyone else's list as well, for every row she drove through was flanked on either side by parked cars. There wasn't a single space to be had, and she was now one of about nine other cars canvassing the lot like sharks in need of a meal. The same was true of the next three lots she tried, and now time was really becoming a problem.

Her first class started at 8:00 am, and it was now 7:39, time for drastic measures. There was one last lot to try, the one she had promised herself she would never park in. The one that, upon the first sight of it, she had nicknamed 'the pit of Hell'. The only bright spot was that it was directly below Nasitir and Storm Halls, which was where her first class was—Anthro 101—and due to the odd encounter with the professor on Friday, she was at least familiar with the building and pretty sure she could find the classroom without much difficulty. That is if she could still breathe.

144

Alicia wasn't terribly surprised to find that the parking lot in question was only half full, even at this late hour. This one was not for the faint of heart, for in order to access the campus, one must first climb up no less than 150 stairs perched precariously against the hillside. Spurred on by her tardiness, she managed to cover the first half of the distance in a few minutes, but then the burning in her thighs and the shortness of her breath stalled her. Nothing short of her mortal fear of being late for her very first college class ever could have propelled her forward, so she was somewhat grateful for the motivation. She crested the last step with only three minutes to find her classroom and get to a seat. Of course, by the time she scurried through the door, the only seats left were in the very front row. She slid into her institutional brown plastic chair just as Dr. Whiteside was clearing his throat and straightening his bolo tie.

"Good morning." He looked about at the sea of expectant faces. "So, you are all here at this ungodly hour to learn about Anthropology, am I right?"

Alicia didn't expect anyone to answer, this was obviously one of those rhetorical questions, but she had the urge to say, "Duh!" She chastised herself inwardly that as a college student she ought not to be so quick to fall on sophomoric responses such as that.

"Of course you are, so let's get down to it, shall we? Let us begin with a question. Can anyone tell me, since you have all chosen this class of your own accord, what precisely is Anthropology?" As he spoke, he began pacing slowly in front of the class, looking expectantly from one student to another.

When he walked in front of Alicia, she discovered she was about eye-level with his belt buckle, the same arrowhead encrusted belt buckle that had caused her anxiety upon their first meeting. He paused in front of her row, and for a brief moment she felt sure he was about to call on her for the answer to his question. Luckily, the boy behind her would be the object of torture instead.

145

"You there, young man in the red sweatshirt, what do you think?" Dr. Whiteside leveled his gaze squarely on the poor guy and waited what felt like a whole minute, but had probably only been a few seconds in reality. Alicia was torn between feeling genuine sympathy for this kid being the first one offered up in sacrifice to the classroom gods, and being supremely grateful that he hadn't picked her.

"Uh, well, it's kind of like Archaeology, isn't it?" It was a weak attempt, but at least he had managed to say something.

"Kind of like Archaeology. Well, in a sense, yes, the disciplines are related, and archeological discoveries can impact and influence anthropological ideas and vice-versa. However, they are also quite distinct. Anthropology studies human beings in relation to distribution and relationship of races, their environmental and social relations and culture. Archaeology is more concerned with studying the material remains of cultures, such as fossils and artifacts."

"So Anthropology studies living people and Archaeology studies dead ones?" The boy behind Alicia was getting a bit braver.

"Sometimes it can be as simple as that. Often, there are archaeological treasures that lead us to further understand the past of a culture that anthropologists are currently engaged in studying. For example, take Native American cultures, like the Inuit peoples in the North. Decades ago, there were anthropologists who made it their life's work to come to know and understand their culture, yet there was already tremendous archaeological material that could be investigated."

"Would the same be true of people from this area, like the Kumeya'ay?" Alicia spoke before she realized she meant to, and was embarrassed at her interruption. Happily it didn't seem to faze the professor.

"It's interesting that you bring that up," her professor said as he turned to her. "There is a wealth of centuries old culture still being practiced on a daily basis in Mexico on the part of the Kumeya'ay Indians. Many people are completely unaware of the culture of Mexico being distinctly different in many of the poorer areas of the country. The largely Castillian

Spanish descendants often live in the more urban areas and run most of the institutions and business enterprises. Those of mixed blood and the pure Indian descendants often live in the more remote areas, and in many cases practice much of the culture of their ancestors still today. The same kind of pottery that was made a thousand years ago is often imported here to sell in tourist shops.

We also have a significant amount of archeological material that is available for study here in San Diego County." Dr. Whiteside paused in his comments, as though he were deciding whether or not to continue in this vein, or move on to another topic. After this brief, almost imperceptible moment, he moved from the front of Alicia's row and resumed his earlier pacing, much to her relief. "For instance, in the desert of Anza Borrego where the Cahuilla people lived and further east into Arizona in the land of the Mohave culture there is much to be seen of other groups.

I'm sure many of you have heard of the ruins in Mesa Verde and other places where incredible fabric of the previous civilizations remains today. Deserts, by the way, are wonderful places for archeological study since they are relatively sparsely vegetated and reveal artifacts rather easily. Areas that suffer significant forest burns also afford a unique opportunity for archeological study…and sadly for pothunters, who easily find artifacts and sell them on the black market." Alicia couldn't help but think of the arrowhead on his belt as he said this.

Her professor continued, "The mountains around Cuyamaca State Park and many locations in the Cleveland National Forest also have much to show us in terms of archeological remains, and in many instances we can couple that with the activities of living peoples of the Kumeya'ay in Northern Mexico."

"Cuyamaca! That's where I live!" Alicia's exclamation was more to herself than intended for the room, but it was just exuberant enough for Dr. Whiteside to hear as he passed by her row once more. He halted abruptly.

"Really? Well then young lady, you live in a very historically rich area. There is much to learn there. I have been trying to work out a permit

147

with the archeologist in the regional headquarters who oversees any studies in Cuyamaca as well. You don't by chance have any "pull" with the park service do you?" He chuckled a bit under his breath.

"No, no, not really. I mean my father is a ranger there, the Chief Ranger, actually, but I don't have anything to do with the park, I mean aside from living in it."

He looked at her quizzically, and for a moment she feared that she had only succeeded in irritating him. But soon the crinkle in his eye that she had first taken for vexation, turned towards mirth, and he smiled, "Too bad. I was really hoping to get a dig started soon. There are so many really important pieces out there, and the longer they go without being properly excavated and safely stored, the more likely they are to be unearthed by pothunters and sold on the black market. That sort of thing happens every day. Even for legitimate collectors such as myself, who would never knowingly purchase stolen artifacts, one never truly knows the history of a piece. Take this belt buckle, for instance." He flashed the mammoth silver and gold oval upwards, displaying the slate gray arrowhead nestled in the middle. The gesture was abrupt and slightly too close to Alicia's face. She involuntarily scooted back several inches in her chair. "Of course, I bought this from a reputable dealer, but one never knows the whole backstory. There have been some very hot items come up for auction lately, I mean some really quality items, but the history and legality of the pieces are not clear. I've even purchased a few things from sellers myself that I wonder about." Dr. Whiteside now looked directly down at Alicia, "Many of these pieces have been from your neck of the woods, too. Kumaya'ay. That's why supervised academic sponsored digs are such a benefit."

She had no idea what to say. She wasn't even sure he expected her to say anything. What could she say? "Oh" or "wow" or something equally pithy and vacuous? She had already spoken out of turn twice in this class, and drawn entirely too much attention to herself on the first day. She wasn't about to do it again.

"Alright, enough of this archaeology tangent and back to the question of anthropology." Dr. Whiteside strode off toward the other end of the classroom, clearly on to a new topic.

Strangely, Alicia couldn't dismiss this new information so lightly. There was something very disturbing about the idea of pots and things, artifacts, pieces of history no less, being stolen from the ground and sold to collectors. These things should be shared with the world. Even scarier was the implication that this might be happening right under her father's nose.

Chapter 18

The green grasses were almost all gone to a wilted and faded yellow as the dog-days of August cooked the vitality out of the pine forest and meadows below Cuyamaca Peak. The pollen and vanilla smell of Jeffrey pine and the lush green of the ponderosas and incense cedars was fading, as well, while Chris Becker sat with the window open at his desk. Atop his well-worn, ancient Prison Industries oak desk sat the curious matchbook cover inside the paper bag. He had taken the precaution to put it in one after taking it home on Sunday since the plastic one Allie had used tended to capture moisture inside. It was good for TV detectives who wanted to show the audience their evidence, but not always good for real life. Fingerprinting it might be helpful, though he doubted it.

He sat staring at it wondering exactly what it meant. He was sure it was the key to opening up something of importance, and he had the uneasy feeling that it was left by Xavier Hess and not some long lost piece of trash missed by the regular cleaning girl at Hillside. With the backlog of forensics requests he knew the low priority fingerprint check would likely take weeks before the Sheriff's Office got around to it. He still only had a rather ambiguous fatality from a cougar at this point, but more and more things weren't adding up. Why was a contractor taking a walk in the woods that morning, why did the bite marks seem off and bother Frank James so much, and finally, what was Hess doing in a motel less than an hour away from home the night before he died?

With the weekend campfire and nature hikes done and many visitors heading home from the campground, things were slowing down in the park. With school starting, weekends were busy and the only long-term campers were seniors usually not intent on raising hell. It was a relaxed time for the staff. It gave a little more time to consider the case. Labor Day weekend would still be busy, but with more schools starting early, the holiday was quieter than when Becker first began working as a ranger. Surprisingly, a trend was surfacing and fewer people saw parks as a place to camp and hike, as video games and other sedentary entertainment gained popularity. Fewer than ten percent of visitors ever hiked the trails anymore, even if they did camp. Many were so out of shape and overweight that a walk to the restroom was difficult enough, which again brought him back to thinking about why a contractor like Hess was in the woods.

Lost in his reverie, he didn't even notice Eric come up the stairs to his office as he was absently examining the panties now officially collected as possible evidence.

"Hey boss…must have been a great night!" Eric said as he raised one eyebrow in amused curiosity. Chris quickly put the items back in the bag.

"No, smart mouth, I'm just "evaluating" some evidence that turned up on the Hess death."

"What is he, a cross dresser?"

"No, they came from the room he was staying in at the Hillside Cabins."

"I see, well, since we're discussing curious situations, you got a minute?"

"Yeah, sure. Take a load off."

151

Eric was young and energetic and Chris could tell something big was on his mind. He had a sheaf of papers in his hand and raised them as he spoke.

"I was down in the basement archives doing a little bit of looking for something we could add to the museum project." Mummifying Dick Savage and putting him on display appealed to Becker, but Eric probably couldn't help him there. One of Becker's successful budget proposals was to modify one of the rooms and the park office hallway to add exhibits along the walls so that visitors had a bit of a nature center to look at. Eric was working on designing an exhibit that described some of the park's archeological resources.

"While I was looking at the accessioning records, digging around in the cabinets to find what is supposed to be there, I noticed that several items are missing. I know they should be there, but I just can't find them. Has anything been taken out by anyone else?"

"Not to my knowledge. What is missing?"

"Well, I didn't do any kind of thorough inventory, really. Once I started noticing that stuff wasn't where it was supposed to be, I looked in other cabinets. Some of the stuff is just crammed in old cardboard boxes making a good home for the mice and spiders. I hope I don't get Hantavirus from all the mice droppings and urine that's down there. Anyway, I for sure couldn't find bone fragments they unearthed when they were building the restroom out at Los Caballos Horse Camp. They found a bunch of pot shards and some arrow heads in that dig, and I can't find any of that either. There was one completely intact pot that was pretty rare when they catalogued all that before finishing the restroom, and it's not anywhere that I can find either."

"Take me down and show me. Besides, if we have Indian bone remains, that stuff needs to be re-interred by law. Maybe it's already been done and they didn't put it in the records."

"No, it's animal bone fragments. Interesting stuff for display, but not anything that's really archeology stuff. They just crammed it down there because they didn't have anywhere else to store it."

Eric and Chris spent about an hour rooting through the material in the basement and checking it against the accession records and came up with several more moderate value items that they couldn't find. Becker was thoroughly pissed by the time they finished.

"Since there is no sign of break-in, it looks like this is the work of someone inside the organization," said Chris. "I'd like you to keep this entirely between the two of us for the time being, until we can figure out what to do to run this down."

"Who has a key to get in here? You gave me the one I'm using."

"Not a whole lot of staff have access, but Val, myself, the Maintenance Chief, the Region Archeologist and Resource Ecologist, and Dick all have keys."

In retrospect, Chris was reminded that that was far too many people to give access to something with an often astronomical value if only to a few select collectors. He had once told Savage that they should reevaluate key access to the basement, and the shop buildings as well, but he had turned a deaf ear to the expense. Locks hadn't been changed for decades, and who knew how many keys were floating around the community. Now with things missing from the shop and from the arch lab in the basement things seemed to be getting out of hand for sure.

"Let me have the list of missing items we've made and the accessioning records. I'll keep them in my office. In the meantime, keep a close eye on this building and the shop for anyone getting in or hanging around when they shouldn't be, especially when no one else is around." Chris took the paperwork and headed back up to his office as Eric went back out on patrol.

Becker turned it over in his mind as he climbed the stairs. He couldn't see any of the staff stealing, but likely one of them was. He really didn't want to have to deal with an internal investigation. They were so disruptive to staff morale. He decided it could wait until tomorrow. He knew he'd have to take it up with Savage's boss, since Dick might be involved. Savage would be mad that he wasn't trusted and told about the missing items immediately. Chris wasn't looking forward to that. Plus he needed to follow up on the Xavier Hess matter a bit more. It was time to talk to Mrs. Hess again and get to the bottom of the motel business. He'd stop and tell the regional director about the thefts after he re-interviewed the grieving widow.

He locked the papers in his desk drawer and headed back down the stairs. He didn't tell the office secretary anything about where he was headed this time. Better to just go. They'd all know where he'd gone soon enough.

He didn't know if Mrs. Hess was at home, but he'd find her somewhere. Once in his Jeep, he pulled out his cell phone while he looked up her home number on the incident report. He was surprised that she answered on the first ring.

"Mrs. Hess, this is Ranger Chris Becker. I wonder if I could stop in and chat with you for a few minutes this morning…say around 11 o'clock?"

"I…I guess so. I thought you asked all the questions you needed to last time you were here." Her voice sounded concerned, but Chris felt there was a hint of irritation and suspicion behind her words. Maybe it was just his suspicion reading more into it than he should.

"Just a few routine follow up questions, and since I am going to be in the area I thought I'd just drop by. Shouldn't take long."

"Can't we just do it on the phone?"

"Well, it's not really convenient since I am driving right now. I'd like to stop by."

"OK, but I have an appointment at noon to get my hair done, so I can't talk long."

"That will be fine, Mrs. Hess. I'll see you then."

Once he was out on Interstate 8 he began formulating how he would approach her. If she knew her husband was at the motel and didn't

154

mention it, then she was hiding something for some reason. He considered a variety of ways to do it, but decided a direct confrontation would be best. Perhaps it would put her off balance enough that she would give him more than she intended in the way of information.

The freeway grasses and chaparral were even more dry and dead than the vegetation in the park. The worst of California fires began in chaparral due to their high oil content and the fact that their dead lower branches were like kindling to a fire. The winds of October would soon be upon Southern California and with the drought conditions they were experiencing, his mind began to wander to dealing with potential major fire conditions. Initial attack on fires was part of his generalist job, but with little in the way of equipment he usually wound up handling traffic control and evacuation once the Forestry Department arrived on scene. Huge campaign fires would see park hand crews assembled to join the fight, but most times that wasn't necessary. Just another problem for a ranger to consider in the average workday, in addition to budgets, crime, campground management, and public education.

Lately, the crime part was certainly keeping him from those other duties, and sometimes he could actually understand why Savage was such a fanatic about keeping him focused on the other parts of his job. Someday soon he knew the time would come when rangers would be split off into just enforcement officers. It was always being talked about. He liked some variety in his job and wasn't looking forward to that time.

When Mrs. Hess let him in the front door he was surprised to see another man sitting on the sofa. His first thought was that she had gotten a lawyer, but that made absolutely no sense.

"Ranger Becker, this is my brother Steve Goodman. You don't mind if he joins us, do you?"

"Actually the things we have to talk about might be stuff you want to discuss in private."

"There is nothing that we could talk about that my brother can't hear."

"Well, if you want him here that's up to you. Some developments in your husband's death have surfaced and I need to understand a few things. First of all, you didn't mention that he spent the night at the Hillside Cabins the night before he was killed. How come?"

"With all the stress of his death it must have just slipped my mind."

"Pretty big event to forget don't you think? Frankly, you don't convince me. Now, how about we try again? Why did your husband stay at a motel when he only lived 45 minutes from where he was going the next day?"

"He was intoxicated. He called me that night and said he had too much to drink at the Hillside Restaurant and was going to sleep it off. He did that kind of stuff sometimes."

He figured it was time to fire the big gun, "Mrs. Hess, do you know who he was having an affair with?"

"What do you mean by that?" Chris could tell she was really agitated at this point. Either she knew nothing about it, or she was covering up something.

"It's a pretty simple question. He was in the Hillside Cabin with another woman, and though I don't know her identity right now, it is only a matter of time before I find out. It would be much easier if you helped me in the process." He knew he was pushing his facts before he verified them, but his gut told him it was the right thing to do.

"What business is it of yours what my husband does? My husband was killed by a cougar. You should spend more time getting rid of animals that run around killing people. I resent your attitude and questions and I want you to leave right now!"

"Well, it's not that simple Mrs. Hess. It looks like your husband may have been murdered. And with that comes a lot of unanswered questions that you are going to have to deal with." Chris knew he was way out over the edge making that assumption when absolutely no one had officially come to that conclusion, but he needed the woman to talk.

"Murder!" The shock on her face was real.

"Mrs. Hess, I need to know if he was having an affair and who was with him that night."

She sat very still on the sofa for several heartbeats, as if she were trying to put things in place in her mind. In the end she decided to open up. Chris noticed her eyes were brimming with tears.

"I have suspected for quite some time that Xavier was seeing someone. He meets a lot of people in his work, so I couldn't ever figure out who it was. I checked his phone records on the bill, but that didn't show me anything. It could easily have been one of the jobs he was working on. Paving some bored housewife's driveway perhaps," she left the remainder of the thought hanging.

"We found a matchbook cover for the Palomino Club. Is that somewhere he frequented?"

"I've never been there and I don't know if Xavier went there or not."

"We believe from a note on the matchbook that he may have had a meeting with someone the morning he died. Do you know anything about that?" Chris was basically writing fiction at this point, but something in his gut again told him that matchbook cover was important, and that the vague scribblings on the back were directions and an appointment time.

She shook her head and looked vacantly through Becker, "I really can't help you. All I had were my suspicions." At that moment Steve's cell phone rang loudly into the otherwise relative calm of the room and he excused himself. Hushed tones could be heard coming from the kitchen, punctuated by the occasional outburst. Presently Pamela Hess continued, "I really thought he would stop seeing her. Actually, that's not even true. I really hoped I was wrong and it was just my imagination. If it was happening, I didn't want anyone to know, you know. I am so embarrassed and feel like a failure at my marriage."

Chris understood first-hand about failed marriage and the feelings of worthlessness and rejection that they caused. His sense was she was telling him the truth, which left him without much in the way of new information. If Hess were having an affair and the forensics did turn out to support a murder, then a jealous wife or husband were always a possibility to consider as suspects. Someone would likely be asking Mrs. Hess a lot more questions.

"Mrs. Hess, I have to ask you one more question. Where were you on the morning your husband was killed?"

"Am I a suspect?" she asked incredulously.

"I'm just trying to cover all my bases, and it is a routine question we will be asking a lot of people in the coming days. In fact, I'd like to know where your brother, Steve, was that morning, too."

"We were both together here. Steve came over for coffee first thing in the morning, maybe around 7:00, before he went to work. He stayed about half an hour before he left to go to Ganglion Instruments in El Cajon. He is their assistant manager."

"Anybody see you guys together here that morning?"

"I don't know, maybe the apartment manager or someone did. We didn't speak to anyone that morning."

"OK, I appreciate your time and I hope I have more information for you soon. If you think of anything that might help please give me a call."

Chris tried the manager's apartment before he left the complex, but no one answered and he saw no one on the grounds. He suspected he'd have to eventually follow up with it, but maybe he could do it by phone. As he left, Chris wondered whether to trust his instincts. They didn't seem like killers, but without some independent witnesses he couldn't rule them out.

He decided to head for the Regional Office to discuss the thefts at Cuyamaca, and then perhaps if he was lucky he might catch both the day shift and night shift bartenders at the Palomino Bar. He was frustrated at the lack of progress he was making and knew he was working on borrowed time. He wondered once again whether he should just take the easy road and call it a lion attack. If the coroner didn't declare this a murder soon, he would likely be in his very own lion's den…and he was no Daniel.

Chapter 19

Even without an appointment, the meeting with the Regional Director Jim Clayton went predictably well. Chris had worked with him ten years before in the North Coast Redwoods and had gotten to know him pretty well and respected him. The respect was mutual. As Becker's supervising ranger, he saw the energy Chris brought to the job and his recommendations probably had a good deal to do with why Becker had promoted out to his first supervising position. Clayton was a deliberate and thoughtful man, and though he had little law enforcement or investigative experience, he recognized a problem that needed dealing with when he was told.

Chris spent a few minutes carefully bringing Clayton up to speed on the thefts of the shop equipment.

"I appreciate the fact that you are alerting me to all this and that you are not trying to freelance," Clayton exhaled as he rubbed what appeared to be weariness and frustration from his eyes.

"To be honest Jim, I really didn't feel I could trust this to anyone else. Something obviously isn't right with this case, and the department climate just isn't right for taking on a   difficult investigation like this.

"What you really mean is Savage is going to tell you to drop it. I've known Dick for years and he's not one to tangle with law enforcement stuff if he can help it. I'm not surprised that with items of little worth that he would just want to ignore it."

Chris studied the floor and said, "I figured if I came to you, that you would be the least likely to stonewall me."

"Good play on words."

It took Chris a moment to get Clayton's meaning. "Oh, you mean the old mine in the park...guess it fits." The Stonewall Mine had been the biggest producer in Southern California in the 1890s and had received little attention from the parks department.

"That mine restoration budget request of yours has been 'stonewalled' for a long time, and it will take your fairy godmother to make it come true." Clayton paused thoughtfully for a moment and said, "I guess I'll take your trust as a compliment, but I doubt the rest of this outfit will take it like that. The Sheriff is really best equipped to handle this and you need to coordinate with them. You also have the rest of your job to take care of, too. I should tell you to just leave it to the Sheriff's Office, but I'm not going to. The S.O. could probably use your help, and I know you. Frankly, I doubt it would stop you if I said leave it alone.

"Hopefully, we'll catch a break here soon and have more of a direction to go," said Chris.

"You continue handling the investigation into the thefts, and if you need more resources, coordinate with me and the sheriff as needed. I can't promise our department can give you much. If you have any trouble with Dick Savage, just tell him to call me."

Chris also felt the need to prepare him for the possibility that the lion attack also might not be what it seemed. He spent a few minutes bringing him up to date and setting out his concerns. That part went the least well, but Clayton wasn't openly ridiculing Becker for his suspicions. While he wasn't given "gung-ho pedal to the metal" encouragement to continue investigating the loose ends of the Hess fatality, at least he wasn't told to

160

drop it. As he left Region Headquarters, he still had the opportunity to make some headway on that situation, so the afternoon found him in the parking lot of the Palomino Club.

The place looked typical for an El Cajon watering hole. The sign featured a cartoonish scantily clad cowgirl on a tan horse installed over a mostly concrete block building with plenty of flashing neon and few windows. Parking was in the back—perfect for those who weren't anxious to be seen from the street. He wouldn't have described it as seedy, just depressing and dark. Only two patrons graced a table at the far end of the room. They were a young couple, and neither of them seemed the least interested in anything but their head to head conversation. He had made a point to slip on a black windbreaker so that his uniform wouldn't be obvious to everyone. Two men were behind the bar, and Chris wondered if he had indeed gotten the staff at shift change.

"What can I get for you, my friend?"

"Actually, I'm here on business rather than pleasure," Becker said, and noticed the man stiffen a bit. "I need to find a woman."

"Sounds like pleasure to me," the shorter bartender said with a smirk, "half of the people in here are in that business!"

Chris had to smile a bit at the humor and being the butt of the joke.

"Poor choice of words on my part for sure. I'm looking for a particular woman who was in here with a guy name Xavier Hess. Do you know him?" Becker passed him the driver's license picture he had earlier pulled from DMV records. The grainy, minimal pixel image was clear enough but lacked personality. Like all mug shots, it was a poor substitute for the real thing.

"Don't need the picture. Xavier comes in all the time. Seen him with a couple of different women over the years, lately the same one a lot. Daytime mostly, usually around now. I figured maybe she was his secretary or something. Guy runs a contracting business."

"Do you know who the woman was?"

"Not well enough to know anything about her. Her name's Lola and I heard her mention she lives here in El Cajon."

"Has she been in here in the last few days?"

"Came in on Thursday, by herself. I figured Hess would be with her like usual, but he wasn't. Sat for about an hour and then left. Didn't look too happy either."

"Look, do me a big favor would you? Give me a call if she drops by again," Becker said, as he handed him his business card.

The bar tender glanced at the card and said, "So what's a Ranger want to talk with her about?"

"I need to give her some of her stuff that Xavier had." Chris wasn't exactly lying since he planned to give her the panties Alicia had found as a conversation starter.

"Why doesn't Xavier do this?" The suspicion and mistrust was clear in the bartender's voice.

"Xavier is not in a position to return anything to anyone anymore. He was killed a few days ago in the park by a cougar. I'm surprised you didn't hear about it."

"Yeah, I been out of town for a long weekend. Killed by a cougar, damn. That's an awful way to go!" He mopped at the non-existent condensation rings and spills on the bar before he spoke again. "You know I just remembered, she might have said her name was Bragdon come to think of it. Lola Bragdon." Chris suspected he knew her name all along.

"Well, thanks. That should help me find her and get her stuff back to her. I appreciate your help."

Rather than use his weakening cell phone battery, he found one of the few remaining phone booths in town and looked up Bragdon's name. L. Bragdon lived only a few blocks away and he called the number. The answering machine picked up and he didn't leave a message. Likely she was at work somewhere. He would probably turn all his information over to the sheriff's office if this became a murder investigation and let them interview her. It was their primary responsibility, although with shrinking

162

agency budgets a number of times concurrent agencies often said it was his agency's responsibility. Reverse turf wars, his ranger staff called it.

He had barely hung up when his cell phone rang. It was Ms. Hess, which surprised him.

"Ranger Becker, you mentioned the note on the matchbook cover and after you left, I went and looked at Xavier's day planner. It did have something interesting penciled in for that morning. 'See SRG', whatever that means. He also had a note about meeting with the prime contractor on the Highway 79 road repair through Julian. He had bid on part of the work for that project. I didn't know he was working on it still, in fact I didn't know if he got the bid, so I'm surprised at the note."

"OK, thanks for calling and letting me know about that." Becker was suddenly struck with the gaping hole they had left in the investigation. "Have you gotten Xavier's vehicle out of the impound lot yet?" Val had located it in the Paso Day Use lot and had the sheriff tow it. If this indeed was murder, this whole thing was messed up because they had spent so much time looking at it as a 'simple' lion killing.

"No I haven't picked it up yet. I was going to have Steve drive me down there tomorrow so we could bring it back here."

"Can I get you to hold off on that until I have a look at the car?"

"Sure, his is a big truck and I prefer to drive my own car, and I probably will just sell Xavier's anyway. Do you think there is something important there?"

"Not necessarily, but it needs to be gone over now that we are looking at this as murder." He was getting farther out on a limb with his claims. Something needed to fall into place soon.

Becker pulled back out on Fletcher Parkway and decided to head for Lola Bragdon's.

Chapter 20

Lola Bragdon lived, like many singles in El Cajon, in a small apartment off Fletcher Parkway. It was upscale with fresh dirt-colored paint and looked to cater to the younger crowd. The poolside was filled with bikini clad sunbathers home early from school or work. San Diego State and UC San Diego weren't a far commute from where she lived, and Becker wondered if Hess had been dallying with a much younger woman. Wouldn't be the first time. Bragdon's ground floor apartment was wedged between the laundry room and the manager's apartment. Becker knocked and got no response. As he was knocking more loudly a second time a woman's head popped out of the manager's apartment.

"Looking for Lola?" she asked.

"Yeah, I guess she's not home. Have you any idea where she might be?"

"I don't think she has been home for the last few days. Last time I saw her I think was Thursday morning. You know these college kids. She probably got a new boyfriend or is hanging out at some girlfriend's place."

"You know which college she is attending?"

"Yes, got it all over her shirts and books and stuff. San Diego State. She's a little old for college. I get the impression she's been working on a four-year degree for about six or eight years now."

"Does she work around here somewhere?" Chris asked.

"How come you want to know? I feel a little uncomfortable giving out that kind of personal information."

Becker realized he still had on his black windbreaker. He pulled it aside to show his badge.

"I'm investigating a case and I need to talk to her. It's really important and I'd appreciate any help you can give me."

"Well sure, I don't know much though. She'd wear one of those Polo shirts with the logo on it a lot, so I assumed that was where she was working now. It was a storage place called Marco's, you know the kind where you put all the stuff you don't need but can't throw away."

"Thanks. If you see her would you give her this," Chris said as he handed her his card. "Tell her to call me ASAP, OK?"

"Sure."

Becker didn't waste more time there other than to check if her car was in the numbered parking space under the apartments. As he expected, it was empty. He knew the storage company called Marco's. It was advertised with a big sign visible from the Interstate. He was there and at the manager's office inside of five minutes.

"Hello, how can I help you," said the perky young employee at the counter. Apparently Marco liked to hire young girls.

"I was hoping you could tell me how to get in touch with Lola Bragdon," Chris said. This time he had left his windbreaker in the patrol rig.

"That's something we'd all like to know. She hasn't shown up for work for the last couple of days and she hasn't called in. I'm really angry about it, too. I run this business on a shoestring and I need my people to be reliable." Chris suddenly noticed the name stitched on her work shirt was "*Marco*." Unusual name for a girl. *Aah, she's the owner, so much for observant police work.*

Chris leaned into the counter. "When was the last time you saw her?"

"Last Thursday. She worked her shift and then said she was going to meet her boyfriend."

"Do you know her boyfriend? How I might get in touch with him?"

"Can't help you there. He's some construction guy she met a while ago. I've never seen him. Got a funny name, but it's not coming to me."

"Could it be Xavier, by any chance?"

"Yeah, that's it. You a mind reader?"

"By any chance can you tell me about her car, like the make, model, license?"

"Sure, that's easy. She had one of those little Honda electric cars. Shaped like a little puke green aphid you'd pick off a rosebush. The plate was one of those personalized things, but I can't remember what it was. Didn't make much sense to me. Most of 'em don't half the time."

Becker thanked her and left his card. He wondered what was going on with Bragdon. Hess was dead and Bragdon was in the wind somewhere. It was odd that she disappeared the same day that Hess died. Could she have maybe not been the woman at the Hillside Resort? Could she have found out about Hess meeting some other woman and attacked him on the trail? Hess's license put him at 210 pounds and 6' 2" tall. Unlikely she could overpower him, but surprise could be an advantage for even the smallest person. He called the Julian substation and deputy Wayne Johnson answered.

"Hey Wayne, are you gonna be around the Sub for the next hour or so?" Chris asked.

"Yeah, I've got reports to write before shift end. Seems like we are having a string of burglaries. Even had someone break into Jack's grocery last night. Really sad when people break into a grocery store to steal food."

"Well, look, I'd like to take a good look at Xavier Hess's car before his wife picks it up. I think something is wrong with this lion mauling case

166

and it might be murder. I'd appreciate your help to see if I'm on the right track."

"I thought it was pretty much a slam dunk. I haven't heard anything from the coroner's office to suggest otherwise." Chris could hear the reluctance and disbelief in Johnson's voice.

"Look Wayne, just give me a chance to test my theory and tell you what I've found out first. I won't take that much of your time when I get there."

"It's OK by me, I gotta be here anyway typing with both index fingers."

"Thanks, Wayne. Would you do me one more favor? Do a search for a vehicle license and put a BOLO out for a missing girl named Lola Bragdon. I think she may be a witness to this in some way. Tomorrow I'll see if maybe the college she goes to can give me information on parents or family that might know where she is."

Becker gave Wayne Johnson all the identifying information he had on Bragdon and headed back to Julian on the Interstate. It was nearly four in the afternoon by the time he made it to the sheriffs' substation east of town.

"We have Hess's truck out back inside the fence. What are you looking for?"

"I'm not exactly sure. We've got bite marks that don't look right for the lion we shot the other night. We've got a guy in expensive shoes walking on a trail at eight in the morning. We've got a note in his room to meet someone, possibly that morning. He's got a mistress who I can't find, and no one has seen her since Hess died. It's just too loose for me. His wife said I could look at the car." Chris knew as he said it all that it didn't sound like much.

"I think you've got a bunch of smoke and no facts," Johnson snorted. "You want to look at the car you are welcome to, as long as the wife doesn't have a problem. Me, I got reports to do. Give me back the key when you are done." He turned and went back into the boxy little trailer that

167

served as the Julian Substation for the resident deputies that worked out of their homes as much as anywhere else.

Becker unlocked the truck and gave it a cursory look. To him it was just another construction worker's truck. Maybe a little newer and more expensive than most, but still plenty of dirt on the tires and a shovel and broom in the back. As he scanned it he noticed plenty of dirt in the bed. Not so surprising for a "dirt guy." He took a sample for no other reason than it was there, and he wanted to be thorough enough to avoid later criticism. He squatted and looked under the truck, which was easy enough with its raised four-wheel drive and knobby oversized tires. Nothing stood out, and as he rose up he came to the realization that he really had no idea what he was looking for. He decided that he needed to just go back to the basics, so he returned to his Jeep and pulled out a pair of latex gloves and his fingerprint kit. He felt like some kid sleuth playing cop every time he used it. Getting good prints was a skill learned best by doing it all the time, and Chris rarely had reason to do that. Then there was the problem that for him, any prints he lifted would be studied by the lab at the Sheriff's Office sometime between the second coming of Christ and When Pigs Fly. He was hoping that the coroner would find some reason to say the death was suspicious and prints from the car could become a priority.

He opened the fingerprint kit. Hess's wife wasn't going to be happy. Fingerprint powder was messy and a pain to remove. Dusting the nasty black powder over Hess's white truck showed few prints, and sitting out in the open for days didn't help preserve them. Oils dried with time and heat and left little behind. He got lucky at several points when prints from a hand that was obviously dirty and greasy made distinct markings. A few other faint ones he was also able to raise with the powder. On the inside he found more prints in better condition in the protected cab, although he expected them all to belong to Hess.

It was a slow process and it was nearly dark by the time he finished. He transferred the lifting tapes to white cards and identified them with location, his signature, date and case number. As he was closing the cab door he noticed at the edge of the driver's side seat a small brown object. On close inspection it appeared to be ceramic, but what struck Chris was the dark smudges on the brown background. It looked familiar to him, but he couldn't place it. He decided to bag it and mark it for evidence. The rest of the cab was surprisingly clean for a work truck. Either Hess was neater than most construction guys or someone cleaned his vehicle for him. Since his wife didn't drive it, then it probably wasn't her. The only odd thing he found was a collection of small soft paint brushes and a whisk broom in the glove box. He bagged and tagged them as well.

Before he left, Chris did a complete photo record of the truck inside and out, including the engine compartment. If they needed more information, he suspected that the Sheriff's team could use their high tech skills and find more useful evidence later. He just hoped later wouldn't be too late. After he put his evidence and collection kit back in the Jeep he went in to return the key to Wayne Johnson.

"Here's the key back. I don't suppose there's any chance you could submit these to your lab and get them faster than if I make the request as an outside agency?"

"You're starting to be a pain. Why aren't you out talking to Bambi or something," Johnson said with a grin. Then his face turned serious, "Is this thing really that important to you? You really feel in your gut something is wrong here?"

"I do Wayne, and I can't prove a damn thing at this point, and I think we are wasting valuable time waiting."

"OK, I'll see what I can do to get this put through a little faster. I haven't heard they are working any murders this week so maybe they'll have time. You gotta know that even most of the burglaries don't get this kind of attention and just get written off for the insurance company to pay. A lot of times they treat us resident deputies as back country hicks, but sometimes we get lucky and they don't put our requests on a back shelf to gather dust. I know one of the women that works in the lab unit, so I'll see if I can charm her. But you owe me."

"I owe you, I won't forget it," Chris said as he headed out the door. He could hear Johnson pecking away on his typing and hoped he would have luck in getting the prints classified and searched.

Chapter 21

The warm Tuscan décor and intimate candlelight of Don Giovanni's restaurant was a stark contrast to what she was used to at the Hillside, or any of the places she usually went out to eat with her dad. This was definitely 'date night' atmosphere—all that was lacking was a lovelorn musician strolling around serenading the happy couples that filled the other eight or ten tables in the cozy dining room. Alicia was glad she and Marcus had agreed to meet there instead of him picking her up at home. That way it felt a little less like a date, and she could leave whenever she wanted in case that became important. She had to admit she was a little nervous. Marcus was becoming something of an unknown quantity. The dark and moody 'bad boy' persona that Alicia had come to rely on had developed a few flaws over the course of the last few days, and she was beginning to really wonder if there was a different person hiding underneath.

Her musings would have to wait, though, as their object had just opened the door. The faint tinkling of the brass bell hanging over the transom alerted the young hostess to her new customer, but before she could offer to help him, Marcus had scanned the small room and seen Alicia sitting at the table in the far back corner. He motioned to the hostess that his party was in that direction and mumbled some sort of pleasantries to her as he walked past.

Alicia managed a slight wave at him when he had first looked her way, hampered partly by the fact that she still felt very awkward and unsure of herself around him and partly due to her surprise at his altered appearance. She had often heard people say 'you clean up nicely' to others who typically don't dress up, and then surprise everyone with their looks when they do. This would be just such an appropriate occasion for the phrase. Marcus, whom Alicia had up until now pretty much only seen in a work setting, now looked decidedly un-workaday. His hair was pulled back in a sleek low ponytail. He wore black slacks and a steel blue long-sleeve button-up shirt. But it wasn't just his clothes that had so changed him, there was something more subtle. Something around his face…his eyes. An openness. Alicia couldn't explain it, but she could see the difference as clearly as if he had taken off a mask.

"Hi, am I late?" He smiled at her and pulled the chair out opposite her and sat down.

"No, no. I think I was early." She wanted to say something about how nice he looked—how different—but she was afraid that it might upset him, make him self-conscious, so she kept quiet about it, trying an encouraging smile in lieu of the compliment in her head, and saying instead, "It's probably better that way. It gave me a chance to look at the menu. Trust me, that's a bonus for you if you're hungry, because I usually take forever to decide in a place I don't go to very often."

"Oh, okay, well have you decided then?" He seemed a bit flustered as he opened the menu, like he suddenly thought he had to hurry to make a decision.

"Not completely, but I've narrowed it down to two or three things. Believe me, that is definite progress." She was glad to see that her words seemed to relax him a bit. Now that he knew she wasn't ready yet, he could peruse the offerings at his own pace. They sat there together in amiable silence, each concentrating on his or her own gastronomical preferences,

172

for another four or five minutes until their waitress appeared to take their order.

"Good evening, welcome to Don Giovanni's. My name is Cynthia, and I'll be serving you tonight. Can I start you off with something to drink?" It was the standard line, something Alicia had said thousands of times by now. It was funny how much more attention she paid to her waiters and waitresses, and how much more she tipped them, now that she was one.

Alicia glanced at Marcus, not wanting to interrupt him if he was poised to give her his drink order, but he was looking at her. Apparently in this situation he was going to stand firm on the 'ladies first' code of conduct. This was definitely starting to feel more and more like a date. If he paid for the whole thing, that would seal the deal completely.

"I guess I'll go first. Could I please have an iced tea, no lemon?" and then, glancing again at Marcus, "are we ready to order food?"

"Sure, I'm ready."

"OK, then can I also have the lasagna with a small green salad?"

"What kind of dressing?"

"Italian, please."

"And for you, sir?"

Marcus ordered veal parmesan and a coke, and then handed both their menus back to Cynthia.

"I'll bring your drinks right away." With that, Cynthia was off, hurrying to refill drinks and get more napkins and a myriad of other things that Alicia was glad she didn't have to worry about just then.

"So," Marcus broke their silence, "how was the big first day?"

"Funny you should ask. I was just thinking how grateful I am not to be at work tonight."

"That bad, huh," he chuckled softly, "yeah, that's why I dropped out after two years."

"Really, I had no idea. What happened?"

"No, no. I asked you first."

173

"Ok, fair enough." Alicia wondered where to begin. She decided chronologically would be the easiest. "First of all, the morning traffic is a bear! I know the tour guide at school had warned us about getting to school early for parking and all that, but what they didn't say anything about was the freeways that turn into parking lots!"

"Sounds like you had a bad start before you even really got started."

"You haven't heard the worst. I had to park in a horrible lot and climb a million stairs!" She wondered if she was laying it on a bit thick. Did she want his sympathy? Stranger yet, was she somehow angling for him to comfort her? She realized that his different look and demeanor had lulled her into a feeling of calm and ease that her previous experiences with him couldn't really justify. Still, she was really starting to enjoy the evening.

"Cardio. Very good for a young person in the morning." That sly Marcus smirk was back, but this time it lacked the calculating manipulative feel. Instead it was more playful, like she was the butt of his joke, but also included in it.

"Very funny. That cardio almost gave me a heart attack! Anyway, I made it to my first class just in time to squeeze into a front row seat thirty seconds before the Professor started his opening speech."

"And what class, pray tell, did you cut your teeth on?"

"Anthropology 101."

"Anthro, huh." His face suddenly took on a cloudier cast, a decidedly more 'Marcus' type of expression.

"Is something wrong?" Alicia felt like the inevitable 'other shoe' had dropped—that she had somehow cracked his carefully crafted façade and that the old Marcus was slowly leaking out.

"No, nothing's wrong."

She could tell he was forcing something down, making a choice of will not to succumb to whatever was trying to upset him, "so, aside from being in the front row, how was the class?"

Before she could answer, Cynthia was back with their drinks, a coaster for each of them, and two black straws wrapped in clear cellophane.

174

"Thank you," Alicia said to the waitress, while Marcus simply smiled and nodded his appreciation to her. When she was gone, Alicia began her answer. She discovered, as she thought, that trying to characterize her experience in that first class wouldn't be easy. "The class was good. In fact the front seat wasn't the problem. My mouth was the problem."

"Whatever do you mean? I can see no problems whatsoever with your mouth. In fact it looks fine to me."

The slight accent on the word 'fine' took all the innocence out of his statement, and sent the blood rushing to Alicia's cheeks. She couldn't believe she had started to trust him, to let her guard down, and here he was, back to his old tricks. She had looked down at the table the minute he had spoken, trying to conceal her embarrassment. She was still focused on her paper placemat, mentally tracing the outline of the boot-shaped map of Italy with her eyes, trying to decide what to say next.

"I'm sorry." It was Marcus who broke the awkward silence. "I didn't mean to make you uncomfortable. I guess my mouth gets me in trouble, too."

"Look Marcus," Alicia was tired of walking on pins and needles around him, and this day had already been too long and stressful for her to be able to stand an entire evening of this cat and mouse, "I have to be honest with you. I'm confused and uncomfortable around you. I'd like to be your friend, but I never know where I stand with you. The only reason I'm even here tonight is that I saw something in your face the other day, when you asked me to meet you here, that made me think I could trust you. Was I wrong?"

When Alicia looked up, that same broken and defeated look she had seen a few days before was on his face again. She instantly regretted her remarks, chiding herself inwardly that this was one of those instances where she probably should have kept her opinion to herself and strived to just 'grin and bear it' as the saying goes.

Marcus seemed to read her thoughts. "I'm glad you said something. Now it's out in the open. You are absolutely right. I do make people nervous,

175

it's not just you. I can see it in their eyes." He paused, and she could see this level of honesty was hard for him. "It wasn't always like this, you know." He managed a wan smile and took a long sip of his coke, as though the icy sweet carbonation could soothe his nerves as well as his thirst.

"You mentioned something about that before, that things haven't always been this way. What do you mean? What has changed?" Alicia saw that same sadness coming into his eyes, and she felt a softening toward him again. He was like a stray puppy whose bite you could forgive when you looked into his sad, lost eyes.

"Well, if I'm going to tell you, I may as well start at the beginning. As you know, I'm not from around here. In fact, we just moved here about six months ago."

"We?"

"Yeah, me and my mom. We moved here from Flagstaff so she could get better treatment at UCSD Medical Center. She has some rare blood disease. It's killing her, actually. But the good doctors over there are trying to ensure that it kills her a bit more slowly. I'm still not sure if that's a good thing or not." Another long sip of coke. "So, twice a week I drive her down to La Jolla for her treatments, and then drive her back up here so she can live in her beloved mountains."

"Oh, I'm so sorry Marcus. I had no idea." That wasn't totally true. Marina had tried to give her a clue. "Why don't you live closer to the hospital, wouldn't that be easier on both of you?"

"I guess, in some ways, but she hates the city. She always has, even though we've lived in it for as long as I can remember. Had to, for *his* sake." He spat the word *'his'* as though it had a bad taste. "Now that we don't have to worry about that any more, she wanted to spend her last months in the wilds, like she did as a kid. Julian was the best compromise we could make. It was wild enough to suit her, but close enough to the hospital to suit the doctors."

"So, who is 'he'? Your father?"

"Yes, my father. Mom's been sick for a little over two years, but did it slow him down? No, he's on the fast track. He's an antiques dealer. An expert, really. Double-majored in Art History and Archaeology in college, interned at Sotheby's in London a couple summers, worked in the Getty Museum, you know, like one of those brainiacs on Antiques Roadshow or something. I used to worship him, wanted to be just like him. I even started out to follow in his footsteps, being groomed for the 'family business' so to speak. That's what I was doing in college those two years—same majors, same classes, same everything as he did. I graduated high school early, at sixteen actually, so believe it or not, if we had stuck to the plan, I'd be at Sotheby's right now." He shook his head slowly, like the thought of that life was so foreign that he hardly could bear to speak of it now.

"What changed?" Alicia was so deeply entranced by his story, and the depth of feeling in his eyes, eyes she hadn't been able to look away from since he began recounting his tale, that she didn't notice Cynthia's approach. Now she was standing next to the table with two steaming hot plates. "Oh, hi," Alicia said as she noticed the waitress and the delightful smelling food, and then, "thank you," as Cynthia placed the large white oval stoneware plate in front of her. "This smells delicious." Alicia hadn't realized how hungry she was until now, but at the first scent of the abundant lasagna, her stomach growled audibly.

"I'll be back to check on you and refill your drinks in a bit. Enjoy."

Marcus hadn't looked up when his food came. He seemed deep in reverie. Alicia took a few bites before broaching the subject again.

"So why aren't you at Sotheby's?"

"She got sick and I saw him for what he really was, a selfish man who cared more about rusty guns and cracked ceramic pots and old bones than he did about the living breathing woman who loved him. I decided then and there that I didn't want to be like him after all. How could a person care more about old things belonging to dead people than they do about the people who are supposed to mean the most to them?" His pain was palpable now, and he vented it by stabbing wrathfully at the pile of pasta on his plate.

Alicia wanted to say something of comfort to him but didn't know what that might be, so instead she let the silence soothe him. They ate quietly for a while. When it seemed that he had calmed, she asked the question that had been bothering her for the last several minutes.

"So where is he now?"

"Don't know, don't care. Cairo, maybe Brazil, shoot, he could be down the street for all I know, and that's perfectly fine with me. He left us, divorced her and shipped out for places unknown. The only real down side is that he took most of his money with him. The sicker my mom got the less she could work. She was a professional chef—worked in several high end establishments, and even a few times as a personal chef to some very wealthy families."

"That's a cool job. So I guess you learned to cook from her?"

"Yeah, basic stuff mostly, nothing fancy."

Alicia's mind went immediately to the little radish rose that she was pretty sure was still buried somewhere in the bottom of her purse. That explains that, she thought to herself, and she realized what a sweetly personal gesture that must have been for him to make something for her that his mother had taught him.

"When she had to quit, I tried to make ends meet by working and going to school, but that was a disaster. I made some wrong choices, but I was a dumb teenager and was really lucky because I hadn't quite turned 18 yet."

"Oh." Alicia didn't really know how to respond to that revelation. She had never gone on a date with someone with a 'checkered past' before. She figured he had gotten involved with drugs like so many teens did. Her father's James Dean reference flashed in her mind. He may have been more right than he thought. She wondered if she should pry into all his sins, but decided to hold back and let him talk.

178

"Needless to say, I haven't felt too good about myself, or anyone else for that matter, for a while. My mistakes didn't help my social skills much." He looked apprehensively up at her, as though he was afraid he had said too much.

Alicia knew that whatever she said next could make or break the moment. She wanted to be friendly, but not too friendly, supportive, but not fake.

"Well, nothing I could say about my first day of college could be half as interesting, however, I promise to tell you sometime about the daring exploits of my mother, and the untold damage it has done to my psyche. I haven't a lot of serious mistakes to confess, but I do bite my nails, does that count?"

Marcus just smirked and rolled his eyes at her. "Very funny." She seemed to have maneuvered through that minefield with the right amount of compassion, humor and aloofness.

The rest of their dinner passed on uneventfully. They had moved into a more comfortable mode of discussion, more carefree and casual, talking about mutual acquaintances and funny stories from school or work. Only once, when Marcus was recounting a particularly long story about a crazy prank the senior class pulled on the freshmen at his high school, did Alicia find her mind wandering back to what he had told her.

She had great sympathy for Marcus and his mother and her situation, but to resort to delinquent or perhaps even illegal activity to try to solve it, well that was something Alicia just couldn't wrap her mind around. It was so foreign to everything her father had ever taught her. And yet, when she had seen the seething rage in Marcus' eyes when he talked about his father—the barely contained animosity he felt toward him—she believed he could be capable of almost anything. Was he a bona fide ex-con? Right across the table from her? She didn't want to think about that, she wanted to give him the benefit of the doubt.

As they finished up their Tiramisu, Cynthia brought the check. "I can take that whenever you are ready."

Alicia handed Marcus a twenty dollar bill with lightning speed.

"No, I've got this one. It's the least I can do after forcing you to sit through my sob story."

She relented, and was forced to concede to herself that this had indeed been some sort of a date, complete with personal revelations and dessert. She just hoped he didn't expect her to let him kiss her or anything. She wasn't ready for that. "At least let me get the tip," she said.

They walked through the big wooden double doors into the cool night air.

"It's starting to feel like fall already, at least at night." She unwrapped the sweater from around her waist and draped it over her shoulders.

"Eight o'clock, not too late. Do you want to walk around town a bit? It sure is pretty at night with all the streetlights. Besides, it's nice to be out here when the tourists are gone!"

She wasn't sure if he was trying to extend their time together, or if he really wanted to walk the town. It didn't matter, though, because she already had homework, and she had to get up and brave that awful traffic again the next morning.

"Thanks for the offer. Normally I would love to, but I can't. Homework. Sleep. These are my recreations now." She grimaced, already missing the summer's lazy mornings. "But, I'm parked on Main down by the Bank. Walk with me to my car?"

"Sure, I'm in that direction too."

They walked down the steep incline from the restaurant to Main Street on the old cracked and lop-sided asphalt. Once at the cross street, though, they turned right onto the well maintained sidewalk, and only had to go fifteen yards or so until they were standing in front of her truck. The street lamps were on either end of the block, so this area would have been much darker if it weren't for the light in the alcove that housed the ATM terminal for Julian Federal Savings Bank. A shadow played in that pool of light as the dark form of a man pulled a receipt from the terminal and began to walk down the ramp toward them. As he got closer, Marcus and Alicia both realized at once that it was Ollie Mahlon. He had two large grocery sacks in his arms, and the receipt from the bank machine was dangling haphazardly from the fingers of his right hand. She could feel Marcus tense up next to her. Ollie stopped several paces away from them, clearly he had recognized them by now as well, and he appeared to be assessing the situation.

"Hi, Mr. Mahlon. How are you?" Alicia wasn't overly fond of him, but she had no reason to be afraid of him.

"Your dad know you're out with him?" He was clearly speaking to Alicia, but he never took his eyes off of Marcus.

Before she had a chance to answer, Mahlon brushed past them, glaring daggers, and something else she couldn't quite pinpoint, at Marcus the whole time. Moments later, they heard an engine fire up somewhere in the darkness down the street. The tires squealed as he raced off into the night.

"That was weird." Alicia didn't quite know what to think. "He seemed mad that you were out with me now. I would have thought he would have been glad, I mean he wants you to stay away from Veronica. Being out with me is away from Veronica, right?"

"Yeah, but it's hard to know what makes him tick."

"And he seemed so mad. The way he was looking at you, I thought he was going to punch you or something."

"Oh, I wouldn't put it past him. He is capable of just about anything if properly motivated."

"Well, I really better get going. Thanks so much for dinner. I had a nice time." And now for the inevitable end-of-date moment. She wished she could just duck in her car and wave cheerily as she drove away, but that would never do. She had to wait out the awkwardness and hope that she didn't have to dodge any misplaced affections. After a quiet moment, Alicia was surprised when Marcus extended his hand to her.

"So, friends?"

"Yes, friends." She accepted his outstretched hand and shook it. She sort of felt like she had agreed to a deal with a used car salesman, and hoped that what she was buying wouldn't turn out to be a lemon.

Chapter 22

Halfway between Julian and home, Alicia's cell phone rang.

"Yes Dad, I'm coming home," she muttered to herself, but when she answered the phone she was pleasantly surprised to hear Michael's voice on the other end.

"Hey Nikki!"

"Hi, how's it going? Where are you?"

"We're still stationed in Biloxi, but we've been pulled off the project. They are sending us back to the base in San Diego for a few days, maybe even a week, so we can pack and prep to ship out for disaster relief in Iowa." There was the din of voices in the background. She could tell he was raising his voice to be heard.

"Are you at a party or something?"

"Yeah, that's all we do around here, party, sunbathe, you know. No, I'm at the airport. We're about to board the flight, but since it was so last minute we have two or three connections. It will take us forever to get back."

"That stinks. Be sure to drink plenty of water."

"Huh?"

"I don't know. Don't people always say that when they are going to fly, that it's good to drink lots of water?" She felt like she was rambling and suddenly realized how tired she was after the events of the day.

"Sure Nick, if you say so," he sounded tired too, "anyway, what I really called for was to say that I should be able to get an afternoon off while we're in town, and I wanted to come up and celebrate your birthday while I have a chance. I know it's still a couple weeks away, but God knows when I'll be back again."

"Michael, that's great! I would love that! When?" The prospect of spending some time with her old friend had given her at least some renewed energy.

"Well, I can't say for sure when. What is your schedule?"

"Monday thru Thursday I'm home from school around five or six. Friday and Saturday I work the lunch and dinner shifts. But don't worry about that. I'll leave the key to our house under the mat, let yourself in whenever you get up here, make yourself at home and I'll see you when I see you? OK?"

"That'll work. Oh, I wanted to ask how the first day of school went, but they just started the boarding call for our flight."

"No problem, we'll talk about it later. Besides, by then I'll have more to tell you."

"True. OK, gotta go."

"Bye, see you soon."

"Take care." And then silence.

The phone call had lasted for most of the remainder of the trip home, and just after slipping the phone back into her purse, she flipped on her turn signal, eased down on the brake, and turned into the long, black driveway. She hadn't been home since 6:00 that morning, but somehow it felt as though it had been much longer. The glow of light emanating from the front room widows gave her an almost nostalgic joy. She couldn't wait to get inside and kick off her shoes, flop on the couch, and just veg out. At this moment the thought of homework was more than she could bear—

especially since she was pretty sure her dad would have a lot of questions about her day, and about her dinner with Marcus. She had left him a note reminding him of her plans.

"Hi, Dad," she pushed through the screen door and dropped her backpack in the corner by the couch. "Do you want me to close the door?"

Her dad was peering at her over his book, "No, leave it open. The breeze is nice. So how was your day?" He put the fringed leather bookmark between the pages and closed the cellophane wrapped cover. She was pretty sure that he singlehandedly comprised at least 50% of the book usage at the Julian Public Library.

"How was your first day at school? I've been waiting all afternoon and evening to find out. Then you can tell me how dinner went."

Alicia was anxious to give him an account of the school day, and hesitant to talk about the dinner date. She considered the interest in dinner a third degree. After all, she was in college now, and her personal life should be her own. She was surprised in a way at the feeling, since she had always told her dad everything that happened in her life since her Mom left. Maybe it was the bad boy image that Marcus had portrayed and she felt her father would disapprove.

"School was fine after I got through all the morning traffic to get there. Jeez! That freeway is a mess, and I'm going to have to get up earlier tomorrow. I had to run to my first class and got stuck sitting in the very front center."

"Oooh, booo hooo! Too close to the teacher, huh! Poor baby," he teased.

"I'm not seeing any sympathy here, and so you may have to read about my first day of school in my memoirs if you keep it up!"

"Ok, truce, no smart remarks. What was your first class, anyway?"

"Anthropology, and it turned out pretty interesting. The professor is interested in Native American artifacts. I mean, duh? I suppose that's pretty natural for an anthropology teacher. Anyway, he wants to do a dig in the park—here!"

185

"Really?" Chris answered warily. He had had more than his share of permit requests for research projects that he had to comment on. The department's regional archeologist would handle it, but Chris was usually asked for input. His biggest problem with it was the fact that it opened up sites to a wider group of people who would then know where artifacts might be found. In the case of college classes, the random students were a complete unknown. If it were just a professor doing the dig, it would be easier to accept and confine the knowledge to someone who supposedly understood the ethical and legal constraints. With several semesters worth of students, the pool of potential violators who might steal from sites or collections escalated dramatically.

"Yes, and he wants me to 'exercise my pull' with the park to get him a permit," Alicia said with a snort.

"Has he applied for a permit yet with the regional office?

"He says he is working with the archeologist, but hasn't gotten anywhere. He seemed a little irritated at how slow they are at approving things."

Chris considered the comment for a moment before answering, "We evaluate requests pretty carefully to make sure they have the qualifications to do the work, and that the scope of what they want to do will actually be completed. In the past we have gotten burned by professors who dig stuff up and haul it off to some dark corner of the college basement where it sits "being studied" for decades. The Prof is supposedly 'writing a book' on it, and basically we never see any outcome, plus we lose our artifacts."

He tossed his book onto the coffee table. "It's bad enough that we have places in the park marked on USGS maps, like Arrowmaker's Ridge, where any yahoo with a map and curiosity can look and possibly take material. When we identify other sites to kids in college classes the word gets out and our heritage gets compromised. We want to learn more, but we lose a lot sometimes in the process. Making pothunting illegal doesn't help a lot when it is so hard to catch them at it or trace material they may have acquired illegally."

"Yeah, my teacher said sort of the same thing. He has this big arrowhead belt buckle that he wears, and he mentioned how he got it legally but he has no idea how the dealer got it."

"Yup, happens all the time," Chris paused, "but now for the big story. How was dinner!" His sly grin was evidence that he knew he was putting Allie on the spot and he was enjoying it.

"It was just dinner, Dad. Not really a date, so don't go making something out of it. I got to know him a bit better. His dad was an art collector and I guess he left Marcus and his mom 'high and dry.' He seems pretty bitter about that."

"Tough on kids to have to go through divorces," he looked directly at Allie, thinking about what they both had to deal with after his wife took off. "Tough on everybody," he said as he looked down at his book.

"Well, the other thing my class and then Marcus' dad made me think of is how Mr. Wong has a really big collection in his office. I don't think I ever told you about it."

"I've never been in his office. What does he collect?"

"I didn't have time to pay much attention, but I did see Hopi carved wooden kachinas, and a leather dress with beads on it. All pure white leather on the dress."

"Sounds like a Navajo wedding dress. They are pretty rare and worth quite a bit of money. I've never seen one outside of a museum," Chris said. "I'm surprised he has one. I wonder where he got it? That's the kind of thing your professor meant when he was talking about his purchase of the belt buckle. Some of these dealers don't just pot hunt, they deal in heavy-duty black market stolen items. The thefts aren't frequent or well known, but they do happen."

"Dad, do you think Mr. Wong could be buying or even dealing stolen artifacts?" She knew her imagination was getting the best of her, but something like that would explain her boss' weird behavior.

"I wouldn't want to jump to conclusions about something like that. And besides, without some report of specific items being stolen, there isn't much you can do to even look into it."

"I'll pay better attention next time I go in his office, although I don't really have much reason to do that, and he got all weird when he found me in there the other day."

"Really? Well, lots of people have privacy concerns that don't rise to the level of artifact theft. Maybe he just had money or something that he was worried someone would grab."

Allie was on a roll, "I bet he is a major dealer in stolen artifacts and maybe even gems from a huge theft ring! Maybe even the Asian gangs are under his control. I bet he can fly through the air like those karate kung foo guys!" They were both giggling.

"Yes, Daniel Wong, master martial arts expert. I think the only thing fast and deadly on Mr. Wong is his motor mouth. I've never seen a guy get so wired so fast and so frequently."

Alicia was still considering the image of pudgy Mr. Wong wearing black pajamas and walking straight up the side of a building as he dodged his adversaries.

"I guess he could have gotten the things he has in his office legally," she said. "For that matter we could consider Dr. Whiteside. He flat out said in the middle of class that he had gotten artifacts that might have been from questionable sources. If he says that in front of a bunch of 'impressionable youths,'" here she paused and mockingly rolled her eyes, "imagine what he might be capable of when he thinks no one is looking."

"Hard to tell. I'm glad you said that though 'cause I'm sure not recommending him for a dig permit, now!" They both sat pondering for a moment before Chris offered, "I was thinking the same thing about Xavier Hess and the things that were in the apartment when I talked to his wife. He had some pretty nice specimens of things, especially a Navajo rug that had to be worth at least $2500 or more hanging on the wall."

"Do you think he got it illegally?"

188

"Rugs are pretty commonly sold from weavers on the reservation. People buy some pretty expensive ones, especially if he bought it from a dealer and not direct on the rez. It looked pretty new, so it probably wasn't anything but a purchase from a legitimate dealer or tourist store somewhere."

"Did you finish off all the pie?"

"Nope, you wanna dish some up for your sweet old Dad, too?"

They finished off the pie in silence, but Chris was wondering about artifacts to himself. Stuff was missing from his basement storage at the park. Wong had high value items in his office. The Hopi kachina's alone could bring $2,000 or more a piece. Then there was Hess. There was nothing wrong with having a Navajo rug on a wall. What bothered him most was the dirt and the bit of ceramic material he had found in Hess's truck. He was pretty sure the longer he thought about it that it was very similar to what a Kumeya'ay pot would look like if it were a piece broken off the curved bottom. Rangers hardly got off the highways and out of the campgrounds any more, let alone made inspections of high value cultural areas in the park. Perhaps tomorrow he should spend a little time in the field, maybe start with a trip to Arrowmaker's Ridge.

Chapter 23

Becker's day started out badly. His Cherokee sat stubbornly in the driveway of his cabin refusing to start. He had the hood up and could smell gasoline and suspected that somehow it was flooding. He decided to go refill his coffee cup inside the house and then come back to see if it would finally start. The coffee pot element had turned off and the brew was tepid. He nuked it and headed back out for the car as the phone rang. He answered and was surprised it was Eric on the line.

"Hey boss, I got a hot one for you. We just received a FAX detailing some pretty significant recent archeological thefts at Borrego, and I also wanted to tell you I went back and finished a more detailed inventory down in the basement. We've got a lot of stuff missing. Much more than I thought. I put it in your box, but I've got to go do the morning camp checks at Paso and Green Valley since no one else is on but me."

"OK, I'll read it when I get there. I'm having trouble getting the Jeep started, so I'm not sure when that will be, and could you tell that to Jane for me?"

It was the better part of another hour and the help of one of the maintenance crew before they found the cracked fuel line and gave up until the part could be brought in from El Cajon. Chris took Val Simpson's Blazer from the shop yard and figured he'd have his rig back before she came back from her weekend. By the time he got to the office it was almost 10 AM.

The report and BOLO alert that Eric had called about were on top of the pile of papers fermenting in his in-box. He scanned the BOLO alert from Borrego and wondered why they bothered sending pictures through the FAX machine. It was so dark and fuzzy he could hardly tell if it was a large clay pot or Rosie O'Donnell. What was clear, though, was that the alert wasn't just about Borrego. Added to it was a detailed account of a series of missing items that the National Park Service and the Bureau of Land Management had put together on sites throughout the southwest over the past five years.

Chris had no idea so many sites had been vandalized and collections at museums had been compromised. Interagency cooperation wasn't good, and this was a perfect example of something that should have had widespread publicity at least among related law enforcement agencies. The Feds rarely paid attention even to other federal agencies, much less ones run by the state or the county, and this was a flaw that would someday have big consequences. Of that, Chris was sure.

He checked down Eric's list of missing items from the basement and noted several Kumeya'ay pots, arrow shafts, beads, arrowheads, and even some raccoon, mountain lion, and deer bones that had been put there because no one knew what else to do with them. It seemed obvious to him that someone who had access on the permanent staff must have been responsible for this. The items weren't extremely high value, but they would bring a little serious money from the right person. There weren't as many missing items as Eric seemed to imply, and Chris thought whoever did it felt they had taken just enough to not have anyone notice that stuff was obviously missing for a long time. It had to be someone who knew that there was no active archeological research going on in the basement by anyone.

Fortunately, the record files with the photographs of the items were still there and attached to the report. Identifying the items should be easy, if they ever found them. He was surprised someone would bother with a number of the small worthless items. Maybe they were just novel and would make nice conversation pieces on the coffee table. Still why risk taking something of no value, unless of course the thief was so sure he wouldn't be caught that there was no risk.

Maybe the bones were used in some sort of pagan ritual. In this day and age of the weird and satanic, and just plain goofy, Chris had heard and seen a lot of the bizarre: A circle of blue rocks on the top of a desert Mesa, a pile of sacrificed chickens under a bridge in the redwoods, not to mention the woman who tied herself to a redwood tree, naked, to protest logging old growth. He imagined a stolen skull with a candle glowing inside, its eye sockets and toothy smile grinning like some weird Halloween decoration.

He tromped down the wood staircase and called Eric on the base station radio.

"R 301, Montane"

"Montane, 301"

"Give me a call as soon as you have a chance." A minute later Jane forwarded a call to him in his office.

"You said you ran some prints on this file you gave me, correct?"

"Yeah, I sent them off last week before I started the inventory. I didn't want to mess anything up while I was rooting around into everything. I got a few good prints." Eric sounded like he was beaming and very pleased with himself on the other end of the line. Maybe they'd catch a break and narrow things down with some prints.

"OK, I'll give a call to the sheriff's lab. I've got some prints of my own I'm hoping to get a rush on if Wayne Johnson was able to light a fire under them for me."

Eric sounded deflated, "Gee, I should have thought of that with my prints."

"Don't worry about it, I doubt it works very often anyway. Hey, do you have time to hike up to Arrowmaker's with me? I don't think anyone's been up there for quite a while and I'd like to see if the site is still intact. It would be good experience for you to see the area."

"Sure boss!" Eric sounded like a puppy about to take that long walk in the dog park without a leash.

"I'll meet you at the end of West Mesa Fire Road at the Japacha Spring in about 10 minutes and we'll hike the rest of the way from there."

Fifteen minutes later they were both working their way around the West Mesa meadows amidst age old Ponderosa's and Jeffrey pines with their fast fading vanilla aroma. The green grass of spring was gone and replaced with California's famous golden grass. It was tall and thick this year from heavy winter snow and spring rain. The forestry fire department loved it that way because they could claim it made the fire danger extreme. Of course if there was a drought and it was short and thin they claimed the fire danger was extreme because everything had been so dry. They had the perfect racket going and funds were never scarce for their operation. Becker envied them.

As they coursed through the meadow and up the steep climb to Arrowmaker's Ridge, Chris marveled at the quiet and the beauty. This was his favorite spot in the whole park. He always felt Cuyamaca was a bit of the Sierra Nevadas lost and floating in Southern California. This meadow was a prime example.

As they crested the ridge it opened into a mini-meadow littered with pot shards. Much of it looked as it had for years, but Chris noted a huge digging operation that had recently been undertaken near the grassy opening's edge. Someone had been carefully working a specific section and sifting and screening the entire dig.

"Well, this is just great!" Chris said with disgust.

"Do you want to set up a stakeout here?"

"Not a very viable option I'm afraid. Likely we would spend days and never see them. Just too hit and miss. Borrego has a wildlife camera that senses movement and begins video-taping. They've been using it to monitor the desert bighorns at the watering holes. I think we could borrow it from their resource ecologist and set it up in one of the trees for a few weeks. My guess is someone drops them off and they dig at night to avoid people seeing them and that camera's low light capability is perfect for that."

"I think we should start documenting anyone who parks in the area so we can cross check some license numbers against names or maybe come up with frequent parkers, too."

"Good idea, Eric, but my guess is that won't give us much, they probably do the drop off and then come back later to pick them up. These guys look like they have a pretty sophisticated understanding of what it takes to get something from a site. They're not someone who came up one Sunday and rooted around with their Swiss Army knife. I suspect they've done enough of this kind of thing to be careful. Still it's worth the effort just in case they are stupid," Chris said as he threw a handful of freshly dug soil on the ground.

"I was thinking about all those thefts on the BOLO we got. One was at Borrego and one was at Mesa Verde and a couple were at the Grand Canyon. I remember Mahlon saying he worked at Grand Canyon for a season, and I know he transferred here from Borrego when our ecologist quit. Maybe he knows something useful about what went on there?" said Eric.

"I knew he was at Borrego for a couple months, but I never heard he worked for the Feds? When was that?"

"I don't know boss, you'd have to ask him. I just know his daughter mentioned it to me once."

Chris wondered if Eric was interested in Veronica Mahlon. He was older, but wasn't that much older than she was. In this day and age a guy five years her senior wouldn't even be blinked at except maybe by her asshole father. Eric was a handsome and buff young guy. In fact he'd wondered about Eric and Elaine at times, as well. 'Interpersonal' relations

194

among park staff was not uncommon, and it made life a pain for supervisors.

"You know Veronica very well?" Chris asked as his eyebrows arched.

Eric flushed red, "I've talked with her a few times. I can talk with Mahlon and see if he remembers anything about the thefts if you want."

"No Eric, let me do that, I need to talk to him anyway." Becker's wheels were beginning to spin. One of the shop items missing was a lithium lightweight battery scene light and a screen for cleaning up native sandy soils when they were out mixing cement and doing mortar work in the back-country on the old Civilian Conservation Corps built trails. It was just the kind of equipment that would be used on a dig site. It occurred to him that the Arrowmaker pothunting might be some locals like Wong or an inside job, too, just like the basement storage seemed to be. "Let's get back and see what we can scare up from the sheriff's lab on those prints."

Both rangers backtracked in the afternoon sun through the big meadow and gave directions to some horseback riders who were hoping to find the remains of the plane that crashed nearby during World War I. All that remained at the site was the motor, but there was always controversy abounding as to what the highly secret plane was carrying. Gold, secret documents, a new weapon, all were suggested, but the cattleman who found the remains several years later always maintained there was nothing there of interest. Still, nothing was left at the site but the motor and that caused people to talk conspiracy no matter what anyone said. He wondered if he had his own homegrown artifact conspiracy going on.

By the time they returned to the office it was near quitting time and Chris wanted to call the sheriffs' lab before they shut down. When he got them on the phone they were especially curt and he could tell they were anxious to go home for the day.

"Can you check and see if you have the results for our print request? That's all I need from you. I know you guys probably want to get out of there."

195

"Actually, that's not going to be a problem. I was just going to FAX them to you before I go off duty. We did the request on the building burglary. The vehicle request hasn't been done yet." Chris wondered why they did them in the opposite order from what they were received. So much for Wayne pulling strings. "The building burg had several good prints and we were able to ID all of them in the system. Considering everyone in the world is not fingerprinted, that was a surprise. We almost never find people in the system when we run them. Only if they've worked for the government or have criminal records already." This was old news to Chris, but he wasn't going to cut her off since she was being so helpful.

"OK, thanks. I'll go downstairs and stand by the FAX."
Becker went down to the lower office where Eric was still finishing up counting campground and day use receipts and getting ready for a bank run before he went off shift.

"They're going to FAX the results of the prints right now," Chris said to Eric as he stood by the machine while it spit out several sheets. His jaw dropped a bit as he read off the information.

"Interesting. The basement report shows your prints, Val's, mine, Jane's, Mahlon's, the Regional Archeologist…and Daniel Wong's."

"Wong?" Eric was clearly as surprised as Becker.

"There goes our inside job theory. I think we need to have a sit-down with Mr. Wong very soon. Have you ever seen Daniel hanging out with any of our people, like maybe Mahlon or Charlie Sims? I never have."

"I've never even seen them speak to each other. In fact I've never seen him spending any time with anyone from the park," said Eric with his eyes wide.

"So, the question of the hour is how did his prints get inside the basement?"

196

Chapter 24

When he swung into the shop yard to fill up with gas, Becker discovered that his Jeep was back in service.

"Got your mount all fed and watered for you," Gus Norton said in his affected cowboy way. As lead maintenance worker he usually wound up with the vehicle maintenance work, and though not a certified automotive mechanic, he usually did well on minor repairs.

"Thanks, Gus, I'll just swap the Blazer out right now."

In short order his gear was stowed in back and he was on the road. His plan was to spend some time checking other known rich archeological areas within the park. Some were close to park roads and others were far off the beaten path similar to Arrowmaker. He started with the closest area with a park road. As the winding pavement narrowed and stretched out across the barren grassy low hills that surrounded Lake Cuyamaca he approached the horse camp areas. Both were near areas that ancient Kumeya'ay groups had used for settlement. Being close to the lake assured food and water, plus back in prehistoric times they didn't have to worry about the ground shifting so much.

When Stonewall Mine was constructed in the late 1800s next to the lake, and actively worked, its depth and complexity were huge. Large pumps had to remove water that seeped into the depths from the lake overhead. When the mine finally closed and the tunnels all filled with water, subsidence began, and every few years huge sections of the landscape would sag suddenly as much as ten feet or more. It made Chris nervous every time he came to this part of the park.

He smelled the campfire and cooking smoke from the 'horsie set' who crammed the Los Vaqueros group camp and the Los Caballos campground along this road. The area was designed specifically for horse use. The Native Americans would have had cooking fires going in the same spots two or three hundred years ago. He thought it interesting that illegal aliens built their fires in these woods now on their way north from Mexico to the promised land. Ironically, most of them were unwittingly descendants of the Kumeya'ay who lived there originally.

Not infrequently, Chris would have to chase illegals through the woods. Rangers and the CHP even stopped a few vehicles now and then in the park that had Mexican illegals stacked like cordwood inside. Once he opened the back of a U-Haul truck just to have 50 people knock him over and run madly into the woods. They searched for them for days and only found a few. He doubted any of them really knew their ancestors had called this their home for hundreds of years, or had any idea that the area was extremely rich in Native American artifacts.

He parked his Jeep on the side of the road and walked out in the field nearer to the lakeshore to inspect one of the sites he knew had been identified by archeologists. If they had their way all the campgrounds would be removed from the area, and though Chris thought that a good idea, he was at a loss as to where replacement sites could be located to meet the identified user need. Park politics being what it was, he knew the loss of a major horse camp would result in a public relations disaster for the park service.

As he scanned the field he noticed obvious sections that had been disturbed. This was not a well-known site to most people. In fact, only a few of the park staff and volunteers were aware of it. Quite a few of the horse patrol volunteer group had heard rumors of moving the campgrounds and why, so he couldn't discount their knowledge about artifacts. Much of what he saw reflected the same type of activity that he had seen on Arrowmaker's Ridge, and he didn't doubt this was the work of the same person or group.

As he moved closer to the campground areas, the digging disappeared. He still wondered who would be so bold as to dig in an area of such human activity unless they knew the schedule of who reserved the camps and when. It was completely deserted in this area for a couple of miles on a night when no one was camped. His ranger staff and visitor service park aids knew the schedule, but it wasn't a top-secret document, so probably any staff member or volunteer could easily take a look at it. Maintenance might even ask someone if it was going to be occupied in case they wanted to do work on the camp undisturbed.

It was obvious he had a major problem going on in the park. He was beginning to think there might be a possible connection between this and the other pot hunting at parks besides his. He drove back to headquarters in the hopes of catching Mahlon in his office. Maybe he could shed some light on what had gone on at Borrego and Grand Canyon. He also needed to talk to Daniel Wong as soon as possible.

As he pulled in to the Dyar House office parking area he noticed Mahlon's vehicle parked next to the County Sheriff's Ford Bronco. Inside the office Wayne Johnson was scamming a fresh cup of coffee from Jane. She even had a donut for him, and he wondered where that had come from. Chris lived on Dudley's Fruit Bars and donuts from the Julian bakery most days, but didn't see any by the office coffee pot.

"Hey Wayne, what brings you here this morning?"

"Your secretary's pretty little face, mostly," Wayne replied with shameless flirtation. *Probably how he got the donut*, Chris thought.

"I also brought some information for you, too," he paused to finish swallowing a big mouthful of the cream filled pastry. "I got a response on that BOLO you wanted put out on Lola Bragdon. They found her laid out as coyote food down out on the south side of Warner Springs. Bunch of Boy Scouts out on a hike with their leader practically stepped on her."

"What happened to her? Do they have a cause of death?"

"Yeah pretty obvious. Lotsa antemortem bruise marks on her, but the bullet in the back of the head was pretty definitive. Somebody just plain executed her. Not sure if it happened there or not, but the deputy who found her said there was a lot of blood and what he thought was brain matter spattered around at the site."

Chris suddenly wasn't much interested in a donut.

"Animal predation was a problem but they stumbled on her soon enough, I guess, to avoid too much of that. Had to run prints on her since she had no ID, but it's your girl."

Jane interrupted Johnson long enough to hand Chris the office ticket receipt inventory, "I need your signature on this while I've got you here."

Becker took the form and ignored her and pressed Deputy Johnson further. "Was there anything else at the scene to give a clue as to who could have done it?" Becker's mind was spinning. This whole thing was getting out of hand.

"Nope. They're working her body for evidence and they worked the scene for hours, but whoever was there with her pretty much wiped out any trace at the scene. You never know though, bodies can give up a lot of secrets when the right investigator looks at 'em. I'll tell you one thing, everybody is *real* curious why you wanted to find her. I mean *real curious,* Chris."

Becker became uncomfortable that Jane and Mahlon both had been standing in the stairwell hall listening to the investigation conversation confidential details.

"Let's finish this discussion in my office Wayne. We need to talk about this a bit."

As Chris passed Mahlon he said, "are you going to be around for a bit? I need to talk to you when I'm done."

"Actually, I don't have time to sit around the office and wait. I've got way too much to do today. If you need me I'll be out reviewing another trail re-route plan below Stonewall Peak off the Cold Spring Trail."

"Can you take a radio with you so I can meet up with you?"

"Sure, but I may be way back there."

"OK." As he started to leave Becker suddenly remembered the inventory form in his hand and realized he didn't have a pen. "Hey, Ollie, can I use your pen for a second." Mahlon's pen was always the subject of ridicule since he never seemed to wind up putting it in the breast pocket like most people. Instead it was clipped below the top button of his shirt. Becker figured he had either been raised by potted plants or else never had a shirt with a pocket growing up.

Becker led Deputy Johnson and the last of his donut upstairs into his office.

"Like I said Chris, we are all real curious about Lola Bragdon. What's the story?"

Chris wasn't sure where to begin so he started with his daughter Alicia.

"You know my daughter, Allie, don't you Wayne?

"Sure, smart kid—works at Hillside Resort, right?"

"Yeah, well she works in the restaurant most of the time but a few days ago she had to fill in for one of the housekeepers who was sick, and she wound up cleaning out the room that Xavier Hess was staying in. She found a pair of women's panties there…and a matchbook cover that had "*Azalea 1/4 mi. ft. br. 8*" written inside. I know it sounds kind of "Mickey Spillane," but I figured truth is stranger than fiction. I went to the bar that the matchbook cover was from and talked to them there. They knew Hess as a regular and they put me on to his girlfriend, Lola Bragdon."

"You never cease to amaze me. Don't you have enough to do?"

Chris ignored the taunt, "When I went to her apartment, she hadn't been there for days. I checked with her employer and she had missed work, too. Anyway, it just seemed strange, and I wanted to talk to her about what Hess was doing up here that morning. It just didn't make a whole lot of sense him being out on the trail. His wife said he was working on a contract bid for part of the dirt work on the highway repair in Julian. Him maybe doing the nasty, and the tawdry little motel tryst made sense, but the rest of it didn't hang together quite right."

"You think she knew something? You think that's why she's dead? Maybe it was just a jealous husband or boyfriend?"

"Yes, I'm sure it could be any of that. But I needed to know more. Now she's dead, and I've got nothing."

"Well, I wouldn't go that far. You've got a nice pair of panties for your trouble," Johnson said as his grin almost split his face ear to ear. "Seriously though, I do think you've got some interesting information, and I'm starting to take your interest in this as a case of more than animal mauling as a possibility. I think it's time we got the detective division brought up to speed on this. I know they'll want to talk to you directly, too. I'll also see where forensics is on their report. A lot of the Hess case hinges on what they say. Let me check in with them and I'll get back to you."

Johnson left Chris in his office playing with his pen. He thought a bit about Lola Bragdon. He had really counted on being able to talk to her and felt he was still hemmed in, with nowhere to go. He was also troubled that his time was being divided with two cases, now that he was working this archeological theft situation. He wasn't even thinking about the car burglaries anymore. He headed out the door and hoped he could catch Mahlon before he got too far off on foot in the backcountry. As he started his Jeep, he keyed the mic on his radio and tried to raise him on the air. There was no answer. He decided just to drive to the Cold Spring parking area and find where his truck was parked and just follow him up into the ridgeline. He wasn't aware of exactly what trail work was being proposed and should have tried to find out where, but Mahlon probably had the only active file copy of the proposal at this point anyway.

As he headed up the highway and approached the "S" curves below Stonewall Peak he saw the ecologist's truck parked in a small turnout below the main parking area a few hundred yards away. Odd place to park, he thought. Once parked, he managed to find the trail along Cold Stream and headed back into the age old oak trees that studded the hillside. Summer acorns littered the ground profusely with no Kumeya'ay Indians to gather them for food. Squirrels just couldn't keep up with the workload. He keyed his mic several times and called for Mahlon but got no answer.

After about twenty minutes of fast hiking he overtook him on the trail and said "how come you never answered me on the radio?"

"Must be busted. Never heard you. I figured you changed your mind."

"You better take it in and try a new battery. If that doesn't work have them look at it. You don't want to be out here without a way to communicate."

"I don't mind being out of communication. Suits me just fine, actually."

"Well look, I was hoping you could help me with some information?"

"What about?" There was a wariness in his expression.

"Well, I understand that you worked Borrego before here and also spent some time at Grand Canyon with the National Park Service a while back. I need to know something about some thefts that happened there. Maybe you heard about them?"

"Don't remember anything special about thefts. Law Enforcement folks didn't spend much time talking with me about stuff. I was just a seasonal maintenance worker fresh out of the Marines. The Feds like to hire their Vets in the park service I guess. We had a couple there fresh from Iraq like me."

"It would have been about artifacts that were stolen from their museum collections. It would be parts of the collections in storage and not

203

out on display. Some of them were pretty high value items as I understand it. Maybe stuff they were afraid they couldn't secure in a display case. You sure you didn't hear about any of that?"

"Is this an interrogation?"

Chris was not totally surprised at his reaction, "No, I just thought you may have heard some scuttlebutt about what went on, maybe who they thought did it, exactly when it happened, that sort of thing."

"Can't help you there Chief. What on earth do you want to know stuff about those parks for anyway?"

Chris hadn't been ready to let the cat out of the bag on the theft from the basement, but he was pressed up against the wall and hadn't planned an answer for this. He mentally kicked himself for it.

"We got a request to keep an eye out for things from their stolen collection, that's all." He congratulated himself on sidestepping the truth.

"Well, sorry, you are on your own I'm afraid. I don't know anything about the theft of pots."

Chris decided to head back to the office and didn't realize until he slid out of the seat in the parking lot that he had never mentioned exactly what had been stolen from the parks. Was it just an off the wall generalization, or did it mean anything that Ollie Mahlon said "pots?"

Chapter 25

"Hey sweetie! How's school?" The warmth of Marina's smile was as welcome a respite from the August afternoon heat as the rural Julian roads were from the hateful traffic she had been battling these last three days. At least that was usually the case.

"Hi Marina. How are things?" Alicia managed a tired smile, then gestured expansively with her arm toward the bank of windows facing Main Street, "what the heck is going on?"

"Oh, the roadwork? Yeah, that sure has been great for business." Her sarcasm was evident. "Thank goodness for our back parking lot, or there wouldn't be anyone here at all!" The last half of her sentence was ratcheted up several decibels as Marina shouted to be heard over the rhythmic thumping of the jackhammer.

"Has that been going on all day?" Alicia couldn't imagine having to listen to that all the time.

"Only since around lunch. They swear the demolition will be done by the end of the week. We'll see," she said as she rolled her eyes, "but enough about this, tell me about school. Any cute boys?" She winked conspiratorially.

205

"Oh brother. I haven't had a chance to even consider that. It's all I can do to find a parking place and get to class! Besides, the homework, oh my gosh, how does anybody go to class all day, do the homework every night, have a part-time job, and have time for any kind of social life?"

"You'll adjust, trust me."

"I hope so, but if the last three days are any indication of what the next four years are going to be like, it's quite possible that coming in here a couple times a week and visiting with you will be the extent of my social life!"

Marina's chuckle was masked by the increase in the jackhammer volume coupled by the jingling bell as the door was hastily pushed open, and then slammed closed, allowing a new customer, as well as a whoosh of hot air and construction dust, into the otherwise calm store.

"What a mess!" Veronica Mahlon spat the words angrily at no one in particular, then looked somewhat embarrassed when she realized she had an audience. "Oh, hey Allie, I didn't see you there."

"Veronica! What's up? Haven't seen you for a while." Of course Alicia knew exactly how long it had been since they had seen one another, and so did Veronica. Something in the other girl's eyes flashed recognition, and Alicia knew that for at least that moment they were both thinking the same thing. She wondered again what it must be like to have a father like Ollie Mahlon, and was grateful that she didn't know first-hand. Hopefully, for Veronica's sake, that whole mess with Marcus and her dad had blown over. Although, if the behavior she had witnessed on Monday night was any indication, those rivers ran pretty deep. Hopefully Mr. Mahlon wouldn't treat every boyfriend Veronica brought home that way.

"Yeah, well, I've been home a lot. My mom isn't feeling well."

"Oh, I'm sorry, what's the matter?" Marina's maternal instincts had been triggered. "Is there anything I can do?"

"No, but thanks. It's her migraines again. She's been in bed a lot, so I'm trying to keep up with some of the household chores." She managed a strained smile, "but it's kind of tough to fit everything in around my work schedule."

Allie couldn't help but make the connection between the number of days Veronica's mother had been ill, and the number of days ago her father had made his very public display at Hillside Resort. She wondered if there were a causal relationship between the two events.

"I can imagine, but I'm sure your mother appreciates your help. Here, give me your list and I'll pull the items for you." Marina took the slip of paper from Veronica's outstretched hand, picked up a basket, and began moving through the aisles as one on a mission.

"They still have you working the night shift?" Alicia didn't really need to ask the question, since she had seen Roni sitting in the cold fluorescent light of the gas station mini-mart as recently as Monday night.

"Yeah, well, you know, I'm the new girl and all."

"I guess, huh." Alicia couldn't help but feel kind of bad about the fact that Veronica was stuck in a 'go-nowhere' kind of job, while she had just started college. Veronica was a good student. In fact, she had gotten better grades in math and science than Alicia could ever hope for, and in an unusual moment of comradery, she had confided in Allie that she had secretly applied to several colleges in the hope of getting a scholarship or something. They had all gladly accepted her, but the financial boon she needed had never been part of it. In the end, her father nixed any hopes she may have had, and told her she better get a job and start helping the family. It didn't seem fair to Alicia, but like her own dad had said a million times, the world isn't fair.

"It wouldn't be so bad if I didn't have to do all the cleaning and shopping and cooking too!" It was clear her exasperation was getting the better of her. "I got off at 5:00 this morning, got home ate a bologna sandwich and fell into bed at about 6:00, and was up at 1:30 cleaning toilets and changing sheets. My dad is going to be furious if dinner isn't on the table when he gets home, but how am I supposed to do that when we can't seem to keep any food in the house? I saw him with three grocery bags last weekend, and where is all that food now? I certainly never ate any of it. All I seem to be able to scrounge up anymore is peanut butter and dry cereal. No

207

milk of course." Her voice had risen to a bit of a hysterical level, and Alicia could see that this had been building in her for a while.

"That's weird, I saw him with a couple bags of stuff the other night, too."

"What? When was this?" asked Veronica.

"Oh, Monday night, outside Don Giovanni's."

"Don Giovanni's? Are you working there too, now?"

"No, I was having dinner."

"Pretty fancy digs for a week night. Chief Ranger pay must be way better than I thought." Veronica snorted a little at the dig, but Allie didn't think to be irritated. She was too consumed with the realization that this conversation may be on a very slippery slope. She wasn't at all sure how well Veronica would take the news that she and Marcus had had dinner together, no matter how platonic it had been.

"Actually, I wasn't there with my dad. I had dinner with a friend from work." At this point she figured it was bound to come out somehow, so she'd rather spin it her way if possible.

"Oh?" Veronica had picked up on the implication right away, and now was merely playing cool, which, Alicia decided, was decidedly better than just freaking out right away. "That's nice. Anyone I know?" Oh yes, very cool.

"Yeah, as a matter of fact, it was Marcus Lundee." Alicia cringed inwardly and waited for the fur to start flying.

"That's cool. Marcus is a nice guy."

Alicia stared at Veronica.

"What?" Veronica asked.

"I guess I was afraid you'd be mad. I mean, you two used to date, and you were talking to him the other day. I thought maybe there was still something there." This was a very unexpected reaction and Alicia found herself stumbling about for the right words.

"Well, 'date' is kind of a strong word, really. I mean we hung out, and I definitely liked him. Towards the end we did go to the movies and

208

dinner a couple times, but it was like almost two years ago, and I was barely sixteen and he was almost eighteen."

"I'm surprised your dad let you guys go out." Alicia had to be careful about anything she said to Veronica about her dad, she had learned that the hard way. She tempered it by saying, "I mean, I don't think my dad would have let me go out in that situation. He's pretty strict about older boys." In saying that, it occurred to her that some of his discomfort in her having dinner with Marcus was the fact that he was a few years older and that she wasn't eighteen yet. Or maybe his fear was that she almost was?

"Well, yeah, my dad is too, but it was different with Marcus, he was like a family friend."

"Really?" Alicia couldn't hide the surprise in her voice. The idea of Marcus being a 'family friend' was pretty hard to imagine if one had witnessed the near brawl that had happened on Saturday night.

"Believe it or not, my dad and Marcus used to be pretty tight. Dad even got him a job in Grand Canyon as some sort of a park aide, but he blew it by getting busted for stealing something. I can't remember what, but it got him fired. After that my dad was really pissed. I guess he figured it made him look bad, you know. After all, he had vouched for this kid, then he turns out to be a crook. Whatever. I never thought Marcus deserved to have my dad turn on him. That's my dad though, a stickler about mistakes and keeping your word, and loyalty and all that." She shrugged her shoulders, and the familiar defeated look she so often wore settled back on her like a comfortable old coat.

"Wow." Alicia wasn't sure what to say.

"Anyway, don't hold the past against Marcus. He's an OK guy. And don't worry about stepping on my toes. He's fair game as far as I'm concerned, and even if I felt differently, my father has made it pretty clear what he thinks."

"Well, OK, good to know, but things aren't like that between us. We're just friends." Alicia couldn't stress that point enough, and yet it didn't seem to be getting through, and she was afraid that the Julian rumor mill would have big red hearts mentally drawn around their initials by this time tomorrow.

"I hate to break it to you, but Don Giovanni's isn't really a 'just friends' kind of place."

The conversation was taking an uncomfortable turn, and Alicia's relationship with Veronica was such that this was more than they had said to each other in the last six months combined. That being the case, Alicia was very relieved to see Marina coming briskly back to the register, two full hand-held baskets wielded expertly around the corner and onto the counter.

"Will that be all for you?" Her lighthearted presence seemed to visibly lift some weight from Veronica's shoulders, and certainly lightened the mood of their serious conversation.

"Yeah thanks. I appreciate you getting it all for me."

"It was no problem." She began ringing the items up at lightning speed. Her usually casual work attitude had been replaced by hyper-efficiency. "How do you want to pay?"

"Oh, here is my mom's credit card."

Marina swiped it and had the receipt in the bag in just moments, and was helping Veronica get all the bags carefully situated so she could still see the ground to walk.

"Now, you be careful on that walkway, they seem to be tearing that up too. Have a good evening." She held the door open for the girl as well.

"Thanks again." She smiled over her bags at the older woman, and then turned to Alicia, "see ya Allie," and then she was out the door into the pounding, grinding chaos of progress.

"I've never seen you work so quickly, you are like a well-oiled machine!" Alicia was teasing, but also wondered why the woman had wanted Veronica gone, as that was the only explanation Alicia could think of for why Marina had rushed so.

"Ha, ha. Very funny." Her look softened, "I know what it's like to have an unreasonable man breathing down your neck. I just wanted to help the poor kid out—get her home as fast as possible. That's all I can really do for her."

Alicia resisted the impulse to follow up on that loaded statement, and instead changed the subject. "Well, she wasn't the only one who needed to do a little shopping, so I better get to it."

Even without Marina's help, or lightning speed checkout mode, Alicia had purchased her items and was walking out to the parking lot in back, carrying her bags, in less than fifteen minutes. As she piled the last parcel into the passenger side floorboards, she was reminded of Veronica. They really had more in common than she liked to admit in terms of family structure. Her mom was technically there, but wasn't terribly effective, leaving Roni and Mr. Mahlon to pretty much run the show alone. How strange it was to see such similar circumstances played out so very differently. Her dad would never buy bags of food and save it all for himself, or hide it, or whatever Veronica's dad was doing.

"What is he doing with all that food?" And then just as she breathed the question into the air, a sickening answer presented itself to her. What if he was giving it to someone else, like another woman? She cringed at the thought of the leopard print panties she had found in that hotel room, and knew that infidelity seemed to lurk around every corner. Ollie Mahlon certainly seemed like the kind of creep that would do something like that to his family.

"Poor Roni..."

Chapter 26

Allie had barely turned the truck's engine over when her cell phone rang.

"Hello?"

"Hey kiddo, where are you?" He was clearly on the road, and the faint strains of her favorite Carly Simon song were fading in the background.

"I just got done buying a few things at Jack's. What's up?"

"I was hoping to catch you before you got home. Let's go out for dinner. I know this great little place near the lake, and I hear the service is excellent." She could hear the smirk in his voice.

"Very funny. Um, ok, well I can put the milk and other cold stuff I bought in the refrigerator there. I don't think Mr. Wong would mind." Although she could never be too sure what would bother him. "Besides, I was going to stop there on my way home anyway to pick up my paycheck."

"Good, sounds like a plan. I'll be there in about 15 or 20 minutes, I just have to do a quick once over of the Paso campground before I go 10-7."

"Does anybody ever go 10-8 or heaven forbid, 11-7?" She knew the code for off duty, but she had always been fascinated by all the other radio codes and jargon the rangers used. When she was younger, she used to think maybe they were all spies, like 007 or something.

"Huh?"

"Nothing, I'll see you in a bit." She was already moving the phone from her ear and starting to close it when she heard a distant "bye" and the connection go dead. She was still idling in the parking lot of the grocery store, so she backed out, rolled to the driveway, and eased carefully to the left around a virtually blind corner. When Julian's Main Street wasn't under construction it was wide, straight, and well maintained, but once you turned from it to any side street, you often had the feeling of being more in a winding alley than a proper road. It gave the place charm, but was hell on the weekends when tourists crammed into every available nook and cranny. Locals did their best to avoid the Saturday and Sunday crowds, cursing them under their breath, yet knowing simultaneously that they were the lifeblood of the local economy.

The ride from town to Hillside was just over ten minutes, so when Alicia arrived she wasn't surprised to see that her father's white park vehicle was not yet among the sprinkling of cars in the long string of parking spaces fronting the building. She parked as close to the entrance as possible, then grabbed her shopping bags and hustled as quickly as she could to the kitchen.

"Whew," she breathed a sigh of relief that no one had bothered to even look at her as she entered, and started shoving her grocery bags into whatever open space she could find in the fridge. Jessie Dickson was the waitress on duty, and she hadn't even looked up from her order pad when Alicia walked in. This was good for Alicia, but bad for business. She would have to find a moment to encourage the younger girl to acknowledge new customers when she heard the bell on the door, even if she was in the middle of something else.

Even though Alicia had only been working at Hillside for two years, she was one of the more experienced waitresses. Most of Mr. Wong's hires were high school girls. They didn't demand the higher wages of more experienced wait staff, but they also usually didn't stay long. The job was harder than it looked. Alicia had started when she was sixteen, and that was about Jessie's age too. Jessie had only been working there a month or two and only one night a week at that, so the poor girl was still learning the ropes.

"I hope Marcus is the cook tonight," she mumbled to herself, "maybe he won't mind all this stuff." She hated trading on their budding friendship.

She looked at her watch. Her dad was due to arrive any minute, that is, if he wasn't standing out in the reception area right now waiting for her. She still needed to get her paycheck, so she walked down the hall and tapped softly on Mr. Wong's door. It was cracked slightly, and she could see the light on, and hear voices. They began low, almost inaudible, but as she stood there for a minute or two, hoping for an opportunity to knock politely, or for Mr. Wong to come out, the voices gradually increased in pitch and intensity. Clearly a fight was brewing. Alicia turned with the intention of escaping before he discovered her lurking in the background. If he was angry, she wanted to get as far away as possible. She spun around to leave, and landed smack into the chest of Marcus Lundee.

"Oof." Alicia stepped back rubbing her nose from the impact with the metal ring on the neck strap of his apron.

"Hey, where are you off to in such a hurry?" He was chuckling softly.

"Shhh! The boss is fighting with someone in there, and I don't want to be a part of it."

"Ooh, really, anything juicy?" Marcus stepped toward the door and put his ear to the crack.

Alicia found herself inadvertently wedged between Marcus and the door, his right shoulder brushing her right cheek, as his arm extended to the other side of the door jam, balancing his weight as he leaned in to listen. She wasn't sure if Marcus meant to pin her there against him, or if she was just a casualty of his curiosity. She suspected the former, boys being boys, and felt an immediate need for some personal space. She tried to carefully wriggle out of the arc of his arm, but in so doing inadvertently nudged the

214

door open more, and alerted Mr. Wong to their presence. The argument immediately ceased and three soft-soled footfalls were heard on the hardwood floor.

"Who's there?" Mr. Wong demanded, throwing the door open violently.

He had reached the door so quickly, that Alicia was still sort of leaning on the door, in mid-wriggle, and the abrupt opening caused her to lose her balance. She was on her way backward, knowing immediately that she was going down and that it wasn't going to be pretty, when a strong arm reached around her waist pulling her back upright in defiance of gravity. Marcus smiled into her bewildered face, then pushed her gently behind him and faced Mr. Wong squarely.

"It's just us, hoping to get paid, but I guess you have company." He peered around Mr.Wong and nodded at the clean-cut man in the well-tailored suit standing near the open safe. "Sorry to interrupt."

The man in the suit didn't reply, he only looked at Mr. Wong impatiently.

Mr. Wong glared daggers at Marcus and Alicia, but stepped back into the room, and grabbed two envelopes from his desk. As he moved to the desk, their view was now unobstructed and they were able to see several interesting art pieces on the desk, and several more in the safe. Some were Native American, some had a more Asian flair, and many Alicia couldn't place.

"Wheeeeew," Marcus whistled, "that's some nice stuff you guys are looking at."

Alicia could only assume that his dalliances on the wrong side of the law must have made him bold, or stupid, or both, because he was obviously taking a risk getting into Wong's personal business like that.

"Take your check and get out of here. The customers are waiting, and you are easily replaced." His anger was boiling barely under the surface now. Veins were throbbing in his temples, and a bit of spittle was launched into the air when he had enunciated his last word.

215

"Yes, sir. You're right." Alicia was pulling on Marcus' arm, as he strained for one final glance at the spoils on the table. He finally let her edge him out of the doorframe not a split second before the door was slammed in his face and the hushed tones of voices could again be heard.

As they walked back down the hall toward the kitchen, Alicia turned to Marcus, "Are you out of your mind?"

"What?"

"Getting so nosey back there. What was that you said 'nice stuff you guys have' or something. Good grief, are you trying to poke the bear? He meant what he said about firing you and you need..." Her voice trailed off, and she realized she may have overstepped her bounds in the conversation. Marcus knew better than anyone his financial needs, and it sure wasn't her place to throw them up in his face.

"Hey, don't worry about it. I was just messing with him. Besides, he should take it as a compliment, that stuff was really nice. Worth a pretty penny too." They had reached the kitchen, and Marcus handed her the envelope with her name on it.

"Thanks. I'm eating here with my dad, so maybe I'll see you later."

"I'll count on that." He winked at her and then ducked into the empty kitchen. In moments she could hear water running as he washed his hands.

As the hall opened into the main dining room, Alicia could see her dad had already been seated and was looking vaguely around for her. She waved and caught his eye. His tension seemed to ease and he looked down at his menu. She was beginning to see that no matter how old she got, he'd always be worried about her.

"Where'ya been?"

"Oh, I was putting the cold groceries in the kitchen, and then I went to get my paycheck. Have you been waiting long?" She didn't really wait for him to answer, but instead glanced around the room for Jessie. She figured she'd give the girl a few minutes, then if she didn't come to take their orders she's take it upon herself to get some drinks.

"No, not too long. Well, I did wait a few minutes to sit. That blond haired girl isn't too observant."

"Yeah, I know. She's trying but I'm going to have to talk to her." Alicia was still scanning the dining room. She could see one table waiting for their check, another with empty glasses in need of refills, and a third visibly looking around for their waitress. Through all this, Jessie was nowhere to be seen.

"Do you want coffee, or coke?" Alicia wasn't going to wait any more.

"Some decaf, if they have any that hasn't been cooked to tar sludge."

"I'll make some fresh, if it is."

Chris scanned the menu for something that appealed to him. The restaurant didn't offer much variety and the burgers were the safest choice. Still, he was in the mood for something a little different. He had pretty much made up his mind to have the enchiladas, hoping they weren't going to be microwaved from out of a box. Alicia still hadn't returned with drinks, and he looked toward the service area but didn't see her. He wondered if she was in the restroom. Chris had used it several weeks ago and the lock mechanism was so poorly maintained that he was locked inside until someone finally heard him banging on the door. He got up to go check and had just rounded the corner to the restroom area in the hall when Allie burst in through the outside door that led to the dumpster off the kitchen.

"He's hurt! Help!" She was crying as she stumbled down the hall with a bloody chef's hat in her hand.

"It's Marcus, Dad, he's out there past the dumpster, and I can't get him to answer me. He's breathing, but he's bleeding a lot from his head." She was shaking. She was probably the only kid in the world that passed CPR and first aid class at age ten, since she had heard her father teach those classes repeatedly. Park life had toughened her, and Becker knew it must be serious if she was this upset.

"Allie, calm down. Go call 911 and get them to send the sheriff's ambulance and the paramedics. I'll get my medic bag and see if I can do anything for him."

By now all the patrons in the restaurant were watching, and Wong and Jessie were frozen at the cash register. A head wound like that seemed odd and Chris immediately wondered if it was an assault.

"Listen up everyone. No one leaves until the sheriff gets here and takes your statements about anything you may have seen. Mr. Wong, please close the front door to keep anyone else out."

"But I have a business to run."

"Daniel, for crying out loud, for once just forget about the money and shut the door!"

Chris got his emergency medical technician bag. As one of many rangers, he had taken the time off duty to become certified in basic emergency medicine and had even become qualified in intravenous therapy and to use a cardiac defibrillator. In the back country medical care was often a long way off when minutes counted. He stepped out the back door and went over to Marcus as carefully as possible without disturbing the area in case it turned out to be a crime scene rather than merely an accident. As he assessed the scene, however, he couldn't imagine how Marcus could have hurt himself this bad accidentally. There just wasn't a mechanism to have accomplished what he saw. The young man lay on the ground behind the dumpster, and the left side of his skull was matted with congealing blood, and bright red blood was still flowing from the wound.

He knew the head was full of blood vessels, far more than most of the body and tended to bleed very freely, but Chris could also tell there was a definite depression in the skull. Injury to the brain was incredibly likely in this case. Becker laid a dressing over the site of the bleed, but didn't compress it tightly for fear of driving possible bone fragments into the brain. The pulse was rapid but regular and he was breathing adequately, but when Chris took his blood pressure the numbers were so low that he started an IV and put him on high flow oxygen. Marcus' brain desperately needed glucose and oxygen to function, and he looked at the dextrose in his bag and noticed it was expired. He mentally kicked himself for letting that happen and hoped the Alpine paramedics weren't so careless.

He stuck Marcus and read his blood glucose level, which so far was normal. He knew that glucose and blood pressure would change radically and soon, and if the pressure inside the cranium rose due to bleeding he would be in dire need of care from a neurosurgeon. At this point there wasn't much more he could do until the paramedics arrived. He wished the proposal to put a paramedic staffed ambulance had already been implemented for Julian.

Having done all he could medically, his cop side took over and he began to survey the scene. There was no blood anywhere else that he could see, which left him with the clear impression that whatever dented Marcus' head was probably not left at the immediate scene. He couldn't see a fall causing this kind of injury. Just in case, he checked the dumpster lid, but saw no blood or hair to indicate that it might have hit the boy, and even if it had there was no way it could have caused that amount of damage to his skull. There simply wasn't anything else around to have done it.

As he checked Marcus' vitals again and tried to rouse him, he heard Wayne Johnson's voice from inside the restaurant. Allie was showing him the way, and being an EMT also, Wayne had his medic bag.

"Did you come in the sheriff's ambulance?" Chris asked. Deputies that were medics weren't so unusual, but backcountry medical transport was an oddity in this part of San Diego County, in that it was provided by the sheriff's department.

"Yeah, Terry is getting the gurney out right now. How serious is he?"

"He hasn't regained consciousness. His vitals are stable, but he is definitely in moderate shock. I have only found one injury, and that is a pretty significant three-inch crush to his skull. Linear in shape, but I don't see anything here that was the cause. The only other odd thing is a lot of redness on both sides of the neck. I think we have a crime scene."

"OK, the paramedics in Alpine were dispatched and we can load him and meet them enroute with our ambulance. I'll need to take some photographs and do some preliminary scene work before we load him. Hopefully, it will only take a minute. I hate to rush a crime scene like this. Will you ride down with Terry and tend to the kid so I can work the scene until we can get some more help up here?"

Deputy Terry Benson wheeled the gurney through the kitchen doorway and he and Becker carefully loaded Marcus onto it while Wayne Johnson began his photos and inspection of the area.

"I'm going to do a cursory look back around the building some more. Hope the kid makes it OK," he said to them as they took Marcus to the ambulance. Chris could see Alicia standing by the door as they maneuvered awkwardly through the tight restaurant hallway and out into the dining room. As they rushed toward the front doors, Chris glanced at the faces of the patrons. He knew anyone of them could be a suspect, yet all registered nothing but shock and concern in their expressions. Allie's face was the hardest for him to look at as she stood woodenly near the entrance.

"Don't worry, we are going to take really good care of him. We will meet the Alpine paramedics enroute and they'll get him the best care. Do you have his family's phone number? I'll need to call someone."

She didn't appear to hear Becker's words as she watched Marcus' still and bloody form on the ambulance cot.

Chris squeezed her arm, "Alicia, I need his parents' phone number. Do you have it?"

She looked up at him with tears in her eyes, "It's just him and his mom. The dad's gone. She is really sick. Marcus is all she has."

"We are doing all we can Allie. He is stable and we're getting him to advanced care as quick as we can. We've got to go now. Do you have her number?" Chris had a hard time keeping the edginess out of his voice. Time mattered. To medics, 'time was brain' in head injuries.

Allie walked wordlessly around the back of the cash register. Mr. Wong had by this time sat on a stool at the long counter and was drinking something from a mug. Chris sincerely hoped it was coffee. A drunk Daniel Wong wasn't going to do this investigation any good. Jessie was sitting at an empty booth in the back with her head down on the table, resting on her folded arms. She looked as if she might be sleeping, but a slight shiver in her frame made Chris think she was probably crying instead. Allie looked in a small vinyl binder in the drawer below the cash register. It contained all the employee contact information for just such an occasion. She quickly found the number and wrote it down on a spare waitress notepad that she also found in the drawer. Chris covered the distance to the register in a few strides and took the paper from her, fearing the moments that might be lost waiting for her to walk back to him.

"OK, wait here and give your statement to deputy Johnson. Don't drive anywhere. Don't go anywhere. Hopefully, I'll be back before closing and we can go home together." With that he was out the door and heading for the ambulance. Alicia watched as the boxy van with its red lights flashing disappeared in the darkening pines lining the highway that stretched ahead to the medical help Marcus so desperately needed. As she watched, she wondered how this could possibly have happened. She thought of Marcus, and of his mother getting that inevitable phone call. Allie hugged herself, realizing suddenly that she was cold. But it wasn't cold from the outside, the evening was pleasant and the AC wasn't blasting. No, this was cold that came from the inside. Fear. Worry. That kind of cold. She wished that she had a mother to call.

Chapter 27

Chris eased his vehicle into a space in front of the Hillside entrance, jerking the gear bar into park and stomping on the emergency brake. This had been a tough day, which had morphed into an awful evening. For the first time since finding Marcus's beaten body, he realized he was hungry. Not surprising, since he and Allie never did have dinner.

Allie. He was worried about her. She had looked so small and lost standing by those big double doors as he and Terry wheeled the gurney down the concrete steps and into the ambulance. He just wanted to scoop her up and give her a big hug, like he did when she was little. He wanted to make her pain go away, make her feel safe. That's what dads do, right? But not tonight. Tonight he had been a cop, a rescuer, able to help everyone but his own daughter.

He slammed the heels of his hands hard against the top arc of the steering wheel. Once. Twice. Three times. He felt better. Actually, he felt oddly drained, as if all the pent up energy and stress and adrenaline of the last three hours in Terry's ambulance, and then in the Alpine ambulance, and then waiting to hear if Marcus was stable, and then the ordeal of getting a ride home had magically been knocked out of him, transferred to the steering wheel of his beat up old pick-up. He had been fortunate to get a lift home from another medic friend who was at the hospital and lived in Descanso, but by then he was so tired he forgot his jeep was at the restaurant and he had to drive his own car to the Hillside.

He peered down the row of sparsely populated parking spaces. He saw the Ford truck Allie had driven, and his own park truck, along with two others he didn't recognize, although he assumed one of them must be Daniel Wong's. Now he was faced with the dilemma of how to get three cars home with only two drivers. He looked up at the restaurant. The lights shown warmly through the red and white gingham curtains. It was hard to believe that just hours ago a young man nearly met his Maker just through those doors.

Chris didn't know what he had expected to find when he went to get Alicia, but the scene that greeted him definitely wasn't it. The dining room was empty and wiped clean except for two round tables in the middle. On one were two half-finished cokes, the remains of a basket of fries, and two glass plates with the remains, judging by the crumbs, of two giant pieces of chocolate pie. At the other, Alicia and Marina sat hunched over examining something. As he approached, their whispering turned to girlish giggles.

"Is this a girls only table, or can anyone join?" He could see now that what they were looking at was a roll of newly developed pictures.

"Oh, Dad!" Alicia hadn't heard him come in, and was startled, "what took you so long?" She threw her arms around him and squeezed.

Giggling or not, he could tell she still wasn't OK.

"Hi Marina. Nice to see you." Chris wasn't sure if that sounded too businesslike, but he didn't exactly know what to say to her in this situation. He certainly hadn't expected her to be here, but now that she was, it really was nice to see her.

"Hi Chris. I heard you all had some excitement here tonight."

"Geez, that's an understatement!" Alicia released her death grip on his neck.

"What are you guys looking at?"

"Oh, these are just pictures from Casey's birthday party last week," She angled the pile so Chris could see. "I thought Allie would get a kick out of them."

Chris looked into her dark eyes and wished with his whole heart that she was telepathic. That he could link to her mind and tell her how much he appreciated her being there for his little girl when he couldn't.

"Yeah, I bet she did." She wasn't telepathic, so that was the best he could do. "Well, let's get home kiddo, what do you say?"

"I was beginning to wonder if we were spending the night."

"Very funny. One problem, though. I drove the pickup here, so now we have three cars."

"How'd that happen?"

"Long story about a short memory."

"I can drive your car home if you want, and then you can give me a lift back here," Marina quickly chimed in.

"You sure it wouldn't be a big problem for you? I promise I'll get you right back here."

"Not a problem, I need to get Casey soon but I have time. I don't work until late shift tomorrow at the store anyway."

Chris certainly appreciated the help, and deep inside he had to admit to himself he was glad to have a chance to keep Marina around a little longer.

"OK, here are my truck keys. It's kind of a beast, are you sure you can handle it?"

"Follow me chauvinist tough guy," she said, as she took off with a smile and an exaggerated sway of the hips, dangling Chris' keys in the hook of one finger.

"See that?" Marina pointed to one of the vehicles Chris had seen parked outside. "That's my other baby."

224

Becker was a bit chagrined. Some detective he'd make. He should have guessed Wong would never drive a raised 1990 Chevy three-quarter ton with off-road tires.

"Not your average 'girl car' I must say," he muttered quietly.

"I'm not your average girl," and with that she swung her hips into the cab of Chris' pick-up and slammed the door.

Chris fumbled out his work keys for the Jeep and Alicia got in the Ford. Both were backing out as he finally got his car started. This wasn't starting out quite like he had expected. It was only a short trip to the cabin, but they were already parked by the time he pulled in front of the garage.

"I didn't mean to come off like your average pig male with my comment about the truck." He stepped out of the Jeep and slammed the door.

"It's OK, my truck is a little over the top, and I only have it so I can get back to my place. The dirt road is a bear when it snows. The truck is overkill, but it was so cheap I couldn't afford to turn it down. It'll do until I find a better place to live."

"Want to come in for some coffee or tea before you take off? Allie makes a pretty mean sweet tea."

"Sure," she said as they turned and climbed the back steps into the kitchen.

"What kind of tea do you like? Dad's a cop and therefore a donut and coffee kind of guy and wouldn't know a good cup of tea if it had a neon sign pasted on it. I've got Earl Grey, orange spice, good old green tea, and some Lipton's black that has been here since two rangers ago I suspect. There's some Mountain Dew if you like that sort of thing."

"What's that you have made cold there in the fridge?" Marina said as she craned her neck around Allie to look.

"It's the green tea with a peach simple syrup."

"Green tea it is then! Can I find some glasses?" Marina asked.

Soon they were settled with their tea and Chris ambled over to the table where they were sitting with a steaming mug.

225

"Is that microwaved Yuban from this morning?" Allie said with disbelief.

"Nope, it's aged to perfection from yesterday morning."

"Yuck, Dad!"

"Hey, I just consider the pot a big thermos, OK?" He was embarrassed that Marina might think him the cheap country clod that he was and changed the subject quickly. "So Marina, where is your place that the road is that tough to get in?"

"I'm down Banner Grade a ways, and the road's not that bad unless it really rains or when the snow and ice builds up."

"I won't even drive Banner Grade if it's snowing," Allie chimed in "it seems deathly dangerous to me."

"Well, I figure if it's my time to go, it's my time to go." Marina saw the quick change in Alicia's eyes as she let the thought hang and realized the conversation was not really a good one considering the night's events.

"Nice people like Marcus shouldn't have things like this happen to them!" Allie said, her voice filled with emotion and her eyes brimming.

"Bad things happen to good people Allie; sometimes they are just in the wrong place. Sometimes they just hang with the wrong people. It's part of the reason why I always make such a big deal about who you choose for your friends. Sometimes they are into things, and you suffer for their acts just by being near them.

"But why does God let that happen? Aren't good people supposed to be protected by God?" Allie was obviously more emotionally affected by all of this than he had thought. This wasn't a conversation that Chris had ever spent much time thinking about or discussing with her as she grew up. He had sheltered her, maybe too much. Maybe a mother could have made a difference.

"Allie, I don't think God reaches down and puts a big silver shield around us. He wants the best for us, but we also have the free will to do whatever we choose. We are put in this world and have to learn to live in a way that is good for us, not damaging. We need to make good choices. He

226

gives us a bunch of good rules to help, but sometimes random things just happen. I can't explain it. It stinks. It's scary. But it can also be amazing. God can use these "bad" things for amazing good." But Chris couldn't help but wonder what could be good about any of this.

Marina was watching Chris through all of this with a look he couldn't quite figure out. Maybe she thought he was being preachy. He wouldn't blame her, it sounded that way to him as well. He thought rather abruptly that maybe she was an atheist and practiced some arcane rituals involving worshipping dead cats. He'd never talked with her about any of that sort of thing. He stopped talking so long that Marina spoke up and he wondered if a mockery of his faith was about to be brought forth.

Marina turned to Allie, "I guess it's all in how we deal with these situations when they do happen that matters, and how we trust that this whole earthly thing is just a dress rehearsal for the real thing. A lot of people look at stuff like this and say '*all things work for good*' like it's part of God's plan, but I think most of the time that is a misunderstanding. Free will was given to us and we have a darned strong habit of using it. We are not God's puppets. The '*all things work for good*' part is that none of it matters if your focus is on *what **God** can do after the bad happens.* You can't let the horrible stuff distract you from what the end game is. It's not easy to accept, I know."

Chris was a bit surprised at how animated Marina was with what she was saying, and thought maybe she had lived some of the horrible stuff she was referring to. At least he guessed he didn't have to worry about any "dead cats" as Allie's cat jumped into Marina's lap.

He chimed in as he sat down, "We all want to think God will protect us from everything if we show our faith in him. People can't accept the idea that a good God would let bad things happen. I think the greater truth is that bad exists in the universe, and God can take a bad situation and allow something really good to come from it. Right now the thing to focus on is that we got Marcus good medical care and brought him to advanced neurological care early. He has a good shot." He hoped he sounded more convinced than he really felt.

Alicia just sat and stared at her tea. Chris could tell she was thinking, and he felt bad. Perhaps he had been too blunt and taken away her hopes and beliefs in what he had said. He knew what he had said was what turned a lot of people away from faith. They couldn't accept a God who should seemingly be so without care about his creation. That was so far from the truth, and there was so much more to it, but tonight was not the night for that conversation.

"Hey, you probably need to get going," he said "I better give you a ride back to Hillside."

"Yeah, it's time for me to pick up Casey and get home," Marina said as she picked up her purse and stood. She gave Alicia a hug. "Don't you worry, Marcus is going to be fine! You just wait and see." Chris wondered at how she could be so sure and encouraging. He wondered if he was way too blunt from all the pain and destruction he had seen in his work. He went out of his way not to make promises he couldn't keep, and Marina had just made one.

Out in his truck and back on Highway 79 Chris was pensive.

"Penny for your toughts?" Marina said, and poked him in the side. Her touch was electric. He hadn't had personal contact, even so simple as that, from a woman in many months. The way her touch made him feel surprised him.

"I'm thinking it is hard to raise a kid. It's hard to not have answers to all the questions and make all the hurts go away every time."

"I think you did pretty good there. She's almost 18 years old and smarter than you think. She was thinking about all of what you said very critically, and I bet you get a surprise from her about it someday. Kids don't forget when their parents are honest and care, and really try. She's lucky she's got you. She could have Ollie Mahlon for a father. I've seen bruises on both his daughter and his wife."

"Lots of people get bruised. Did they say they were hit by him?"

228

"No, and I can't prove it. But I'll bet you he did."

Given all the rumors, Chris would have to watch closer for those signs and follow up on it, he thought with a sigh. Though there wasn't much he could do without a complaint.

"Well, I hope you are right about Marcus getting better. I couldn't bring myself to promise her that. The dent in that boy's head looked pretty nasty to me," said Chris.

"Maybe you should pray to that God of yours just in case," Marina said as they pulled up next to her truck.

"OK, and I'll also pray you really can handle that truck all the way home!" Becker said, and was tempted to give her a hug but didn't. She surprised him speechless with a quick kiss on the cheek as she jumped out of his truck and got in hers. She gave him an exaggerated wink as she gunned the engine on her vehicle and pulled out on 79 and headed north.

As he drove home his thoughts turned to Marcus and he wondered why he had been beaten so badly. Was there some other background to him they didn't know, or was he just in the wrong place at the wrong time. Hopefully, Wayne Johnson and the sheriff's department could come up with an answer.

Alicia was waiting at the back door as he got out of his Jeep.

"So what do you really think happened? Somebody beat Marcus up for a reason. Why?"

"I don't know Allie, I have been thinking about it all night. You know him better than I do. What was he into? Was something going on that none of us saw while we were in the restaurant tonight?" As he said it, Becker realized he still hadn't had dinner. He opened the cabinet and dug out a container with trail mix in it, and they sat down.

Becker looked at Allie with her chin in both hands supported by the kitchen table. "I suspect Marcus has an enemy somewhere out there. It could be any number of people. Daniel Wong is a disagreeable guy at times, and seems to worry about money a lot, but he is a businessman. I'd worry about my business if I were running one too, I guess. Still, the secretiveness with the artifacts that he collects and keeps in his office makes me curious." Chris thought to himself, *especially since we had some things taken from the basement storage at work and one set of prints down there were Wong's, even if someone was just showing him around because he was interested in archeology and anthropology, it was still suspicious.*

He got up and topped off his coffee cup to warm it, "Still, I can't see why he'd hurt Marcus." He realized he had no more reason to connect Daniel to Marcus than he did to the car burglaries he'd put on the back burner.

"This whole thing could be the work of outsiders we have no knowledge of, but so much of the time 'if it looks like a duck, it is a duck' holds true and we should look at the locals that raise our suspicions. Then there's our missing artifacts. I can't see how Marcus fits into any of this. Ollie bothers me because he isn't very forthcoming about stuff, is an absolute jerk, and also worked at a couple of parks that were the victims of serious archeological thefts. He also has a history with Marcus that has a real cloud on it, and his prints are in the basement at work. Why? I can't see him having much reason to be in there. In fact I am surprised he was ever issued a key."

"Then there is this whole mysterious death of Hess which doesn't seem related to this except that everything is happening at the same time. With Marcus we have three totally separate major crimes going on at the same time. Happens all the time in the big city, but not so much in a place like this. Makes me suspicious that it's all one crime. Hess collected antiquities, too, so he's in the club as well. Then there are the initials in his day planner. The first and last initials, S and G, match Steve Goodman, Hess's wife's brother. Where is he in this mess, if anywhere at all? And for that matter, could Hess's wife have killed him in a jealous fit. I'd like to find out if Goodman's middle initial is "R" like on the note and what he was doing the morning he died. Did he plan to meet Hess, and deal with him over his cheating on his sister?"

"Why would Hess meet his brother-in-law so secretively? That doesn't make any sense at all," Allie said.

"I can't say I disagree. Just another piece of the puzzle, and then there's Lola Bragdon's underpants, we wouldn't want to forget them, now would we," and with that, Chris dumped the last of his coffee and turned to Allie. "It's late, you need to get to bed. You've got school tomorrow and I've got work, let's see if we can get some sleep." He was already feeling he shouldn't have discussed so much of the cases with her, even though she had been involved in some of the critical information gathering.

Allie was silent and stone-faced. She didn't move to go to bed. She didn't move at all. Chris froze mid-step and turned to his daughter.

"What's wrong kiddo?"

"I have to find out how he is doing, Dad."

"Who, Marcus?"

"Yeah, I have to know that he's going to be OK." She stood slowly, looking frail and weak in the darkened room.

Chris wanted say something, to do something to comfort her, but he knew that nothing he could say was what she wanted to hear.

Chapter 28

Thursday, August 22nd

Chris Becker got up early Thursday morning and felt gritty with red eyes that were burning. He hadn't slept well again. Thoughts of how all the unrelated facts fit in the puzzle kept running through his head all night. To make matters worse he had consumed all the two-day-old coffee in the pot for their late night discussion and didn't have any to make a new pot. He decided to skip breakfast and get coffee and a donut at Hillside. Besides, it would give him an opportunity to talk with Daniel Wong.

Wong was looking out the restaurant window as Chris parked his Jeep. His gaze seemed unfocused on the forest beyond.

"Morning Daniel, enjoying nature this morning? Pretty nice view from your front dining area."

"Yes, I like the mornings the best here. Cool, and the shadows make it even greener than it usually is. Plus the breeze on the lake makes lots of ripples and the ducks are busy on the water. Then all the fisherman come and ruin it."

"You don't like fishermen?"

"Not these kind who work the lake in their boats. True fishing is done with a fly rod!" He smiled nostalgically, like he was reliving some distant memory then seemed to visibly shake himself back to the present. Chris had a hard time imagining Wong with a fly rod wading in the water.

"What brings you in so early? I never see you here in the mornings."

"I'm out of coffee at home and I need a donut fix. You got one?"

"Yes, several freshly delivered."

"I also wanted to ask you a question."

"Oh?" Wong's face darkened with what seemed to Chris like concern. He was a very private person, and it was obvious that questions were an invasion to him, no matter what they were about.

"Yeah, we've had some items come up missing from our archeology lab in the basement of our headquarters. We figure it's some recording error or just plain incompetence and someone put the stuff someplace else."

"What could that possibly have to do with me?"

"Well, we ran fingerprints in the lab since we had to consider it as a possible theft, and among the prints we found inside the lab was one of yours." Chris looked at him steadily.

"Are you suggesting I stole something from your lab?" Wong's face had clearly moved past "darkening" and was in full "how dare you" mode at this point.

"Hold your horses, Daniel, it's just an odd thing that I have to clear up. Investigations come up with stuff like this all the time, and it all has to be checked out."

"I didn't take things from lab." Becker noticed how Wong started leaving words out of his sentences when he got upset. He figured it was some kind of retrograde stress effect since learning the language when he first came to this country, and he went back to speaking pidgin English and leaving out words when he got upset.

"I'm not saying you did, Daniel. It's just that the prints are there. How come? I mean, I know you like Native American artifacts. Allie tells me you have a few beautiful ones in your office."

233

"You think I have stolen items in my office! You come and look! All mine! All legal." His sentences got even shorter the more excited he became.

"I'd love to see the items you have. They're probably really nice. I'm more interested in how your prints might have gotten in the lab in the first place. Maybe we should start with that, don't you think?"

"My life is my own business!" Wong declared with icy emphasis.

"Daniel, when your fingerprints show up in my lab, your life just became my business. A crime has been committed and a lot of people's lives will get brought into question. I have a right to ask these questions, and I need your answers."

"What happened to 'incompetence' or 'misplacing' the items?" Wong's excitement was verging on out of control.

"It's one of many possibilities. Now why are your prints in the lab! It's a simple question."

"I went there with Jane. She is my girlfriend now. She saw my collection and offered to show me the items in lab. I don't like people to know my personal life. Who I date is my business."

"Now see how easy that was? No one needs to know anything. I'll just verify it with Jane and we're done. Simple as that." Chris wondered if the fact that Jane was not Asian was part of Wong's reticence. Old-country traditions sometimes die very hard. He wondered if he would be as concerned about how people viewed him if he really wound up dating Marina, since she was of Hispanic descent. Somehow he didn't think so. Maybe it was because those from Mexico had been part of the southwestern U.S. culture for almost 500 years and were so much a part of America, and California especially, that no one thought twice about it. We'd already fought three wars with Asian peoples that still were in recent memory. Perhaps Wong had had his share of prejudice and bad reactions.

"I still resent you coming in here making accusations about me."

"That's your privilege Daniel, but I have a job to do."

Chris left a five-dollar bill on the counter and turned and headed for the door. He was sure Daniel Wong was boring death rays into his back as he left. He doubted that Jane would contradict Wong's story, but still he needed to talk to her about it. He headed to the park headquarters.

He knew something was wrong the moment he pulled into the lot outside the Dyar House Headquarters. Jane was standing at the door.

"What the hell did you do to Daniel?" she asked. "I've never heard him so mad before."

"Daniel's got a thin skin, Jane, he'll get over it. I'm sorry if it's caused you any trouble. I needed to find out why his prints were in the basement as part of my investigation into what happened to all the missing stuff down there. He told me you guys are dating and that you took him down to show him the things there since he is a collector."

"Yes, I did. What's wrong with that?"

"Nothing, and don't you go getting a thin skin on me, too. How did you get in there anyway?" He brushed past her and went into the reception area.

"I borrowed a key from Dick. I asked him if I could show a friend around in there."

So much for security thought Chris. "Is Dick in yet?"

"Yes, and Daniel wanted to file a complaint about you with him, so get ready."

"Oh, great," Chris muttered as he started to clomp up the narrow stairs to his office. He could hear Savage on the phone, and his "I will be sure to investigate your complaint thoroughly" as he hung up the phone didn't sound encouraging. He knew he'd done nothing wrong, but Chris could never tell how Savage would react. As a manager, his boss was more into protecting his own ass than doing what was right and standing up for employees. Becker knew he was in for a chewing out no matter what. He didn't even bother to try to go past Dick's door and get to his own office, he just stood on the threshold of his boss's room and waited for him to hang the phone up.

235

"Why do you insist on causing problems and upsetting people!"

"It's called investigating a crime, Dick…it's kinda why they pinned these shiny silver things on our chests. I never accused Daniel of anything. I just wanted to know why his prints were in our secure basement archeology lab storage area. He's the one who got upset, mostly because he had to admit he was dating Jane, I think. Go figure."

"What are you talking about 'investigating a crime,' what crime?"

At this point Becker had stepped into political quicksand. He had not informed Savage about the missing items because his prints were in that basement as well as the others. He wondered if he had let his dislike of the Superintendent lead him down the path of making him a potential suspect. At this point he would have to bring him into the mix. *Damn Daniel for trying to make waves.*

"We've had some items go missing from the archeology lab in the basement. I ran prints and Wong's came up, for that matter so did yours."

"Oh, now you are accusing me of a crime!" Savage was red faced."

"I'm not accusing anybody. I'm just following the information I have. On top of that, you gave a key to have Daniel come into a secure high value area. You are one of many variables. So is Jane."

"That's what's wrong with you young rangers, all you think about is police work."

"That's not all I think about, but right now it is what I'm doing and it needs doing whether you like it or not."

Savage held Becker's eyes for a moment and then looked down at his papers on the desk. "It's still not going to go away. He wants to complain to the governor."

"Oh, come on Dick, everyone wants to complain to the governor, and we both know the governor doesn't give a crap about any of those complaints. You just have to write a letter explaining the circumstances and it all goes away."

"I'm still going to have to do a full internal affairs investigation with an outside source since there are allegations of racial discrimination."

"What! That's ridiculous. I never said a word about anything like that to him." Chris wondered if Savage was making it racial on his own by forcing his interpretation on what Daniel said. He doubted Daniel would accuse him of something racial, even if he had been more angry than it appeared on the surface.

"Well, that doesn't change anything. We'll still have to turn it over to Internal Affairs in Sacramento."

"Great, let me know when they want to do the 'beat me with a rubber hose session.'" Becker turned to leave. "I'll be in my office for a while reviewing yesterday's reports."

"Before you go, what is happening with the Hess mauling accident? Are you still wasting time digging into that?" Savage was still sticking to the posture that it was an "accidental" animal encounter and it almost made Chris finally irritated enough to tell his boss off for once and for all. He mustered all his self-control and just said, "I'm still waiting for the coroner's official report and then I'll complete the 'accident' report for you to review." The less said the better. Fortunately, it seemed to be enough for his boss and Chris took the cue and headed for his own office.

Once inside with the door closed he took a deep breath and tried to figure what the next logical step would be. He considered his conversation with Allie from the night before and realized that there was still a big question surrounding who Xavier Hess was planning to meet. That notation in his day planner '*meet SRG*' was confusing as heck. On a hunch he picked up the phone and asked the dispatch center to run a records check on Steve Goodman, by first and last name. He wanted to find if his middle initial was "R." About an hour into his paperwork Jane brought up a background check on the only Steve Goodman in the San Diego area. It proved to be an approximate age match. The information was surprising in two ways. The middle initial matched, and Steven R. Goodman had been arrested for felony assault but the case was dismissed.

He decided to do a full background records check on Marcus Lundee, Xavier Hess and Ollie Mahlon as well. There were too many questions about too many people and it was time to get serious about finding out more about them. For now he would give Daniel a pass. He felt Jane had cleared him, and no doubt if he did a check on him some IA investigator would see it as some form of harassment and racial discrimination.

By lunchtime he had all the records in front of him on his desk. What he found was interesting but didn't really help as much as he'd hoped. Mahlon was ex-army, which surprised him, no criminal record, which kind of surprised him, too, given the man's temperament. Xavier Hess was army too, which made him even more curious. Marcus had no record, but since he was only nineteen, he could have had a string of juvenile offenses, and those records were harder to get at. That fact needed to be followed up on a bit more. He was still a bit suspicious of Marcus, and a bit uncomfortable with Allie having hung out with him.

Becker watched through his office window as Val Simpson drove up in the parking lot below and quickly went downstairs to talk with her before she came inside. She was busy gathering campground receipts up from the front seat as he stepped out the office door.

"Hey I've got a favor to ask you if you have some time," he said as he walked over to her Bronco.

"I've got to do a bank run once I drop off the campground 453s." Everything in government had a number from rangers to camp tickets. Government speak was one of the first things a ranger learned.

"No problem, I need to go calm Daniel Wong down. Seems I upset him by asking why his fingerprints were in our basement. I'm hoping by now he's rethought his request of Dick to have me hung by a tall oak. Maybe spending money for an early lunch at his restaurant will make it all better. Money always seems to make Daniel happy."

"Just why were his prints down there, and why were you fingerprinting the basement anyway?"

Chris rolled his eyes and sighed, "Long story. We've got some missing artifacts in the basement. I'll fill you in on all the details later, but for

238

now it seems he has the hots for Jane, and it's mutual. She wanted to impress him with our collection since he likes collector art and antiquities," Chris said, as he helped her by taking the money bag. "Anyway, I can take the bank deposit. I need you to do me a favor and find out the details about this little gem." He handed her the yellow rap sheet on Marcus. "Does he have a juvenile record, did he steal something, what did he steal, when, where, all that kind of stuff. Also, what army units Hess and Mahlon were in and when. What kind of stuff they did and the like."

"Marcus? Isn't he the kid that works at Jack's? The one that got hurt so bad at Hillside last night?"

"Yeah, cleans up at Jack's and he cooks for Wong," he paused, "and occasionally takes my daughter to dinner." He took a deep breath and tried not to sound too protective. "Busy boy. Allie says he needs the money to help take care of his mom. Gotta admire that, but I'm still more than a little curious about him, especially with him getting thumped and left for dead for no apparent reason." He took the money and started for his Jeep. "See what you can dig up. Tell Jane I'm off to the bank and then to get lunch. Whatever you do, keep this quiet, and don't let Dick know or he'll chew your ass. He's already been snacking on mine this morning."

"Will do."

"You probably ought to go up to the sheriff's substation and see if you can do it there out of everyone's sight and hearing. Maybe you'll get more traction there anyway."

Chris made the run to the bank, and as he pulled out of the lot he flipped his phone open and dialed the number for Mrs. Hess. His curiosity about her brother wouldn't go away.

"Mrs. Hess, this is Ranger Becker. How are you doing?"

"I'm doing as OK as can be expected, I guess. It still feels so strange with Xavier not around. I get really depressed sometimes. Steve has been really great and comes over all the time."

"That is great! I was actually calling about Steve. Can you give me his phone number? I need to ask him a couple questions."

239

"Sure," She hesitated, "but what can he possibly tell you?"

"Well, it may be nothing but I'll have to ask him first." Chris knew the answer to his next question, but he had learned from experience that sometimes asking a witness or suspect the same questions later often gave slightly different answers. "How did Steve spend his time the morning your husband was killed?"

"I already told you, he was here with me having coffee early that morning before he went in to work. You aren't suggesting he had anything to do with this?"

"No, but you know how this works. I have to ask all sorts of offensive questions of people just to rule out everything."

"Oh. Yeah, I guess it must be difficult at times for you and everybody you talk to."

Becker wrote down the number she gave him and he dialed it. He still wondered if Goodman had time after his coffee with his sister to wind up in the park with Hess.

"Ganglion Instruments, this is Steve."

"Hey Steve, this is Ranger Becker. I'm just cleaning up my report and realized I forgot to ask you where you were the morning Xavier was killed."

"I was here at work all day. Started answering phones even before my shift started at nine."

"Who can I talk to in order to verify that."

"My boss, George, was here that morning. I can transfer you, but what's this all about?"

"It's nothing, just details that have to be entered in the report so everyone can rest assured I did a complete job. If you can transfer me, I'll be out of your hair."

Becker spoke briefly to Steve Goodman's boss, who confirmed he had been at work the whole day in question. Frankly, Chris was relieved that it turned out to be a dead end. Mrs. Hess didn't need any more family trauma. He also decided to set aside questions about Goodman's assault

240

charge for the time being as probably not relevant. He drove back to the park and had parked in the Hillside parking lot and noticed Wong watching him out the restaurant window. Time to cowboy up and see if he could make nice with him.

Oddly, Daniel was actually taking orders and serving the patrons himself. One guy with his multi-pocket vest looked like a fisherman out for the day on the lake. The other Chris recognized as a lizard-looking local who was more often in the alcohol intensive part of the restaurant in the evening hours.

"How come you don't have a waitress? You cooking too?" Chris asked. He knew there were at least three other waitresses other than Alicia. He had seen the newest one, Jessie Dickson, working the past few days. There was also Hannah Mooreland, a sweet girl in her early twenties living with her parents in town until her Marine husband came home from deployment in Iraq. Then there was Neela Jones, a cranky, hard living woman in her forties who didn't want anyone to know her story, and someone who Chris knew Alicia preferred to avoid. Happily, since Alicia usually worked weekends and Neela usually spent her weekends on a bender, they rarely worked together.

"Darn people have no work ethic these days," Wong said as he flipped open his order book.

"The new girl I hired just quit with not even a day's notice!"

"Wow, with Marcus in the hospital you really are short-handed." Chris hoped Wong didn't mean Marcus had a bad work ethic because he was in a coma in a hospital.

"Yes. Have you heard anything about how the boy is doing?" Complete sentences from Wong were a good thing. At least he is calm and showing concern about Marcus.

"I'll just have a cheeseburger and coffee, and no, I haven't gotten any word yet. I was going to call this afternoon but I wanted to talk to you first."

241

"About what?" Daniel called as he rounded the counter to the grill area and flopped a patty of what appeared to be 90% fat on the iron top.

"I just wanted to apologize again about having to question you this morning. I know I upset you. My boss said you complained that I was discriminating against you because you are Asian."

"Never said a word about anything racial. That's nuts! I was mad that you thought I might be a thief. I'm not mad anymore. You've got a job to do and I overreacted a bit. I'm the one who needs to apologize. You never accused me of anything."

"Well, just so you are ready, my boss is trying to make it into a big internal affairs investigation, and they will want to question you."

"Don't worry, I'll set them straight. Sounds like your boss is out to get you?"

"Dick and I don't see eye to eye all the time. It's just part of life I guess."

He spent the rest of his lunchtime in silence watching Daniel handle the restaurant by himself. The man's skills as a cook were not all that bad either, and as Becker finished his burger he saw that both Val and Wayne Johnson were pulling into the Hillside parking lot. Val had a sheaf of papers, as did Wayne. They obviously were coming to find him, and from the hard and drawn look on their faces, it was serious business.

Chapter 29

Becker came down the steps of the Hillside restaurant and met Val and Wayne by their vehicles. The parking lot was empty, but he still felt uneasy talking in the open.

"If you guys have something important, perhaps we should all take a seat in the sheriff's department Bronco. It's almost as big as my living room and nearly as comfortable." He opened the door and climbed in the big front seat and waited with anticipation as the others got back in. Val was the first to start.

"I was surprised at how easy it was to come up with most of this information I found. I have a Lieutenant friend in San Diego PD who had contacts with the military from his service time. He put me on to the right folks and I found that both Hess and Mahlon served at the same time in the Army. I figured they didn't know each other since Mahlon was an MP and Hess was in the Engineers, but then I realized they were billeted in the same duty in Bosnia for a while and it turns out Mahlon was a low level flunky sergeant doing facility security for the engineer unit that Hess was in. He stands a good chance of knowing him, but it gets better. His discharge is a "general" type rather than "honorable" and he only served four-and-a-half years. It's often a polite way the military gets rid of "undesirables." They told me that could be anything from a guy who just doesn't get the discipline to a real head case. Criminal behavior usually results in "dishonorable." It's harder to get in the records to find exactly what he did to cause the discharge, but the guy I talked to said it was probably mental. If he was always fighting the system or just plain too aggressive with his brothers in arms, they'd toss him. Personality disorder isn't helpful on a battlefield environment apparently. Guess they're afraid you're gonna shoot your own guys."

"What about Hess?" said Chris.

"Hess was a heavy equipment operator. Got discharged after four years of service with an "honorable." Not much more on him. And I couldn't find anything more on Steve Goodman. But here is where things get really interesting. Marcus Lundee worked at Grand Canyon a little over two years ago on a maintenance resource management crew. Guess who his boss was?"

"Ollie Mahlon?"

The look of surprise on Val's face was priceless, "You get the prize!" she said. "Seems Mahlon helped him get on the payroll under one of those disadvantaged teen conservation group programs where they help the park do resource or structure improvement projects. He was assigned at one point to do repointing of the mortar work on a historic building that housed a museum collection. Some stuff turned up missing and they went through a big investigation. Eventually Marcus admitted to stealing the stuff. They fired him and he went through a few months in juvie lock-up since he had no prior record."

"Interesting information, but if the kid never wakes up we're not going to find much out. One thing bothers me about all of the Grand Canyon information. I asked Mahlon specifically if he knew anything about the thefts in Grand Canyon, since I had heard he had worked there. He said he didn't know anything and hadn't even heard anything about thefts there. Said the law enforcement types didn't talk much with him about anything. He had to know about one of his own crew getting grabbed and he had to know about the theft. Why did he lie to me?"

Wayne broke in, "that's my cue I think—I got your fingerprint request back on the Hess vehicle and the prints they hadn't finished running from inside the truck came back to Ollie Mahlon. I would be really interested how he explains his prints being inside of a locked pickup truck. And I know it was locked because I was the one who inventoried it before it was towed."

"What do you think Chris? Maybe Marcus could be good for your missing stuff in the basement, too, if we can connect him to being in there somehow," said Val.

Chris shook his head, "We've got nothing that puts him there. No prints, no nothing. Still, his background makes him a dark horse in this story. Hopefully we'll be able to question him at some point. I need to follow up with the hospital."

The Bronco was getting stuffy and hot with the windows rolled up in the afternoon heat. "Maybe we should split up. I need to get home and take care of some personal business, plus I'll call the hospital and see how Lundee is faring. Let's not tip our hand just yet. Val, you quietly find out what Mahlon is up to today."

"I already know, I think. I saw him in Julian just before I left to come here. He was going into the Julian Hardware store. No clue what he was doing after that, but I bet he's not going to get out of town very easily. They apparently finally renegotiated the subcontract to tear up Main Street and have started the work."

"And I'll bet you anything that Hess was the contractor that they dropped!" Chris slapped the dash as he said it. "Look, see if you can get a location on him and then call me on my phone. Don't use the radio. Wayne, I assume you want to update your detective division on all that we've found out."

"I'm heading back to the substation to call them right now. Oh, by the way, I forgot to tell you that the final coroner's report came out, and I have a copy here for you." He handed it to Chris and waited while Becker scanned the report. It was several pages long and about the third page in Becker looked up quickly.

"Antemortem bruising and a unique mark on the back of the neck they say looks like a ball point pen or something." He looked at the ceiling of the Bronco and muttered, "Holy crap, I should have realized this a long time ago. I am so thick, we've been looking at this all wrong! Hess can't spell abbreviations very well! And the bones…the damn jaw, and I think I know who stole our jawbone." He turned to the others, "I don't have all the details of why worked out in my mind yet, but I think the "what" is pretty clear to me. Wayne, how soon can you get another couple of deputies?"

"I can get the one that's on duty pretty easy. I think he is over at Warner Springs right now, so maybe a half hour if he's not into something. Otherwise I'd have to get the sergeant to call one of the other guys in from home."

"Good, I think we may need to move fast. Do me a favor, Wayne. Call Caltrans when you get back to the substation and find out for sure who the contractor was that they dropped for the excavation work on Highway 79," Chris paused and chewed his lower lip, "and I really need to talk to Marcus Lundee."

"You gonna tell us what you think is going on?"

"Yeah, but no time right now!" he said as he got out and slammed the Bronco door and headed for his Jeep.

Chapter 30

Alicia didn't know what she had expected from Marcus once she got to the hospital. Her worst fear was some sort of 'death-bed' style declaration of love. What really awaited her was in many ways far more disturbing, and left her with only one course of action. She had to call her dad. Now!

Hospital regulations forbade the use of cell phones inside the building, so Allie had excused herself and found a windblown concrete balcony with railing reminiscent of prison bars, bare of every comfort save a scarred folding metal chair. She brushed it off with her hand, whisking away a few leaves, but doing nothing for the years, perhaps decades, of grime seemingly embedded into the enamel paint. She plopped down anyway, feeling suddenly too tired and small to carry the burden of information that had so recently been unleashed onto her. Flipping open the phone, she pushed the speed dial number that would connect her to her father.

The ringing stopped after four or five, and went straight to voicemail. His phone was either off, which it never was, on vibrate, which was rare, or had been left in the car, which was all too possible. She hit the speed dial number again. On the fourth consecutive try, he actually answered.

"Hello, this is Chris," it was an odd way to answer the phone, she knew, but she had become accustomed to it when he didn't know the caller. This was his business voice, which meant he hadn't had the time to check the name of the caller before he answered.

"Jeez, Dad, it's me. I've been trying to call you for the last ten minutes. Where are you? What are you doing?" She hadn't intended to sound frantic, but it was no use, damage done.

"Allie, what's wrong?" All his senses were on alert, and the business voice was gone. She had succeeded in freaking him out.

"Dad, don't panic, I'm OK. I'm at the hospital…"

"WHAT!" Clearly he was panicking.

"No, Dad, I'm fine. Listen, I need you to come down here right now. I mean it. This is important." Her voice had inadvertently dropped a notch or two and taken on something of a conspiratorial tone.

"Allie, what is going on?"

She didn't want to tell him over the phone, and she was afraid he might not come if he knew it was to talk to Marcus, but she knew that he had to hear what Marcus told her for himself, and to be able to ask his own questions.

"Dad, just trust me. It's important and," she sighed and decided she had to give him something, "it's about the case. Marcus is awake, Dad, and you've got to talk to him about what he told me."

There was a beat of silence.

"I'm already on my way and I'll be there in 45 minutes. Don't move." And then he hung up.

*　　　*　　　*

It actually took 48 minutes for Chris to pull into the crowded hospital parking lot. Alicia was certain of this because she had looked at her watch at least two dozen times in those long minutes, willing the second hand to move faster. Finally he was here, and she stood up from the cold metal

248

bench outside the ambulance bay where she had been waiting for the last half an hour, and hurried toward him as he rushed from the far left of the lot where he had parked.

"Dad!" Alicia shouted and waived her arms wildly over her head to get his attention. "Dad, over here!"

He finally heard her and put his hand up to his forehead, shielding his eyes from the low sun as he searched in the direction of her voice. He saw her almost instantly and waved as he leapt over a narrow island of low-cut boxwoods and jogged up to her side, talking even before he had reached her.

"Allie, what is going on? What are you doing here? Why aren't you at school?"

"Calm down Dad, I didn't ditch. The professor didn't show up for my first class today, and then I usually have a long break. However, technically I'm ditching now, but I think the circumstances warrant it." She had laced her arm through his and was leading him through the front doors of the hospital and toward the cluster of elevators across the lobby.

"Yeah, about that," he had stopped right in front of the elevator doors and tuned to face her squarely, putting his hands on her shoulders and looking down into her vibrant green eyes, "when are you going to tell me exactly why you so desperately wanted me here?"

Just then the elevator bell dinged, signally the arrival of the car to their floor. The doors flew open and three nurses, an angry man in a suit and a young mother with a screaming little boy flooded out. Chris and Alicia filed in, along with an older gentleman, and Allie pushed the button that would take them to the floor of the intensive care ward. They rode to the sixth floor in uneasy silence, knowing they couldn't continue their conversation with an audience, no matter how indifferent he might be.

As they stepped out into the quiet hallway, Chris scanned for a place to sit, and gently steered his daughter to a vacant waiting area overlooking the gravelly roof of the opposite wing of the hospital.

"OK kid, enough is enough. Spill." His face was deadly serious and she knew it was time to lay it all out for him.

"You're right, Dad. I'm sorry I've been kind of cloak and dagger about this."

"Kind of, you're a regular Deep Throat!"

"Huh?"

"Nothing," he put his arm around her, "Come on Allie, you know you can trust me."

"It's just," her eyes got an almost imperceptible glassy sheen, and her voice thickened slightly with new emotion, "it's just been a really weird week, ya know?" She leaned her head against his shoulder like a little girl, and he kissed her warm hair. It smelled clean, like oranges and something else he couldn't quite place. In the midst of all this craziness, he hadn't really had the chance to see all this from her perspective. A murder so near her home, having to clean the hotel room of the victim, and then being the one to find her friend's beaten body would have been a lot for anyone, no matter how tough they were. And Allie was usually tough. She had been forced to be, growing up as she had. But this might be too much, even for her.

They sat there silently for a moment, him giving her the time to just be vulnerable, without having to talk about the fact, and her trying to delay the inevitable. Finally, she decided there was no point in waiting any longer.

"Dad, promise you won't get mad, or flip out, or jump to conclusions if I tell you what Marcus said?" She had leaned her head back so she could look up into his face.

"That's one of those loaded questions that parents, and peace officers, don't like agreeing to, but I do promise to hear the whole story before I decide anything, how's that?"

"I guess that's the best I can get, so here goes." She sat up straight, kind of shook herself, and was suddenly all business. "First, you need to understand that it was Mrs. Lundee who asked me here. I mean, sure I called the hospital to see how he was doing, but when the nurse put his

250

mom on the phone, she begged me to come here right away. I guess he had been asking for me." She looked sideways, waiting for a reaction, and she wasn't disappointed.

"Sheesh," Chris mumbled under his breath and rolled his eyes.

"Yeah, I know, I thought it was a little 'romance-movie-of-the-week' myself, but when someone is beaten and left for dead, if you're the one they ask for you go, right?"

"Right, when you put it that way, I guess."

"So, when I got here he was unconscious or asleep or something. I guess he's been kind of in and out all night. The doctors were really optimistic and said the swelling in the brain was not as bad as they feared. They said he might come completely out of it anytime. I took one look at his mother, and I could tell she had been up all night. I told her I would sit with him if she wanted to go home or get something to eat or something. So, she actually took me up on it and went to the cafeteria for a while."

"I'm not sure you did her any favors then…hospital food, yuck." Chris made a face like he had just bitten into a mushy banana.

"Well, it's a good thing she left, because Marcus really woke up about 10 or 15 minutes later, and I don't know if he would have felt comfortable saying what he said in front of his mom." She raised one eyebrow and cocked her head to the side as she paused for effect. Chris thought she was enjoying having the informational upper hand over her father. He also wondered if she enjoyed watching him squirm at the discussion of her possible romantic entanglements, something he had largely been spared due to her self-imposed anti-steady-boyfriend policy in high school. He noted with some trepidation that that blissful time was likely drawing to a rapid end.

"OK, quit stalling, let's have it."

"Well, at first it was kind of gushy. He said how glad he was to see me and reached for my hand. He held it for a while. I told him how glad I was that he was all right, and that I had been worried, we all had. He looked so quiet and nervous, I thought he was going to propose or something."

251

Alicia was looking down at the floor and absentmindedly picking at invisible lint on her pants. It was a nervous habit Chris had noticed in her whenever she was trying to act like something was no big deal, when that really wasn't the case at all.

"Lord, kill me now."

"Calm down. He didn't. In fact nothing I had imagined could have prepared me for what he did say." She looked up directly into his face now, "Dad, he said he was responsible for Xavier Hess's death!"

"What! Wait, what?" Chris's head was spinning, torn between the immediate panic at the thought that his daughter had been out with a murderer, and the nagging voice of reason after talking with Val and Wayne that told him this didn't make any sense at all.

"You promised you wouldn't do anything until you heard the whole story! Dad, you promised!" She had both her hands in his now, sitting knee to knee, her nervous eyes probing his face, her fear mirroring his confusion.

"Hold on, just hold on." The cop in him had finally gained control of his parental instincts, and the facts were rising to the surface of his consciousness. "Marcus admitted to you that he murdered Xavier Hess?"

"Well, no, not exactly. He said 'It's my fault, it's all my fault. I am responsible for that man's death on the trail.'" And then he said something really sad, "I guess I deserve this for what I've done." He couldn't finish because the floor nurse came in to take some blood and do some other tests on his head or something. He made me promise I'd wait and come back to his room later. I told him I'd go get an early dinner and be back in a while. That's when I called you."

"Wheeeeew," Chris let a long breath of air escape from his thinly pursed lips. "Well, that only leaves us with more questions than answers, doesn't it?"

"The only way we are going to find them is to ask Marcus." She glanced at her watch and did a quick mental calculation. "I bet he is back in his room by now."

They found Marcus indeed back in his room, with his mother sitting in the chair next to his bed, reading to him from what turned out to be the Sports page of the newspaper. When she heard them come in, she looked up from the article and smiled at Alicia.

"Hello, did you have some food? Marcus mentioned you went to eat while he was having his tests." Her kind visage turned mildly quizzical as her gaze passed from Allie to Chris, "Who have you brought with you?"

"Hi, ma'am, I'm Chris Becker," he took a step over the threshold and leaned in to shake her outstretched hand, "Allie's dad," he knew the uniform could sometimes be intimidating and he hoped he could put the woman at ease. He would need her co-operation if he hoped to get any information out of the boy. He could just see it in her eyes. She may be sick herself, but the wolfish instinct of a mother was alive and well in her, ready to pounce. "I was one of the first responders who handled your son's case last night. In fact I was the one who rode in the ambulance with him and I called you enroute." He hoped this would turn the tide of her suspicions.

"Oh, thank you!" She was gushing now and moving to hug Chris, "thank you so much." The hug was a bit uncomfortable, but at least it was 'mission accomplished.' He could probably have gotten her to rob a bank for him now. It always amazed Chris how simple it could be to put someone at ease and get them on your side in an investigation, if you just treat them the right way, even if you haven't just saved their son's life.

"I'm just glad I was there to help. Listen, I was hoping I could ask him a few questions about last night, is he up for it?"

"Yeah, I'm good." The voice wasn't exactly feeble, as it came from the pale form in the bed, but it wasn't exactly Marcus's normally strong tone either. "Actually, mom, could you go check on my dinner. I'm getting kind of hungry."

"Sure son. Are you sure you'll be alright?" Then, turning to Allie, "will you be sure to stay with him?"

"Of course, Mrs. Lundee, we'll stay with him. Don't worry."

253

Chris graciously held the door for the woman, ostensibly because her hands were full of newspapers and her purse and an old navy blue zippered cardigan, but in reality he did it so that he could casually shut the door behind her. This conversation needed to be private and uninterrupted if at all possible. Walking up to the young man in the bed, he noticed how pale his skin was, and that his thick dark hair hung in dank locks like some star football player who had just taken off his helmet to talk to the press. Only, this wasn't going to be Marcus' victory speech.

"Hi Mr. Becker," Marcus was the first to break the uncomfortable silence, "I guess I'm not surprised Allie called you." Allie had circled the foot of the bed and was easing up the other side as he spoke. He was talking to her father, but looking straight at her. Something in the tone of his voice and the look in his eyes belied his words and made it clear that even if he wasn't surprised, he was hurt.

Allie took a step back, unsure how to react. She felt compelled to defend herself and her actions, yet knew that at the moment there were bigger issues at hand. She struggled for the composure to keep quiet.

"Marcus, Allie tells me you said some pretty serious things a while ago. She says you might want to talk to me?" Chris tried to sound as friendly and encouraging as possible without making the boy any promises he couldn't keep. He felt as though he should warn him, but reading him his Miranda rights wasn't needed since this wasn't yet a custodial situation, nor was he clearly the focus of an impending arrest...yet.

"Yes sir, I'm tired of all this, and it's time to get it all out in the open. It's gotten way out of hand."

"Let's just start at the beginning, shall we? Just tell me what you know. He had shifted into what Allie always called his 'cop mode' and made the metamorphosis complete by extracting a small tablet of paper and miniature pen out of his back pocket and was holding it. He didn't want to start writing in it yet because sometimes that halted the flow of information.

Alicia instinctively took a step closer to the bed and laid her hand lightly on Marcus' arm. She felt the need to be protective of her friend in the

254

impending interrogation, but at the same time felt a sense of dread lest he reveal something that made him alien to her. Chris eyed her hand on the boy's arm, conscious that the familiarity of the gesture was unnerving to him, but choosing to ignore it. Instead he waited. Waited for an answer. Waited for the truth. He was very good at this part.

"Well, I know you want to hear about what I think happened out on Azalea Trail, but that isn't the beginning."

"What?" Chris didn't have a lot of time or patience for games.

"You said 'start at the beginning.' Well the dead guy isn't the beginning." Marcus used his right hand to smooth the hair back from his face, and to then prop himself up a bit more in his pillows. Chris noticed he was careful not to move the other arm—the 'Alicia' one, at all.

"Fair enough. What is the beginning then?"

"Well, that would have to be a couple of years back in Grand Canyon National Monument. I took the rap for stealing some stuff that was never recovered in return for a bigger cut of the profit when it was sold." Marcus was looking down at the thin beige hospital blanket, twisting the oxygen tubing that fed the cannula he was still wearing in his nose. "I'm not proud of that, Mr. Becker. I just want you to know that all the things I am going to tell you, well, I'm not proud of any of it. But I will also admit that if I had to do it over again, I don't know that I could choose to do any different. My mother is sick and my dad left us flat. I just didn't have any choice. We needed the money."

"I'm not here to judge you right now. What I need are the facts. I know about your record in Grand Canyon." A swift inhalation of air was heard from Alicia, but Chris didn't even skip a beat as he pressed on, "I also know you paid your dues. Are you saying you didn't actually steal the stuff?"

"No, the stealing part was never something I could bring myself to do. I took the blame that time because it was my first offense and I was still a juvenile. I gave a bunch of bogus names of who it was sold to, and said I'd spent all the money, so nothing was ever recovered. The judge went easy on me."

255

"Is murder your thing?"

"Dad!"

"No!" Marcus struggled to sit up, but only made it about six or eight inches off the pillow before falling back again, "No, absolutely not!" The effort of the movement had exhausted him and he struggled for breath. "I had nothing to do with that, and ever since that day I have been trying to figure a way out, but I can't. I'm in too deep." He let out a long breath that seemed to come from his very core. A sad, defeated breath. Chris should have been hardened to the emotional blackmail of criminals, but he couldn't shake the feeling that this kid could be saved. This kid wasn't one of the bad ones yet. And he didn't have to take his own word for it; obviously Alicia thought there was good in him, too.

"Ok, let's back up, just for the record, and you tell me exactly what part you have been playing in whatever is going on."

"Basically, I'm the concealer. I'm the guy who hides the stuff 'til a buyer is found." He looked up at Chris, seeming to accept the weight of his complicity. "I always knew it was wrong, but it seemed like the ends justified the means. But that was before. I never agreed to be a part of murder. He should've known that. But he didn't care. He said I was in too deep now. I was just as guilty as he was. But no way! I never hurt anybody!" His body had tensed and he emphasized this last by slamming his fist on the bed. "He wanted to move the stuff and it got to the point that Xavier and I both wanted out of the whole thing. I even talked Xavier into going to the cops with me. He probably threatened him with something like that, and it got him killed. In the end I guess he didn't like the choices I was making in friends." Marcus glanced at Alicia as he said this, then closed his eyes and lay slowly back down on the bed, as if every muscle in his body ached with the effort. "I suspect he thought I would tell Allie what was going on and she would tell you."

Chris had held his peace during this little speech, but he could contain his urgency no longer. "Who did this to you Marcus? Who is this guy you are talking about? If you are really going to come clean, I'm going to need a name."

This had really only been a formality. Chris already knew the name Marcus was going to say. Yet, even being prepared for it, knowing it, there was something primal that congealed in his bones, something vicious that ignited within in him when the boy's pale hand again came up to brush the hair from his bruised and battered face.

"Mahlon. It was Ollie Mahlon."

Chapter 31

Outside the hospital Ranger Chris Becker wound their way through the sea of cars in the parking lot. Fortunately he had parked fairly near where Allie had parked the pickup and it gave them a chance to talk.

"Wow, I can't believe all he told us. It scares me pretty good, Dad. In my wildest imagination I never would have thought that he could be involved in anything like this. And what was that business about 'you already knew about his problems in Grand Canyon.' You didn't say a word to me about it. What if he'd been a serious felon?" Allie's voice had an edge to it Chris didn't feel was warranted.

"I only recently found out, and anyway it was part of an ongoing investigation that I didn't feel would be wise to reveal outside the department investigating team. Besides that, the court judged him a candidate for a pretty minor punishment and apparently felt he wasn't a serious threat. You know I can't talk about everything I'm involved in when it is a criminal investigation, especially when it reveals personal information about people. That's the kind of stuff that costs officers their jobs."

"I still think you should have said something! Just some kind of warning."

"OK, point made. Let's concentrate now on what we have to do with what we know. First and foremost I want you to go home. I need to go and submit a warrant so I can search Mahlon's house and hopefully arrest him while I'm there. I don't really need the warrant to arrest him based on Marcus' accusation, but I don't want to screw up the artifact search without one, and it's going to take a while to get it worded properly and then find a judge at this waning hour of the afternoon who will sign it."

"OK, Dad. When do you think you'll be home? Should I wait up?" Allie said with her door open and keys in hand.

"I'm hopeful I can get to the park by 7 PM or so, and with luck I'll have the arrest and search team with me, and we can move in on Mahlon. That may take quite a while, so don't wait up."

"OK, please be careful!"

"I will, now you get going."

Chris didn't wait to watch her leave as he headed for his Jeep. His plan was to get to the Sheriff's detective division and use their office to write up the warrant and get them involved in the action. Since he was the declarant for the warrant based on Marcus story, they would need him to go before the judge. He had come this far and didn't want to just turn it over to the sheriff's office, he wanted in on the arrest of Ollie Mahlon.

The afternoon was late by the time he brought everyone up to speed and had the paperwork filled out. He had one of the detectives read it to make sure it was good enough to get the judge's approval. He was no fool about the fact that writing search and arrest warrants wasn't his specialty, and all he needed at this point was some liberal crank judge to turn him down. The detective thought it was fine and gave him instructions on who to contact at this hour at the county building. Chris took off for the courthouse to make his case before the judge. The detectives on duty said he should notify his rangers and that they would notify Wayne and then "everyone would do the deed together" once Chris showed up with the warrant. Chris was pleased there was no turf war on the issue, and perhaps because Ollie Mahlon lived in the park and worked for the park they somehow felt obliged to keep Chris involved. Whatever the reason he was relieved.

The Judge turned out to be a remarkably cooperative young man. Chris wondered how on earth he had made judge so young. He carefully read Becker's narrative on the warrant, asked a couple of basic questions of fact and then signed off on the search and arrest of Mahlon for felony assault and battery, burglary and homicide. The detectives had told him that since he was writing the warrant anyway, and the information spoke to the assault and the murder as well as the thefts, he better include those parts just to cover himself.

So, Becker found himself back at the detective's offices at 7PM.

"We got Wayne Johnson and one other patrol deputy from Julian plus two of us from the detective division. Wayne suggested we meet in Julian to form up."

"OK, I've called two of my rangers in and they can meet there. How about at 8PM?"

"Sounds good," the senior detective agreed as he lit a cigarette and took a long draw. Chris wondered if he detected a sense of heightened excitement in the man. These guys must have done this a thousand times. Could they still get a rush out of it? He knew he was feeling a bit more heartbeat in himself for sure.

They all headed down to their vehicles, and Chris took the opportunity to bring Val and Eric up to speed on his phone on where and when to meet.

"Take the same vehicle, I don't want to chance Mahlon seeing a caravan driving up the highway and get spooked for some reason."

His phone battery went dead as he was about to flip the phone shut. He mentally kicked himself for not charging it and quickly grabbed an extra sheriff's portable radio from the detectives before he drove into the rapidly darkening late August evening. He knew this was going to be an interesting night and hoped nothing would go wrong. What could go wrong? They had a good, coordinated plan. This would be a slam dunk.

260

Chapter 32

The drive home seemed almost short to Alicia, even though she battled traffic all along Mission Gorge Road leading back to the freeway, and then drove in fits and starts from Grossmont until the Lake Jennings exit. There the road finally opened up, and she could go the speed limit up the steep incline to Alpine and beyond to the turn off to Highway 79. She cruised on mental autopilot, taking the route more from muscle memory than from conscious effort.

The events of the day still reeled in her mind, and she just didn't seem to be able to get a firm grip on them. She felt like a little girl chasing butterflies. Her thoughts flitted around in her mind, just out of reach, and she was powerless to capture them. Most of all, she couldn't quite get a handle on how she felt about things. She was upset about Marcus that was for sure. It was frightening to know that her friend was mixed up in continued criminal activity. She was also pretty angry with her father. All the "official business" in the world couldn't persuade her to keep something this big from him. She resented the law enforcement world that kept her in the dark sometimes. But the thing that shook her most was the knowledge that Veronica's father was probably a murderer, and was certainly the one who put Marcus in the hospital. She could hardly imagine how Veronica would take the news and what this could do to her family.

The shrill ringing of her phone broke her reverie and brought her mind into focus. Alicia's first impulse was reach across the seat and into her purse. She fumbled for the metallic pink phone, and had nearly flipped it open, when she remembered what her dad had said—no talking while driving. She reluctantly kept the phone closed, but did steal a brief glance at the caller ID on the screen. It was Michael again. She was starting to feel bad about ignoring so many of his calls, but the best thing about their friendship was that she knew he would always understand. She did, however, vow to herself that she would call him back before she went to bed. Although it would not be before she made herself a turkey sandwich and took a long hot bath.

The east-bound two lanes of I-8 changed to one as she exited onto SR 79 and began the long, winding trek through Descanso, up the S-curves, and down past Green Valley and Paso Picacho campgrounds to the meadow and her small cabin. It somehow seemed as though it had been days since she had been home, and in the waning light the old homestead took on a feeling of refuge and safe haven that her youthful mind rarely considered. Still, it was never as comforting to come home to an empty house, and she wished her dad were home.

Alicia parked as close to the walkway leading to her front stoop as possible. She had that uncomfortable feeling she always got coming home to an empty house, but it wasn't fully dark yet, and somehow that made a significant difference. She had always been afraid of the dark, ever since she was a little girl, but this dusky twilight was different, a bit curious, somewhat mystical, almost alive with possibility. She had often thought this should be called 'the witching hour' instead of midnight getting that label.

Tramping up to the door, carrying her purse and her school backpack, she fumbled with the ancient lock and finally pushed through the door into the shadowy back porch. Dropping her bags where she stood, she fumbled for the light switch on the wall by the door, but apparently the bulb had finally burned out. Her cat came out from the kitchen, undoubtedly having uncurled herself from the couch cushion bed she had likely occupied the entire day, and simultaneously yawned and meowed vigorously her displeasure at the duration of her master's absence.

"I know kitty. You were lonely. I'm sorry." She petted the silken fur, then proceeded to scratch obediently behind the cat's ears. "Who has the upper hand in this relationship? I clean up after you, feed you, even trim your nails, and what do you do for me, hmmm?" She rubbed the soft fur under her chin, lifting her kitty face upward to look into her bright green eyes. "Yes, yes, I know. You provide love, and homey ambiance, and much needed fur on my favorite black jeans."

The rumble in Alicia's stomach indicated that this bonding moment was over and that what she really needed was some dinner and to get the kitchen lights on. She kicked her bag out of the path of the door, then gave the door a shove. The expected solid slamming noise was instead replaced with a soft thud, as though perhaps the floor mat was in the way of the jamb.

Immediately the error registered in her subconscious and her senses peaked. Before she had even turned around completely she knew something was wrong. Instinctively her eyes scanned the door, looking for something that could account for it not shutting. Her eyes locked on the meaty fingers curled around the edge of the door, a foot or so above the knob. Her breath froze within her. She was instantly aware of every inch of her body. It was as though even her hair had individual nerve endings. *This*, she thought, *must be how a rabbit feels, right before the cougar strikes.* All this in the split second before the door flew open with such force that it swung the full arch of its hinges and smacked heartily into the adjacent wall. Alicia suspected who it was before she even saw him.

Ollie Mahlon loomed like an angry bear in the threshold, oddly framed by the pinky-mauve dusk. The cool evening breeze carried a few fall leaves in through the open door as he stepped deeper into the unlit mudroom. Without even thinking about it, she took a step back, trying to re-establish as much distance between them as possible. Mahlon noticed, and paused mid-step. He sneered, slowly, calculatingly, as though a thought was spreading in his brain as the oily grin spread across his face. The thought must have bloomed to full force because the sneer turned to a chuckle. Alicia's blood went cold in her veins. If she had ever doubted the connection between Man and animals before, she didn't now. She had never seen a more vicious stare on any predator than she saw in the face of Ollie Mahlon, nor could she deny her desperate impulse to run.

"Mr. Mahlon?" Alicia's voice cracked despite her best efforts to control it. She had heard of people talking themselves out of situations like this. She just had to keep her head.

"Mr. Mahlon," his tone mocked, but there was no mirth in his eyes, "you put on a respectful show, little girl, but what have you and your boyfriend been saying about me!"

"My boyfriend?" She tried to sound more innocent than terrified.

"Don't play around with me girl. I know that Marcus Lundee has been telling tales. Did you relay that pillow talk to your dear old daddy?" Mahlon had stopped advancing on Alicia, which was a relief because she now felt herself to be rooted to the floor as solidly as if she were one of the old pines in the yard.

"Marcus hasn't said anything about you, and he and I are just friends. I don't know what you are talking about!" Alicia tried to keep an even tone to her voice, but with each word she felt her pitch rise. Panic was setting in quickly. She needed to keep her wits about her, but her mind was feeling thick and fuzzy with fear.

"Ugg!" Clearly she had said the wrong thing. Mahlon lunged at her with wild anger and closed the distance between them in one huge step. In one deft movement he grabbed the base of her hair in his left fist, painfully tight against her scalp, and angled her face to look up into his. The rough fingers of his right hand cupped her chin, forcing her mouth shut hard. When he spoke his mouth was mere inches from her face, spittle flecking her cheek with his every word.

"Friends! Ha! You aren't just friends. I saw you coming out of Don Giovanni's that night!" He was shouting now, and Alicia was so close to him now she could feel his body shaking in anger. She had known Veronica long enough to have seen the bruises that nobody talked about. Now she knew without a doubt how they got there, and she was realizing that she was going to be next. She couldn't think of anything to say to defend or deflect his accusations, and it didn't matter anyway, so securely did he hold her mouth. Her fear and desperation sent hot tears to the corners of her eyes, even as she tried to will them away. They began to crest her lid and trickle toward her hairline as Mahlon released her jaw and slid his rough hand down to her shoulder, cupping it in his beefy paw and squeezing the tips of his blunt fingers deeply into her flesh. She let out a sharp yelp like a dog that had been whipped, but his shouting drowned her out.

"Tell me! Tell me now, you spoiled little brat!" Whatever grip on propriety and reality Mahlon had seemed to be evaporating quickly. "I saw you out back of the restaurant, I know you talk to him all the time! You saw me there too, didn't you!" His eyes were glazed and little beads of perspiration pricked out on his forehead. He released her hair and cocked his hand back for the inevitable blow. Alicia squinted her eyes in preparation.

And then the amazing happened. From the corner of her eye, and somewhere behind her in the kitchen, a hand and then an arm shot out and grabbed Mahlon's hand in mid arc. He was so shocked he let go of Alicia's shoulder and stepped backward toward the open door, as the now full form of a man came out from the adjacent room. Alicia's mind raced, trying to make sense of facts that seemed out of place. Who was this person, why was there someone else in her house? Mahlon suddenly seemed off kilter and unsure. It was one thing to menace a girl, or even a young man alone, but now there were two people in a situation for which he hadn't prepared.

In the shadow of the darkened entry with his back to Alicia, the mystery man took another step toward Mahlon, and without a word, raised a short length of 2x4 which Alicia immediately recognized as the makeshift

265

doorstop she used to prop open the back door. In a moment of clarity, Ollie Mahlon seemed to weigh his options carefully, then he spun on his heels and ran down the steps two at a time. The man turned, dropping the 2x4. The outside porch light shone clearly on his concerned and bewildered features. He took a step toward her and looked searchingly into her face.

Relief and adrenaline sent mixed messages and her legs turned to rubber beneath her. Alicia collapsed on the floor, any strength in her gone. Even before the first sob bubbled to the surface, Michael's strong arms engulfed her. She knew he was talking to her, saying something, but she couldn't make sense of the words. Her mind spun and she just hung on to the sound of his voice like a lifeline to reality. Presently, her breathing calmed and the tears passed. How long they sat, quietly, with her head on his shoulder and his arms around her, cradling her like a wounded animal, she couldn't say. Finally, after what felt like hours, but was in reality probably only a minute, she straightened up and looked into the face of her rescuer.

"Michael. What are you doing here? How did you know?" In her mind he had been elevated from adopted brother to superhero status in the span of a few moments.

"Would you believe me if I said it was the Bat Signal?" His familiar crooked smile broke a jovial line across the otherwise somber features of his face. He was trying to lighten up the situation, but his true concern still colored his every expression.

"Very funny. No, really, what are you doing here?" The purely random luck of the situation began to dawn on her. A chill ran down her spine as she contemplated how the encounter with Mahlon could have gone.

"Don't you remember? I called and said I'd be coming up here. One of the other crewmembers lives on the reservation out at Warner Springs and his folks picked him up and gave me a ride here from the airport since it's on the way. You said 'make yourself at home' and told me where the key is kept, remember? Anyway, I tried calling a couple times on the way up the hill. When I didn't get you I figured you were in class or something. It's been a long week, so I thought I'd get some shut-eye before you got home. I was crashed out in the back bedroom when I heard the door slam and then voices. I could tell something wasn't right. I figured I'd see what was what."

"Well, so much for your nap and your quiet evening in the mountains." Alicia smiled wryly.

"What was with that guy? Should we call the police or something?"

Alicia suddenly came to her senses. "My Dad! We have to call my Dad right now!" She raised herself to her knees and grabbed the receiver from it from its cradle on the wall frantically dialing the number, but it went straight to her father's voicemail. She kept dialing it but with no success.

Chapter 33

Becker was chewing a nervous lower lip most of the way to the Julian substation. Swoop and grab operations in a warrant search and an arrest were not common elements of his job, and the fact that this was one of the park employees was sure to make news. Dick Savage would be mad for sure about not being kept in the loop and getting the bad press, and he would find a way to make Chris pay for doing the right thing.

The typical government way of disposing of problems was to fire them quietly in return for no prosecution. Usually, there was a stipulation that they couldn't ever come back to work for the department, but often the law breakers would show up in other state departments a few months later. It was a stupid way to do business, but in Chris' opinion that was what California government had become from top to bottom: often ineffective, generally partisan, hugely wasteful and even corrupt in many cases. The fact that it still functioned at all often surprised him. He often wondered if it would survive much longer without a real economic crisis and revolt.

In Ollie Mahlon's case justice would be carried out without any deals. The assault on Marcus would see to that. Hopefully they could tie him firmly to the Hess murder and if they could find the stolen artifacts in Mahlon's possession, he was sure the DA would prosecute to the fullest on that as well. To Becker it seemed archeological crimes were becoming trendy and popular to bring to trial in this era of self-centered pseudo-environmentalism that gripped California's yuppies. To the DA it meant more votes on election day. Sometimes it seemed murder and rape were often less motivating to voters than shutting down a large Mall development or busting someone digging up rare plants or old bones and pots to sell.

His Jeep and the detective's unmarked unit were the last to arrive at the sub on the southeast side of the hamlet of Julian. All the officers were crowded in the small substation office drinking coffee out of Styrofoam cups as Chris came through the door.

"All right, looks like we are all here," said Wayne Johnson. "I think we all know each other?" A chorus of assents and nods followed, and Wayne spread a small map of the park out on the table.

"This is where we are going to serve the warrant. This time of night Mahlon should be home. Chris, would you sketch a diagram of the shop yard and how the buildings and houses are placed so everyone is familiar with the layout."

"Sure, it's pretty easy. He has the big stone house in the front of the Paso maintenance yard. It's the one right next to the inholding that has the Division of Forestry's stone fire station complex. It's a square two story with a door in front and one in back. Rear access is off the shop yard itself, so one unit will need to go in the rear to manage that exit side of the building. I'd say put yourselves on the C/D side of the structure. We should have another person on the A/B side corner to watch those areas and to keep the firefighters out of the way. The sheriff's office has agreed that I will be the one to serve the warrant. I'm going to use Eric and Val to clear the rooms and do the primary search for weapons and stolen artifacts. Wayne and I will most likely take Mahlon into custody ourselves. Wayne is incident commander.

"One thing I want to emphasize is I've never seen Mahlon with a weapon, but he has service time in military police work, so I would lay bets he is well armed. As far as I'm concerned this is an armed entry, and I expect he may try to resist. There is a wife and daughter in the house who we have no reason to believe are involved in any of this. In fact some statements lead me to believe they are virtually abused prisoners in a manner of speaking. What we do know is that Mahlon is nervous about the investigation and his reason for the attempt on Marcus' life was to silence witnesses. I suspect if he hadn't heard Allie, she's my daughter, calling for Marcus and coming out the back door of the restaurant, he probably would have had time to finish the job."

Wayne Johnson spoke up, "OK how about one detective on each corner and Chris and myself will go in the front door with one deputy and the other deputy will be outside the back door. You guys on the corners be especially careful about crossfire conditions with each other if this thing goes sour." The others nodded their agreement and Wayne chose who would go to each post. The whole group filed out to their vehicles.

Ten minutes later the entire group swung into place in unison on both sides of the building, and with guns drawn they did the "knock and notice." Chris was not surprised when Rose Mahlon answered the door, and with a fresh bruise under her eye.

"Rose, we need to speak to Ollie for a minute."

"He's not here, Chris."

"OK, Rose I'm sorry to intrude like this, but we have a warrant for his arrest and to search the house, so we'll need to look around."

"Well, he's not here," she repeated.

Wayne Johnson turned to her, "Do you know where he went?"

Chris motioned to Eric and Val to begin their movement through the house.

"It is important that we find him," Chris said "Do you know which way he went when he left?" It was only the two-lane highway that fronted the house, so that limited the possibilities down significantly in the backcountry of San Diego County.

"What is this all about, Chris?" she cried, "What has he done?"

"Marcus identified him as the one who beat him up the other night and said he's been stealing archeological items from parks. He's also been indicated in the murder of Xavier Hess who was killed here on the trail recently."

Rose Mahlon sat down with a heavy thump into the thick sofa cushion behind her. She was breathing heavily and obviously shocked by the charges.

"I can't believe this," she said. "He has his faults, and it isn't always easy to live with him, but I can't imagine him doing this. I have no idea where he went, and I didn't notice which direction he headed. He was pretty mad," she said as she pointed to the red welt on her cheekbone. "He didn't like the way the steak was cooked. Seems like everything upsets him lately. He gets that way when he is stressed, but I never saw anything out of the ordinary that was getting to him. Now I see why."

Eric and Val came out from the long hallway with Veronica Mahlon in tow.

"We didn't find anyone except Veronica," said Val, "do you want us to start the detailed search for the missing items on the list, Chris?"

"Yeah, get to it and I'd like both of you to stay here with both of them in case Ollie comes home. And don't let him surprise you!" It seemed to Chris seeing the regular park vehicles near the house and shop yard would not alarm Mahlon like sheriff's vehicles might. The element of surprise might make taking him into custody easier.

"Wayne, can I talk with you and the others outside?"

The deputies and the detectives gathered around Becker's Jeep.

"Look, he doesn't have too many choices. He could be in the park, which I doubt, but I'll alert the night ranger to be on the lookout anyway. Mahlon could be in Julian or headed down the hill. If he's down the hill we

271

aren't gonna have much luck finding him ourselves," Chris said as he opened his vehicle door.

Wayne Johnson interrupted, "I suggest we put out an all points bulletin for him while my deputies check for him or his car in Pine Valley and Descanso. I can cruise Julian and Harrison Park."

"I'll go with you to Julian as well, if that is all right with you. That way there'll be two of us near each other if anything develops," Chris said.

Wayne nodded, "OK, everyone knows what to do? He's driving a blue 1985 Chevy van." Johnson rifled through the papers in his hand and rattled off the license plate number for the group.

"OK, let's hit it," Becker barked as he slammed his car door.

Headlights and brake lights swung in all directions as tires squealed off into the night. Becker was nervous. The whole thing was in the wind now. Taking him at the house would have given a measure of control, confinement and predictability. This was totally without a framework now. So much for the slam dunk!

Chapter 34

Chris made a quick pass through the village of Cuyamaca, which was little more than the main highway and a littering of houses sprinkled up a steep slope above Lake Cuyamaca, which provided drinking water and an occasional fish. He found no sign of Mahlon or his vehicle. Sergeant Johnson took Harrison Park, which was a subdivision mid-way between the park and Julian. It was one of those slapped together unregulated areas that had developed with extremely poor building code standards and roads that were little more than one lane drives in most places. It was home to a Catholic outdoor camp, tiny cabins and deteriorating mobile homes. One small country store held court in the middle of the community for those who needed more smokes or a loaf of bread. It took more time to search that area, and so Chris leap-frogged Wayne and headed to Julian.

He passed the gated community of Julian Estates. The sheriff had agreed to go through the adjacent trailer park, called Pinezanita, although Chris could see most of it from the road and didn't observe any sign of his quarry.

Once in Julian, he headed west on the main street, having agreed that Wayne would handle the eastern side of the area. Once he was a block into town he saw that the street was almost impassable due to the construction that had started. That would obviously make things more difficult for him. He hadn't been in town in several days and was shocked at how much had been ripped out for the highway repair already. Heavy equipment was working with bright lights everywhere. Pavement was down to bare earth and the excavation was continuing much deeper in several places. Cars were being routed onto C Street and over to the junction on Highway 78 that took them past all the downtown businesses.

It didn't take long to spot Ollie Mahlon's van parked improperly and obviously hurriedly on B Street. He continued to cruise the side streets and swept the whole town except for Main Street while he grabbed the handi-talkie to get Johnson on his radio.

"Wayne, I've spotted his van on B Street just south of Main. So far I haven't seen him anywhere in town. I need you to break off and meet me. I'm gonna go into Jack's, so it'll look like I'm just shopping in case he sees me."

"OK, I'm down Banner Grade a little bit, and it will take me about ten minutes to get back to you if I don't run code."

"That's OK, I'll sit tight. We don't want sirens."

Chris found a place to park on the edge of the construction two doors down from the market and hoped they were still open. It was late and he couldn't remember when they closed on Friday, and he sure didn't want to just stand out front. Fortunately, they were open, but he was surprised to find no one was at the register. He looked at his watch and realized the store should be closed already according to the hours posted on the door. He cruised the aisles as though he were looking for something special. He rounded the shelves at the rear of the store and turned toward the separate back room that held the laundry and house cleaning retail supplies.

As he walked the hallway that led out to the alley door, he heard muffled voices. He turned his head left and right and was still perplexed at where they were coming from. He went back out to the main grocery area and saw no one. The store was only about 40' x 60' in size so he figured he should be able to see anyone talking inside. The exterior bank of window panes fronting the store didn't reveal anyone, and he figured the common stone wall of the adjacent buildings surely wouldn't transmit voices easily.

He went back to the rear portion of the store and actually looked out the back alley door. Marina's truck was parked behind the store, but no one was in sight there or behind any of the stores. The small door off the rear sales area was unknown to him, even though he had been in the store many times. He suspected it held an office, and standing to the side and cracking open the door, he saw a moderate sized storeroom and a desk with a computer on it. The computer screen showed an effusion of greenish blue glow that was the only light in the room. It was enough to see no one was at the desk. The muffled voices were louder here and Becker risked a quick click of his gun belt flashlight to sweep the room.

It was empty, but what he did see gave him chills. Papers we scattered and stock knocked off the shelves. It looked like signs of a possible struggle. What was even more strange was on the wall opposite him he had seen, in the brief flash of light he had used, some kind of exit. There appeared to be an open door and a descending stair hewn right into the rocky earth below. He moved near to the open door and could see faint light deep in the hole that appeared to head out below the front of the store and under Main Street. The voices had stopped, but he was sure now that they had been in this secret cavern.

Whoever was down here was in a strange place at a strange time of night. The trashed office set his senses on alert as well. He considered Marina's absence and her truck still sitting in the lot. With Mahlon still on the loose in the area Chris couldn't discount the possibility that he was here for some reason. What was more troubling was where was Marina? One of the muffled voices sounded possibly female. He didn't want to wait for Deputy Johnson, though he knew he should. He couldn't walk the steps down without them seeing him long before he had a clear view of what was going on. He had a sick feeling. He couldn't help but wonder why Marina, or someone, wasn't out manning the store since the front entrance was still open. Even with all this construction, there were bound to be customers.

Second by second he was becoming convinced she was down there and might be in danger. Being the wilderness survivor that he was, Chris remembered putting a signaling mirror in his shirt pocket along with a tiny BIC lighter in case he ever needed it to start a fire. Past incidents where rangers faced being lost and facing hypothermia were not lost on him, and Chris vowed to be prepared for those kinds of emergencies if possible. Now, he realized he might be able to slip the mirror inconspicuously down the first step and see what was reflected below without being noticed. When he fished it out of his pocket and carefully angled it down he saw a tunnel with a few dim bulbs at ceiling level and dozens of boxes of what he suspected were store supplies stocked neatly along the hard rock surface. Now he could see where they must store their stock. It never occurred to him, but obviously they needed storage space for deliveries, and to survive the competition of stores off the mountain, Jack's had to be buying in bulk.

No one was in sight in the crooked tunnel, but he knew they had to be near, and he slowly and quietly descended the earthen stairs. No movie cliché crumbling rock or unsure footing gave him away, and he slipped in behind the edge of the boxes lining the wall in front of him. One was already open and what he realized in the dim light was he was staring at a priceless Santa Maria style pot, two partially packed Kumeya'ay Indian pots and a lion skull. Marcus had mentioned hiding the stolen goods for Mahlon, and Chris mentally kicked himself for not asking where. His excuse was Marcus had said Mahlon was moving them all as fast as he could, so he didn't follow up. He was surprised to see any of them still here.

He could clearly hear a woman's voice now, and he moved to where the tunnel bend obscured his view ahead. There was a heavy wooden frame and what looked like a wall that was evidently really a door. When he looked briefly again with his mirror the image was dimly lit, but he could clearly see Marina with her back against the rough granite and her hands apparently tied behind her back. As he did so he also noticed something odd. Quite a few of the boxes were old and yellowed, and every one of them was some form of alcohol. There were fancy whiskeys, cheap wine, and many boxes with bottles that had no labels or information on the box containing them at all.

A set of legs protruded from a line of more crates and boxes with the torso bent over invisibly doing something behind the stacked goods. No more than twenty feet separated Becker from the duo and he drew his service pistol, and with it aimed forward, he stepped into the light of the tunnel.

"Keep bent over and bring your hands out behind your back!" Chris barked as Marina's head snapped left and looked at him with unbelievably wide eyes.

"Chris, he's got a gun." The momentary look in her direction caused him to feel more than see the movement out of the corner of his eye as the figure took cover and turned and pointed a gun at Marina. Chris was surprised Mahlon hadn't taken a shot at him. It would have been the smartest thing to do. Why he chose to threaten Marina made Chris wonder whether there was some hesitation in Mahlon about killing after all, or maybe he only had a line of sight on her and not him while he cowered behind the boxes.

"I'd be more than happy to shoot her right now, Becker." Mahlon sneered. "I don't have a whole lot to lose here at this point." Chris was tempted to shoot and hope he penetrated to boxes and their contents, but worried Marina might still get hurt, so he decided to play dumb.

"I just came in to buy some bread Ollie, what the hell is going on here. Have you lost your mind?"

"Is that your 'bread buyer' in your hand there? I usually use cash or a credit card if I'm strapped. I've never had to take bread at gunpoint."

"Cut the crap Ollie! What is Marina doing tied up in here? And what is this place, and for that matter what are you doing? Put the gun down."

"No can do. This has gone too far. I guess your daughter hasn't told you much after all. I was worried about her and Marcus, and him talking too much. Stupid kid told me he was not going to help me move this stuff."

"Look, whatever has happened can be worked out," Chris said, although he knew full well nothing of the sort was possible with a good outcome for Mahlon.

"Nope, it's done now. Sorry she had to be involved, but Marcus was supposed to get this stuff out of here. It was a great place to store it all if Cal Trans hadn't decided to actually do their job for once." Mahlon jerked his head toward the noise and vibration of the heavy equipment above. "I figured Hess might be able to avoid digging deep enough to open this place up, but the idiot got greedy and lost out on the contract bid. Kept talking about how he didn't like what we were doing, and threatened to go to the cops. I thought I could get all this stuff out of here before they discovered this tunnel for the highway repair, and I would have if Marcus hadn't chickened out on me. It would have all worked out. Dummies didn't have a clue how big this was and how much money we could have made off this."

"Are you saying you had something to do with Hess getting killed? And what stuff are you talking about?"

"There's no point in continuing to talk. I've said too much already. I don't have time to play around. You need to drop that gun, Chris."

This was where it really got tough. All the movies showed the police giving up their weapon. The reality was: drop the gun and you were most likely dead. In real practice the rule is "never give up your gun." Chris could only hope he could distract and shoot before Mahlon reflexively shot Marina, or maybe Sgt. Johnson would pop around the corner and change the odds.

Vibration above in the street was shaking dust from the ceiling and walls as Chris said, "Sure, I'll just set my gun down and you let Marina come over here." Chris bent over slightly thinking he would fire and lean back behind the cover of the wall before he bent over further, but he could see Mahlon wasn't taking his eyes off him. If only Marina would move and distract him somehow. No matter what he wasn't giving up his gun.

"Don't try anything funny. Just put the gun down and step back from it. Stay where I can see you."

Becker heard the words, but his focus was consumed by the barrel of Mahlon's gun pointed straight at him. The room telescoped down to that few inches that circled the tip of the pistol—the shadowy depth of the barrel, the perfect cylinder of metal, inert and innocuous in its own right, but cold death in the hands of a person trained and willing to use it. He knew there were other elements to the scene, but they had faded into the fringes of his conscious mind. This kind of stand-off was not likely to end well for either of them. He tried to stay calm and stall for time so his mind could work out a solution. He closed his eyes, forcing his breathing to slow, forcing his mind to focus. He had to get his head back in the game. Holding his slightly bent position he tried again to talk Ollie down.

"OK, I'll level with you. We know what you were up to. I've got a warrant for your arrest. You know you don't have a chance here, Ollie. Cops are everywhere looking for you. There're others coming in here right behind me in minutes. No matter what you do, you won't get out of here tonight unless you walk out with me." Chris hoped his voice sounded more sure of this than his own heart was, not just for his sake but for Marina's too. Wayne Johnson *was* on his way to back him up, but there was really very little chance that he would make it down here before this thing had played itself out. Chris tried to ignore the cold ball of fear growing in the pit of his stomach. He thought of Allie, and more than anything else that steeled his resolve.

"I'll take my chances. I'm not going to prison. Now put the gun down!"
Becker realized that perhaps Ollie was afraid that Chris could shoot him even if he shot Becker first. It dawned on him suddenly that Mahlon might actually be scared. He wasn't sneaking up on kids and smashing their heads here. It was an even fight, and that wasn't Mahlon's style. This fact might just prove to be the edge Chris needed. He straightened up just in time to see Mahlon pull back further as his eyes widened.

279

The reality of the scene unfolding in the underground tunnel had somehow seemed out of sync with the world above, but the connection between the two was suddenly brought back into alarming focus. Yet still, Chris' awareness of the real world seemed to return to him in stages: the rumbling noise of the highway workers and their equipment overhead that suddenly seemed deafening, the veil of fine dust that seemed to cloud his view, the suddenly distinct and unmistakable shifting in the ground beneath him. A moment later, one of the heavy equipment night crew on the street repair project dropped several inches into the tunnel with the entire front end of a bulldozer blade while attempting to dig out the road base for the new asphalt. Dozens of small rocks dislodged and Marina reflexively let out a scream as Mahlon looked up. It was the mother of all distractions and the opportunity Chris needed. He fired. Once. Twice. Just for a moment Mahlon turned his gaze from the collapsing roof to look at Chris with a brief expression of surprise before he slowly collapsed forward like a deflating balloon. Chris moved in quickly and grabbed the gun out of Mahlon's hand, but he could see there wasn't much need. The special fragmenting jacketed hollow-point bullet had hit him squarely in the neck and Becker could see it had exited through the back of the head. So much for the chest shot he had been aiming for. The man's eyes were fixed and staring. Becker felt for a pulse and detected nothing. It was over.

Becker had no time to breathe a sigh of relief, or to fully realize the weight of what had just happened, however, as another shower of dirt and pebbly debris rained down on his hunched over form. The need for self-preservation took control and he reached out for Marina in the semi-darkness.

"We should get out of here before the whole roof collapses! They probably don't even know this is here," he shouted to Marina, as he reached around her and pulled her to her feet. Together they stumbled toward the stairs. His timing was perfect, because much of the remaining roof started to collapse behind them as they reached the stairs. Coughing and sputtering they emerged from the dust cloud into the upper-floor office and continued running until they burst through the back door and into the cool evening twilight.

Chapter 35

Three days had passed since the death of Ollie Mahlon in the underground tunnel. It had been a whirlwind of official statements and reports. It took half of the first day to dig his body out and piece together the timeline of events. Dick Savage was trying to keep his head above water with damage control, and somehow blamed Becker for all his troubles. The Regional Director was genuinely frustrated with the fact that Chris had needed to do most of the investigation behind the back of his boss, and that Savage was so out of touch with the realities of his job responsibilities. It was doubtful that Savage would lose his job, but Chris suspected that an involuntary transfer to a less desirable posting might be in the offing for his boss as a result of all this mess.

Yesterday had been a pretty violent dressing down in Savage's office, with him revising the whole structure of his instructions to Chris in order to try and blame him somehow for all his troubles. He even accused Chris of trying to get him fired by going behind his back to Region. In some ways Chris had to admit there was a grain of truth in that, and he felt removing Savage sure could be a really positive change for the department.

282

The death of a park employee at the hands of another was headline news in the papers, and as usual they spun the story in the most unflattering way they could. Now Chris, Allie, and Marina sat together for the first quiet day they'd had since this all began. Chris had almost lost both Allie and Marina, and that fact still shook him to the core.

"It's just pots and stuff, Dad! Who would do all this, kill Mr. Hess, beat up and nearly kill Marcus, break in here and try to do who knows what to me, and then take poor Marina hostage over something like that?"

Chris got up from his seat on the couch near the swamp cooler and said, "Yeah, and don't forget Hess's girlfriend, Lola Bragdon. Apparently Ollie felt for some reason that she knew too much and killed her too. At least that's the current theory. He couldn't handle the idea of being caught—too much at stake. There was some very valuable stuff in that cache, stuff that is hard to move undetected in the art market and needs the right unscrupulous buyers.

He'd let Marcus take the fall for him before when things went bad, and this time he couldn't pull it off. I suspect getting kicked out of the military didn't do his self-esteem any good, and like so many people, he felt the world owed him something, and he just decided to take it. Frankly, I think he was becoming more mentally unhinged all the time. I think crimes of violence tend to follow the "three R's." Random, Relatives, and Riches. Killing for money may not be as common as the other two, but it certainly happens. Just the fact that he came here to hurt you," Chris paused for a beat to maintain control. The thought of what could have happened to his little girl still made him virtually blind with fear and rage. "It shows how illogically he was thinking and what risks he was willing to take. The man had gotten to the point where he was just plain crazy."

Allie nodded her head for emphasis, and stretched her feet out onto the coffee table, stifling a yawn as she spoke, "No argument here. That guy is a complete nut-job. That being said, putting all the loot in that tunnel probably seemed like a good idea at the time." She stretched her long slender arms to the ceiling and pointed her toes yawning fully as she

283

relaxed the stretch and curled back into a cat-like ball, "it's all so spooky and creepy—a hidden tunnel leading to an old speakeasy hidden in the basement of the building across the street. I can't believe no one knew about it! It's been down there for what, 75 years or something!"

"Well, I suppose someone knew about it. That building is on the National Register of Historic Places. I walk past that plaque on the front of Jack's every day, and yet I never really thought about the history of the place—at least not until I was almost part of it!" Marina piped up from her cozy armchair in the corner.. "It almost didn't turn out so well for any of us. I shudder to think what would have happened if that tunnel had collapsed the rest of the way even 30 seconds earlier." Marina spoke calmly, but the truth in her words hung quietly in the air a moment longer. "You know, I sure didn't know that tunnel was even there. You mentioned storage, Chris, but Jack's doesn't buy bulk because the inventory doesn't move fast enough before expiration. That heavy wall at the end just looked like a wall to me. With the old Eagle mine just up the street, I guess there could be tunnels everywhere."

Becker headed for the kitchen and said, "That wall must've looked that way to the Federal Revenuers, and from what I can gather they never busted the place during prohibition."

"That's the interesting question, Dad. What is the history really? What went on down there? Who could have spent time in those musty caverns?" Allie's eyes were as big as saucers as she imagined famous mobsters, ladies of ill repute, sullied politicians, "Marcus told me yesterday that he was the one who told Mr. Mahlon about that tunnel in the first place. Apparently his dad—you know he was into history and art and archaeology and stuff—anyway, he had somehow stumbled upon it years ago while he was in Julian researching Civil War stuff. The memory of it stayed with Marcus and he made the mistake of relaying the story to Mr. Mahlon one day, and the rest, sadly, is history I guess."

"Well the real sad part in my mind is that the collapse pretty well destroyed everything, including the remaining artifacts that Ollie had hidden

284

away in there so no one would connect them with him. There was some beautiful stuff from Grand Canyon and other places besides the material from here. Turns out they're putting an estimated value of nearly a million dollars on everything.

One thing that wasn't destroyed was that lion skull that he took from our collection in the basement. Forensics tied the DNA on it to Xavier Hess all right. Pretty ingenious of him to choke Hess out like he did and then use the jaw afterwards to make it look like a cougar killing. Getting behind him around his neck and using the carotid restraint arrest hold that rangers use must have been something he saw us practicing in our monthly training. It cuts off blood supply to the brain and doesn't leave any real marks to speak of—and it would put Hess out long enough for him to crush the windpipe with the jaw, especially if he applied the hold for longer than recommended. Problem is, since Ollie only had the maxilla and not the mandible, the jaws matched on both sides of the bite. A cat's mouth just isn't made that way or it would never close the bite properly. Everybody was so damned desperate to call it a lion kill that it was almost missed. I have to thank Lt. James for noticing the discrepancy and the fish and game biologists that did the necropsy, or we would never have figured it out," Chris shouted this last bit over his shoulder from the kitchen of their cabin as he refilled his day old coffee into his favorite cup.

"I'm surprised the coroner was not more on the ball about it as well, because the impression of the top of the ball point pen on Hess's body was a dead ringer for the one always clipped in Mahlon's shirt. It was one of the first things that really convinced me it was murder. He must have pressed it against him pretty hard while he was choking him from behind, maybe even enough to crush the windpipe a bit if he was applying the restraint hold improperly. Not too many cougars carry a ball point pen. Just shows how prejudging circumstances can lead you way off on the wrong path."

Stepping back into the dining room and heading back toward his spot on the couch he said, "If Mahlon had managed to kill Marcus, he might have pulled the whole thing off anyway. We would have had a hard time tying him directly to anything. If you hadn't gone looking out the back door of the Hillside Restaurant for Marcus that night, I'm sure he would have finished him."

"Makes me shiver just thinking about it," Allie said into her cup of tea as Chris sat down. "It's amazing how fragile life is, and how almost losing people you care about," she paused and squeezed her dad's hand, and then looked over to Marina and smiled, "can put things into focus for you. I could have lost you, Dad. We all came so close to this having a very different ending." She was quiet for a while, and then said "One good thing is that I think Marcus has gained some much needed focus, too. He's likely going to get probation in return for his cooperation during the critical phase of this case, at least that's what the assistant DA told him."

"So, any idea what his plans are now that he has this second chance?" Chris was hoping that whatever plans they were didn't involve Allie too seriously.

"What, Dad, are you worried about his intentions with me or something?" Alicia was teasing him, enjoying his discomfort, "no, don't worry. Unfortunately, he and his mother are moving closer to La Jolla so she can be nearer the doctors, and so that he can hopefully get a job and soon return to school."

"Well, I wish them all the best, but isn't that going to be a while off? I would imagine he has quite a bit of recovery to do before a move and a new job."

"Yes, and with his mother's illness, he's going to need some help. That's why I offered to come cook and do some light housework for them until he feels better. I should be over there several times a week, really getting to know him better." Allie stifled a giggle and winked at Marina.

"Oh brother!" Chris rolled his eyes and shook his head, more to play along than out of consternation. How could he disapprove of his daughter's big heart.

Marina was sitting next to Allie, and Chris noticed how truly pretty she was. She wasn't like those he had made a career of dating all his life—

and ultimately marrying—but maybe it was time for a change. At least it was time for a girlfriend, and he liked the prospect across from him a lot. And the little girl stepping into womanhood next to her was pretty neat, too.

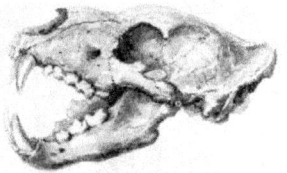

Acknowledgements:

Writing a book is a huge undertaking in any circumstances, but when two people are working on the project together, across hundreds of miles, the enormity of the process is especially compounded. This isn't something that can be accomplished without the help and support of many people.

Greg: Most other authors that we spoke with commented that writing jointly with someone else was a complete failure for them. Agreeing on what was to be written, how it should be portrayed, etc. was constant friction for them until the project fell apart. Those that didn't quit indicated that one of them wrote and the other just pretty much proofread.

I have to give enormous credit to Wendy for her creative thinking and incredible writing ability and the talent she had for blending my narrative with her own contributions. Every chapter has both of our dirty fingerprints on the passages, and we would often remark weeks after writing a section in the book that we had trouble figuring out which one of us wrote it. On a personal level, I couldn't ask for a greater gift than my daughter, and this co-authoring experience gave me a great deal of pleasure that I wasn't expecting.

Thanks go to my son Bryan Picard for his caring concern, great ideas, and for photography and cover design assistance. He is the son I always wanted. I also would like to thank those who spent time with helpful suggestions and thoughtful criticism like Michael Rea, Stephen O'Brien (who also taught me what standing up for what's right means), Ron Angier (who also kept me sane every day at work with his energy and humor), Bill Ramaley (whose calm wisdom, wit and professionalism guides more people than he knows), Angie Edrington (whose encouragement and help was critically important), and Jeanne Baird (who also kept me out of trouble with the continual business details of work that always go uncredited).

Wendy: Before I begin thanking all the people who supported me through this project, it seems fitting to thank my partner in this undertaking—my dad. You were my first and truest friend. The greatest joy in this process was that I was working with you. Further, I would like to thank my family, first and foremost, my ever-supportive husband, Jeremiah, who has put up with a wife glued to the computer screen, for hours on end, with little complaint. Thank you for believing in me. You never doubted that I could actually finish this book. In every way imaginable, your love has changed my life. Equally supportive were my two sweet daughters, who showed their enthusiasm by arguing who would be first to read it "when Momma is done." You inspire me daily.

I would also like to thank my friend and mentor, Michael Rea, for the many hours of discussion on everything, but especially writing, and for his invaluable formatting help. And last, to my friend, Stephen Van Dyke, the real-life Michael, who has saved me, literally and figuratively, more times than I can count.

Wendy Picard Gorham finished her Master's Degree in American Literature and has had a fascination with books and writing all her life. She lives out her love of words daily by teaching high school literature and writing. This is her first joint writing project, and having grown up in parks, she knows her subject well. She lives in California with her husband and two daughters.

Greg Picard finished his Bachelor's Degree in English, specializing in creative writing. After getting his Master's in education and counseling, he worked as a high school and college teacher, counselor, park ranger, editor, firefighter/medic, railroad brakeman and historian as well. He has written travel articles and short essays, and this is also his first jointly written novel. He makes his home in the Rocky Mountains of Colorado.

www.ingramcontent.com/pod-product-compliance
Lightning Source LLC
Chambersburg PA
CBHW070314260626
47160CB00003B/838